Praise for Eleanor Hyde's previous Lydia Miller mystery IN MURDER WE TRUST

"IN MURDER WE TRUST is great fun. [Hyde's] humorous take on the decadent, affluent New Yorker and his parasitic periphery makes for delightful enjoyment."
—MARISSA PIESMAN

"New York and Southampton, fashion and passion: [Hyde] weaves a terrific tale of greed, deception, and murder. Lydia Miller is contemporary and clever—a stylish and suspenseful delight!"
—MARILYN WALLACE
Author of *The Seduction*

"Oh joy! A likable heroine and a logical plot. Lydia's appeal lies in the fact that she's a normal New Yorker (if that's not an oxymoron). Smart, but not smug, and no braver than she has to be, she's the kind of character Hitchcock would have liked—the believable mortal who's summoned to adventure."
—LINDA STEWART
Author of *Sam, the Cat Detective*

"A very stylish debut."
—ANNETTE MEYERS
Author of *These Bones Were Made for Dancin'*

By Eleanor Hyde
Published by Fawcett Books:

IN MURDER WE TRUST
ANIMAL INSTINCTS

ANIMAL INSTINCTS

Eleanor Hyde

FAWCETT GOLD MEDAL • NEW YORK

A Fawcett Gold Medal Book
Published by Ballantine Books
Copyright © 1996 by Eleanor Hyde

All rights reserved under International and Pan-American Copyright Conventions. Published in the United States by Ballantine Books, a division of Random House, Inc., New York, and simultaneously in Canada by Random House of Canada Limited, Toronto.

http://www.randomhouse.com

Library of Congress Catalog Card Number: 95-96171

ISBN 0-449-14941-2

Manufactured in the United States of America

First Edition: August 1996

10 9 8 7 6 5 4 3 2 1

PROLOGUE

September, Labor Day

They were practicing slam dunks, Gary Grillo and his next-door neighbor, Kathy, whose short white shorts kept creeping up. When she gave them a furious tug down, Gary knew his father must be somewhere nearby. He started missing shots.

"That's not how you do it," Dad said from behind. "Watch this." He grabbed the ball from Gary, dribbled it on the tarred driveway, and tossed it through the hoop over the garage door.

"That's how you do it, isn't it, honey?" he said to Kathy's legs. Then: "Come on, kid," he told Gary. "We got work to do."

"Hey, it's Labor Day."

"Labor Day's when you labor," his father said. Asshole.

"One of these days," Gary said to Kathy, behind his father's back, and drew a finger across his throat.

Parked in front of the house was a big semi. "Three tiers," Dad said proudly. "Borrowed it from my drinking buddy, Deets."

"What for?"

"That would be telling."

Gary climbed into the truck on the passenger side.

The cab smelled of grease and gasoline. His father got a can of Bud from a cooler near his feet, twirled the radio dial to a ball game, and took off.

Gary tried to figure out what his dad was up to. He wore his green work coveralls with the deep pockets. Did that mean

1

something illegal? He'd already served time for working in a chop shop.

Gary casually opened the glove compartment.

"Keep out of there. That stuff belongs to Deets."

"Not these," Gary said, holding up a pair of work gloves. Rubberized for high-voltage wires. "You using them today?"

"Nah, they were in my pocket."

Mountains rose to his right. Green, wooded. Occasionally the sun came out, skimming the tops of the pine trees, but mostly it was hidden behind the clouds, a kind of yellow smear.

They left the expressway and started climbing. Why? Nothing up here but vacation houses. Burglary? His father wasn't that dumb. He knew people didn't leave until after Labor Day. But maybe he'd heard of someone who had. A telephone lineman might hear things like that. The houses were isolated. Just mailboxes or arrows with names pointing up some long lane.

His father lit a cigarette and smiled over. "Still want to know what we're doing?"

"No."

"That's good, since I'm not going to tell you."

"That's what I figured," Gary said.

"What we're doing is making money."

"Legally?"

"Let me put it this way. It's not *il*-legal. Just don't shoot off your mouth about this."

"So if it's not illegal, why can't I talk about it?"

"Because I said not to. I could've got Deets. You want to go to college and be a computer engineer, you need money, right?"

Wrong. He wanted to be a biologist. "Right."

Smoldering butts stank up the cab. Gary stuck his head out the window and breathed in the pine smell. They kept on climbing. Up, up, and up. The road was rutted, bumpy. They passed an arrow saying COATES, farther on another saying GONDOLA, then a large white sign lettered in black: CONSERVANCY — NO TRESPASSING.

"Listen, you want to make money on your own? There's

some flowers up here. White orchids. Put them in a gunnysack, give them to me. Ladies' hair, something like that."

"Ladies' tresses? They're rare. You can't pick them. They're on the endangered list."

His father laughed. "Where do you get that shit?"

"Coach Kline. He's our biology teacher."

"Yeah, well, tell Coach Kline to stick to coaching."

The minute the truck pulled into the clearing, Gary knew where they were. The old stone quarry. He and Kathy sometimes bicycled up here, but they came up the other way.

Kathy would sit on Suicide Rock, a big white boulder that overlooked the water in the quarry pit, speculating on why her grandmother had jumped.

His father parked the truck near the quarry pit and checked his watch. "Where is he? Makes me mad as hell when people are late. Your mother is a prime example." His voice was thin, edgy. His Adam's apple worked overtime. He spun the radio dial, running staticky stations together.

Gary heard it first.

"What the hell?" Dad said. Then: "Jesus, it's Tanner!"

Birds flew up from trees, scattering in different directions.

The siren screamed up behind them. An ambulance. White with blue letters. East End Hospital. Gary had never heard of it.

A big man in a white jacket jumped out. He had a beer gut, a bushy red beard, and a greasy pigtail.

Gary followed his father down from the truck, lagging behind, keeping his distance.

"Greetings and salutations," Tanner said, his voice high for someone his size.

"What's that for?" Gary's father nodded at the ambulance.

"Camouflage."

"Some camouflage with the siren going."

"Just funnin'," Tanner said, smiling through his beard.

Gary, standing some twenty feet away, heard strangled sounds coming from the rear of the ambulance. There was a smell like a backed-up toilet.

"That all you got?" Gary's father nodded at the ambulance.

"What'd you expect on short notice? Why'd you bring a kid?"

"This is my boy. He's helping."

"Who we working for, man? Where you taking these?"

Gary's father patted his pocket and smiled. "Secret. For my eyes only. I don't know where they come from and you don't know where they go. That's the deal. Why we get the big bucks."

"Yeah? No lookee, no loadee. This time I wanna know."

"No one sees this but me. Let's get to work. It smells like shit."

"That's what it is," Tanner said. "Shit. You'd shit, too, in their place. Gimme my money."

"Not till we've loaded the truck."

"Up front, as per usual. Otherwise I take off," Tanner said, and headed for the ambulance.

Gary's father took a wad of bills from his coverall pockets, peeled off half, and pocketed the other half.

Tanner's eye twitched. "Gimme what you put in your pocket."

"I give you half since you only brought half a load."

"I get what I always get." Tanner stepped toward his father, his eye twitch worse. Dad didn't budge. Gary braced himself. Tanner looked over at him, then walked around Dad and opened the rear door of the ambulance.

The smell made Gary sick. He was going to throw up. He tasted his hamburger, the onion he'd had with his hamburger, his whole lunch. He even tasted breakfast.

The slats on the crates were close together, so that he couldn't see inside. The sounds were worse than the smell. Shrieks like in a horror movie. Panicked cries and whimpers.

"Don't worry, they won't bite," Tanner said, and winked. "People's pets. The best kind for experiments. Too tame to fight. Catch," he said, throwing a crate at Gary. Gary nearly dropped it. A bloody paw squeezed out at the bottom. Almost unheard in the confusion of barks was a small feeble yelp.

Gary took the crate and ran, hearing footsteps behind him, his father yelling, and a high voice, shrill with fury, cursing.

A minute later iron fingers dug into his shoulder. He was spun around and found himself looking into eyes with tiny red crisscrossing veins. One twitched. "Drop that crate, you little faggot." Gary dropped it on Tanner's feet. Hard. He was sorry to jolt the animals, but gratified to see the surprise and pain in Tanner's face.

Gary took off, his sneakers skimming the earth.

The footsteps were behind him again by the time he reached the woods. Two sets—the one lagging behind would be Dad's, the nearest Tanner's. Gary was glad he'd practiced running for track all summer. Coach Kline said he was a natural. Okay, okay, he could outrun two beer bellies.

But a woods wasn't a track. He plunged through bushes and cleared a log. A thorn hooked his T-shirt. Jerking free, he ran on.

After a while he risked a look over his shoulders, and saw only branches and underbrush. No green coveralls or white jacket in sight. He'd outdistanced them. They'd given up.

He couldn't stop them from what they were doing, but that didn't mean he had to help. A tree seemed as good a place to hide as any. He swung up to a comfortable branch. He was catching his wind when he glimpsed a patch of white in the distance.

Too late to run.

Tanner came into view, running crookedly, breathing hard. Gary could hear him from where he sat. And see the small glint in the palm of his hand. A knife . . . Holding it so it barely showed. Tanner moved softly. He stopped under the tree like he knew. Gary pressed against the trunk. *Don't look up. Please.*

Tanner moved on. Gary let out his breath.

He wasn't sure how long he stayed in the tree. He waited until what seemed like forever, allowing them time to load the crates and drive off, his dad giving up on him.

He climbed down and started back.

Just as he became convinced he was going the wrong way, Gary saw grayish daylight ahead. He crept toward the clearing. The ambulance was gone, but the truck was still there. Maybe he could talk Dad into taking the animals to a shelter. He dismissed the idea. Not a chance.

He couldn't hear any animal sounds. Even in all this quiet. His dad would be in the cab drinking beer, getting drunker, meaner, and madder. Yeah, well, I'm bigger, Gary thought.

His father wasn't there. The ignition key was missing. He must be searching for him in the woods. Now was the time to let the animals out. Dad was already sore at him, so what the hell?

Bracing himself for the stench and the cries, Gary walked to the back of the truck and slid the gate up.

Empty. Except for some old rags.

Gary went over and sat on Suicide Rock, and skipped stones. No use looking for his dad, they'd miss each other. Dad was bound to come back soon. It was getting dark. Chilly. Gary tried not to think of that small bloody paw.

The birdcalls became fewer and fainter. But the woods came alive with animal scufflings.

Down below, the water lay in shadows. Still. Not one ripple. Black water in a jagged stone bowl. He skipped another stone and heard a thunk. Leaning over, he looked down. Something caught his eye.

It floated, belly up, like a very large, very dead fish. His father's coveralls. The pouches of the large deep pockets, water-filled, stuck up like fins. Beyond the finny pouches he saw a pale blob, half-submerged in the water.

The earth tilted and went out of focus. He got to his feet feeling dizzy. A thousand thoughts he couldn't hang on to whirling, flying out and up, scattering. If he'd stuck around, Tanner wouldn't have killed Dad for the other half of the money. Or was it to find out where Dad was taking the animals? Or both?

He'd wanted his father dead and now he was. Everyone had heard him say it. Mom, Kathy, the kids at school.

But a lot of kids said the same thing. Only their fathers didn't end up floating in a quarry pit. No one would believe he hadn't done it. No one but the one who'd killed him.

If the police didn't get to him, Tanner would, since Gary

was the only person who knew Tanner did it. He'd come looking with that knife. Tanner could be on his way back to get him right now.

A twig snapped. Gary tensed, and searched the darkness for something white. But that was dumb. Anyone would know enough to take off a white jacket at night. He suddenly realized he was a target in a white T-shirt. He stripped it off, shivering as the night air struck his skin, and rolled the T-shirt up tight. He couldn't throw it away. No one would pick up a bare-chested hitchhiker.

Provided he made it alive to the highway.

CHAPTER 1

Lydia sifted through the press releases, hoping to find something worth mentioning in her column "chic to chic" for the fashion magazine *gazelle*.

Her assistant, Gillian Smith-Markham, a British import, stood in the doorway wearing a black Mizrahi coat. "I'm on my way, wish me luck," she said.

Her pale redhead's complexion appeared even paler than usual.

"Don't do it," Lydia advised.

"I'll be in safe hands. Dr. Malmener is a first rate doctor with an international practice—in the States and in Switzerland, where he runs a very posh spa."

Apparently, Gillian didn't know that *malmener* meant "mishandle" in French. Now was not the time to enlighten her, Lydia thought.

"He promised it wouldn't hurt or leave any noticeable scars.

I can still wear a bikini," Gillian said. "That's why I'm getting this. Nigel and I are spending Thanksgiving in St. Thomas."

"You British don't celebrate Thanksgiving."

"Nigel is from Kalamazoo."

"The last thing you need is a lipo, for God's sake. You're not fat. You're not even overweight. And a mere baby."

"But you recommended it in your column."

It had come back to haunt her. So far, she knew of four women who'd had lipos since last month's column appeared. And there were all those readers out there she didn't know of. "I meant flabby women who were sick of fat thighs," Lydia said.

"I'm flabby," Gillian insisted. "I better be off." She gave a half wave and left.

Lydia sighed and shook her head. Gillian was twenty-four, eleven years younger than she was. Lydia blamed the lipo thing on the sick business she was in. Fashion distorted a woman's sense of reality, playing up to her sense of inferiority, magnifying flaws that could only be remedied by clothes, makeup, diet, or cosmetic surgery. Which was why she was getting out of this racket.

She could hear her boss's foghorn voice, five doors down, still holding forth on the phone. Lydia had been waiting all morning to tell Milke Forte, the editor in chief, that she was quitting, but Milke was either on her phone or out of her office.

Lydia returned to the press releases, bypassing paeans to a new body rub, another new perfume by yet another designer, and a lipstick called Chameleon, purported to flatter the wearer, be she blond, brunette, or redhead.

"Goddammit, she wasn't there."

Lydia looked up to see Regina Fellows, the beauty editor, high-heeling into her office, dark hair flouncing indignantly on her shoulders, fire in her eyes. She flung herself into the chair opposite Lydia's desk, displaying a lot of leg, her thick ankles cleverly and expensively concealed in Blahnik boots.

Lydia wondered how Regina and Gillian could afford designer clothes on their salaries. Were they on the take, accepting gifts from designers? If so, Milke would have a fit, maybe even fire them for a practice she considered unethical, even though it was common in fashion magazines.

"Who wasn't where?" Lydia asked.

"Laura Haddon, that's who. She didn't show up for the shoot. We waited on the steps of the Metropolitan for over an hour. Six of us. God knows how much it cost, considering what Davis Whalen, that bloody Aussie, charges."

Lydia felt a sudden ache. Davis Whalen had become the magazine's big-time fashion photographer, replacing her husband, Mark, who had died just four months ago in August.

"We kept calling to see what was keeping her, but all we got was her damn machine," Regina complained.

"I'm surprised. Laura's a pro. It's not like her not to show up. She's been modeling for how long now?"

"Since before I was born."

Lydia refrained from comment.

"Where else can I find a mature, fifty-something model who still looks good?" Regina wailed.

"Cheryl Tiegs?"

"Booked. Besides, Davis Whalen wants Laura. I wish I knew her secret. She hasn't even gone to that Chinese cosmetic surgeon who did such spectacular things for Jackie. Someone told me she's utterly terrified of going under the knife—Laura, that is."

"I did," Lydia reminded her. "She told me at an arts benefit. She said she was 'showing,' meaning she was showing her age."

"I know what showing means," Regina said, sounding irritated. "We did have to do a few touch-ups the last time. I'll give her one more chance." Regina pulled Lydia's phone toward her and punched out a number. After listening a minute, she yelled, "You're through, lady!" and hung up.

"Doesn't it worry you?"

"What?" Regina said, her attention diverted as she pawed through Lydia's press releases looking for something she could steal for her own column.

"Laura Haddon not showing up. Something could have happened."

"Knowing *her*, she probably ran off with some boy toy who's spending all her money. Listen to this," Regina said, picking up a press release. " 'Anima restores the user to dewy youth without the risk, pain, time, or expense of a face-lift. Cleopatra would have killed for it.' Do you believe that crap? You're not using it, are you? In your column that is, not on your face. I can tell you're not using any anti-aging thing just by looking at you."

Lydia was tempted to tell Regina she didn't need it as much as she did since she was at least five years younger, but held her tongue.

"I'm merely sorting the possibles from the impossibles. If you want it, take it."

"I don't take spurious claims." Regina raised her head and listened to the silence. "Milke's off the phone, finally. Wait until she hears about Laura Haddon's no-show."

"Hey, I've been waiting to see her," Lydia said, but Regina was already highstepping down the hall to Milke's office. "I'll only be a minute," she called over a shoulder.

A half hour later Regina left. By that time Lydia had applied fresh lipstick and darkened her too blond eyebrows, emphasizing the winged one that gave her a snotty look—a good defense in dealing with snotty people like Milke. "The only person you have to be nice to is your hairdresser," Milke claimed.

Lydia picked some blond hairs off her black cashmere turtleneck and floated them toward the floor, only then becoming aware of how absurdly she was behaving. Why worry about her appearance on a job she was leaving?

The phone rang the minute Lydia stepped inside Milke's office. "Darling," Milke chortled from behind an antique desk that stood on tiptoe. "I've been waiting! Guess what happened?" It wasn't Lydia she asked the question of but her caller.

With a long cigarette holder that looked like a prop from a Noël Coward play, Milke pointed Lydia to a delicate chair, also on tiptoe. A curved glass window overlooked skyscraper tops, visible as far as Wall Street, jutting into a hyperbolic blue sky—a dream backdrop, just as Lydia had imagined New York to look from the movies she'd seen as a child.

Milke was thin and small-boned and bore a certain resemblance to Coco Chanel, a fact she played to the hilt, wearing little black suits with gold chains and long strands of pearls, a silk flower pinned to her shoulder, and beige low-cut shoes with black toes to make her legs look longer. Her blue-black hair was cut thirties style, an era some people claimed Milke dated back to. Milke didn't look old, just ageless, like the well-preserved people Lydia saw in Palm Beach, Newport, and the Hamptons—wherever the rich hung out.

Milke was making her famous phone noises—oomphs and whoops and snorts—unintelligible to any eavesdropper. Lydia had heard others imitating Milke, not in fun, unfortunately, but seriously, as if Milke set a style in noises as she had in clothes for over the past half century.

Milke pushed an open magazine across the desk toward Lydia. A newsmagazine. Lydia couldn't tell which one, since the magazine was folded. Continuing her phone chatter, Milke tapped her cigarette holder on a yellow-highlighted news item headlined the SUCCESSFUL WOMEN SYNDROME.

"Read it," Milke mouthed. Lydia read. The item was short and described a new look labeled either Frozen Face or The Trance, increasingly prevalent in women. "I first noticed it in models, actresses, and TV anchor women," Dr. Paula Waxberg, a neurosurgeon at Memorial Hospital, was quoted as saying. "Lately, it seems to have spread to other women—politicians, trial lawyers, and CEOs. Women in power positions. At first I attributed it to too much plastic surgery, but many deny ever having undergone it." T. D. Bledsoe, author of *How to Get in Touch with Yourself*, attributed the look to facial paralysis. "When people put up a phony front, the facial nerves rebel and refuse to respond."

"Well, what do you think?" Milke asked, now off the phone, eyeing Lydia with bright little bird eyes. "If it promises to be madly exciting or something scandalous, you could write a piece on it. You're always complaining that I don't give you a chance to show off your journalistic skills."

Lydia took a deep breath. "I'm leaving, Milke. In two weeks."

"Leaving!" Milke cried, as if Lydia had insulted her. Maybe she had—the ultimate insult, defecting from the magazine. "After all the years I spent grooming you for your job?"

"Neil had something to do with it," Lydia said. She'd been Neil Underwood's assistant for two years until he quit to write a play that would stand Broadway on its ears. Five years later he had yet to finish it.

Milke tangled her fingers in the strands of pearls and chains, and touched the Russian cross she always wore around her neck—whether for decoration or religious reasons, Lydia wasn't sure. For a moment Milke looked her age, displaying an emotion Lydia seldom saw: distress. She'd hoped Milke might show some regret that she was leaving, but she wasn't prepared for this.

"Whatever salary they promised you, I'll meet the offer."

"Money isn't the problem."

"Oh, that's right, I forgot you came into a fortune."

"Not a fortune, but it does afford some independence."

Milke was referring to Adam Auerbach, who'd died just a month after Mark, making this the worst year of her life. "Adam was never a boyfriend. And it's no longer a fortune. Half of it went to estate taxes and what's left I split with his ex-wives. But it does allow me to pick and choose."

"And you choose to leave here? I didn't know you were so unhappy. I thought you liked it. You were so wildly excited when you first came to work on the magazine."

"It was all very glamorous for a kid from Smalltown, Ohio. Meeting the rich and famous. Going to shows in Paris, Rome, and Milan. Telling women how to look and what to wear. Even if it was a lot of crap, they listened. I had an audience."

"Now you have a bigger one."

"I told them wrong. My mission miscarried."

"See what you did? You drove me to smoking," Milke accused her, inserting a cigarette into her holder and lighting it. "I didn't know you had a mission, sweetie. Tell me. I'm intrigued."

Lydia shrugged. She wasn't about to bare her soul to Milke and be mocked.

"Well then, who is it you're going to work for? *Elle*, *W*, *Vogue*, *Bazaar*, or *Mirabella*?"

"Nora's Ark."

"Is that some dyke magazine, darling?"

"It's an animal shelter. A woman named Nora Coates founded it. She's dead. Her son runs it now."

"An animal shelter! You can't be serious. All those smelly creatures! Whatever are you thinking of?"

"I'm thinking of abandoned animals, that's what. I've wanted to do something about it ever since I was a kid and people dumped them on our property. We lived on the out-skirts of town, near a woods. I guess people expected their sheltered pets to forage for themselves. I took them in and kept them in Dad's warehouse—he was in the moving-and-storage business—until gradually they overran the place and he put a stop to it." Lydia stopped herself. Her golden rule was: Try Not to Bore Others As They Would Bore You. "You don't really want to hear this," she said.

"Oh, but I do. You never mention your childhood."

"Neither do you," Lydia didn't say. "Okay, you asked for it. My father said the animals could stay only until I found them homes.

"I managed to find a lot of homes for a lot of animals, but it backfired. People started dropping off more. I'd cry all the way to the ASPCA, where I knew the animals' fate would be sealed forever, and vowed that when I grew up I'd do something about it—so now I have the chance, and I am."

"Darling, don't get me wrong. I love animals, too. I'd be bereft without my little Minou. But you're overdoing it. You'll turn into one of those sour-faced do-gooders who go around looking miserable because everyone else isn't as miserable as they are."

"At least I won't be encouraging women to starve them-selves or have stupid, needless operations so they can dress like teenage hookers or belly dancers or parade around in something strapless, frontless, and backless. People in the fashion business don't wear such ridiculous clothes. So why don't we preach what we practice?"

"Darling, you can't ignore the designers and expect to survive in our shark-infested waters. What is it that you want to say?"

"That women should develop a sense of themselves, their own style. That style is more important than fashion."

"Stay on and say it. I give you my word, I won't touch it."

Lydia shook her head.

"When do you start your new job?"

"After Christmas."

"That's two months away. You can stay until then."

"I'm going home to see my family. My nieces and nephew won't recognize me if I stay away any longer."

"I'll make a bargain with you. Give Nora's Ark a whirl, and call me in six months. By then you should know how you feel. In the meantime we'll see how Gillian pans out. If she's good, you'll no longer have your column, but something with a little more clout."

"I'm as high as I can go."

"I started this magazine from scratch and I want to leave it in good hands."

"Milke, you're not considering retiring?" Lydia asked, unable to imagine Milke in any setting other than this one, with Manhattan stretched out around her.

"God, no, sweetie. I admit I'll be looking over your shoulder and getting in your way. But I'm not the monster you people here think I am—just a workaholic who expects everyone else to be. Do you know what happens when people like me retire?" The question was rhetorical. "One day we're fawned over, sought after, every little word quoted. We're the royalty of the fashion world—we can make designers or break them. We're invited to the biggest and the best parties and get the best tables at Le Cirque, Four Seasons, and 44. The next day it's phfft. Finis. Gone." Milke snapped her fingers.

"The friends we thought loved us for ourselves alone, and not purely for business purposes, disappear—they're paying homage to our replacement. We no longer count. We're no longer any use to them. I'll become just another little old lady, a target for taxi drivers and bicyclists. Lonely and ignored. Lucky if someone shows up at my funeral. You're right, dear. Take the time off, save your animals. See your family. My family is here. And sentimental old lady that I am, I thought you were part of it."

"We can meet for lunch."

Milke gave her a look.

Lydia got up from her chair, feeling something close to tears. She circled Milke's desk and kissed her cheek. "Okay, we'll talk later. Maybe I will come back," she said, not believing it for a minute. She berated herself for the rest of the day for not being firm with Milke, who, after all, might have been trying to manipulate her. Just say no.

In the evening, she told Kramer all about it on the phone.

"Hey, you led with your heart instead of your head. Of course I wish you'd do that more often," he said, sounding wistful.

Lydia wasn't sure how she felt about Kramer, who was nothing like the goofy, skinny Kramer on *Seinfeld*. Her Kramer—hers?—was on the chunky side, sensible and sensitive, traits not only surprising in a man but even more so in a cop—a detective with Suffolk Homicide. She'd met him last fall during that terrible business with Adam.

Kramer lived out on the Island with his eight-year-old daughter, so they didn't get together often. Except Lydia was the one who always came up with the excuses. It was too soon after her husband's death to become involved with any man. Kramer understood this. His wife had died in an automobile accident when his daughter was an infant. He'd confided to Lydia that it was only in the last few years that he'd been ready to commit to a relationship, which seemed to be what he was suggesting now. She promised Kramer she'd see him when she got back from her visit.

Two weeks later, after she left *gazelle* and before she left for Ohio, Lydia visited Carolyn Auerbach, one of Adam's former wives, at Oak Grove, a fancy funny farm in Connecticut. Carolyn had a tendency to flip out when the world was too much with her. Lydia didn't know the official name of Carolyn's illness—Carolyn wouldn't say. She suspected Carolyn was a manic-depressive, since her spirits either soared or plunged. On the other hand, she might be a paranoid schizophrenic, considering how wildly suspicious she became of people, especially Lydia.

This time, though, when Lydia visited her, Carolyn was fine. She hugged Lydia and said how happy she was to see her. "I'm being released Saturday, isn't that great? And making all kinds of plans. Wait till you hear."

One of Carolyn's plans was that Lydia would rent the top floor of her town house. "I started renovating last spring, so it should be ready by the time you get back. You'll have your own private entrance—"

Lydia cut her off. "Thanks, but I've found a terrific place on Central Park West. It's on the sixteenth floor and has a glassed-in sunroom that looks down on the park, where the trees look like broccoli. I'm moving in when I get back. The present owners promised to be out in a month."

"Maybe they won't move," Carolyn said hopefully.

"They have to." Lydia mentally crossed her fingers. The closing wouldn't take place until she returned.

Just before she left she called Neil.

"It's back to Brigadoon," she said, referring to her hometown—Elvira, Ohio—where things never changed.

"Poor you," said Neil, who was from Grosse Point and detested the Midwest. "For how long?"

"A month. I'll be back the day after Christmas."

"I'll miss you."

"Here, too."

Both agreed to get together when she got back, and both knew better. Neil considered New York dangerous, which was how she felt about the Hamptons, freaked out by her terrifying experience there last fall. In the meantime, while she was deciding whether to sell the house in Southampton she'd inherited from Adam, Neil and his longtime lover, Steve, were house-sitting for her, Neil at work on his play. The timing had been perfect. They'd been house-sitting in East Hampton for

Gabriella, a fashion designer, who'd returned from Milan to reclaim her converted barn.

Lydia left for Ohio on a Thursday after the evening rush hour, rolling off the George Washington Bridge into a psychedelic New Jersey sunset. "Maybe we should just keep going. Life on the road," she said to her dog, Colombo, who sat in the passenger seat beside her.

Colombo looked eagerly out his window, game for anything. He was orange and white and shaggy and looked like a huge toy dog from F. A. O. Schwarz. He'd belonged to Adam, who'd named him after the rumpled TV detective, Columbo. A stickler for getting things right, Adam had insisted on spelling the dog's name with an *o* instead of a *u*, which he'd said was the correct spelling in Italian.

Lydia stuck a cassette of "All I Wanna Do Is Have Some Fun" into the tape deck and sang along with it, bopping along in her third-hand Datsun. She didn't have to keep any commitments, she told herself. She wouldn't be arrested if she didn't call Milke in six months, see Kramer when she got back, or even visit her family if she didn't want to. All she had to do was have some fun.

CHAPTER 2

"We're back," Lydia told Colombo, entering the George Washington Bridge and leaving New Jersey behind.

She'd been driving all night. Her eyes felt grainy, her mohair sweater scratchy, and her jeans too tight. Colombo dozed on the leather seat beside her. He'd had enough of being on the road. And she'd had enough of Ohio. She loved her family, but . . .

Lydia went out of her way to drive past her new apartment building on Central Park West. She'd been all set to move in on her return and was bitterly disappointed when her broker had called her in Ohio to tell her that the present owners, an older couple, had postponed moving out until after New Year's. The closing date was rescheduled for January 4. In the meantime she'd reluctantly arranged to stay at Carolyn's place.

She drove through Central Park, passing bare-branched wintry trees. It was Monday, the day after Christmas, and the sun was trying to break through the clouds.

Lydia found a parking space on Third Avenue and Seventy-fifth, a block east of Mortimer's, where she'd promised to meet Regina Fellows, her former coworker at *gazelle*, for lunch. Mortimer's was a theatrical, old social register and Eurotrash hangout, seldom frequented by fashion people, which was why Regina had chosen it. "I don't want anyone in the business listening in," she'd said in a phone call to Lydia in Ohio. "I have a very serious matter to discuss."

Lydia was puzzled by the call since she and Regina had never exactly been buddies.

Before heading to Mortimer's, Lydia ran her fingers through her hair, shrugged into her brown suede jacket, and took Colombo for a brisk but brief walk then returned him to the car. "I won't be long," she promised.

She paused for a minute to admire her brand-new red Corvette, which she'd bought in Ohio on the premise that she was less likely to get ripped off in a small town where shady car dealers were generally known.

Entering Mortimer's, Lydia was surprised to see that instead of being sent to the outer Siberia of the back room, Regina was royally seated at a table in the first room among the ladies who still went to lunch, the social register crowd clad in Adolfos and knit suits. Who did Regina know? Was she a friend of the owner, Glenn Bernbaum?

"You look a mess," Regina said when Lydia sat down

across from her. Regina had new copper glints in her dark hair. Otherwise she was her usual thin and trim self in a sexy outfit by Todd Oldham—Hollywood and rock stars' favorite designer—and too much makeup. Regina seemed to think it incumbent for a beauty editor to go heavy on the stuff she wrote about.

"You'd look a mess, too, if you spent a night on the road."

"Weren't you scared traveling at night, a woman alone?"

"Not with my trusty dog and cellular phone. So what is it you want to discuss?"

A waiter appeared at their table. He was tall and good-looking with a long Roman nose. Probably an actor between jobs. Lydia ordered breakfast—eggs Benedict and tomato juice.

"Fettuccine, limestone lettuce with shallots, and another of these," Regina said, holding up an empty martini glass.

"Martinis? Since when?" Lydia asked.

"Since your former assistant took over. There's no restraining that brat. And Milke thinks she can do no wrong. Gillian's her fair-haired girl, as you once were. Only I will say, in your behalf, that you were never as obnoxious and devious as this kid."

"I've always found Gillian very cooperative."

"But you didn't know the nasty things she said about you behind your back."

"But I heard of some of the things you said," Lydia didn't say. Lydia was beginning to be sorry she'd agreed to meet Regina. This back-stabbing business had been one of the reasons she'd left. "Well, what do you expect me to do?"

The waiter set down their drinks.

"I thought you might give me some tips on how to handle her," Regina said, taking a sip of her martini. "But I see you can't help. Or don't want to." Suddenly Regina's heavily lined eyes lit up. "Don't look now, but isn't that Prince Pavlos and his bride?" she whispered, nodding at a nearby table.

"I can't tell one prince from the other. Who is he?"

"Merely the Crown Prince of Greece," Regina said, excitedly. "She's the American heiress, Marie-Chantal Miller. All

the chic people attended their wedding in London last year—
Queen Elizabeth; Valentino; Carolina Herrera; Princess
Benedikte; Laura Haddon, God bless her; Pia Getty, and
Prince Kyril and his wife, Rosario Nadal."

"Gee, I'm sorry I missed it."

"You know what you are?" Regina asked. "An inverted
snob."

The waiter, who had arrived with their food, winked at
Lydia. Maybe he approved of inverted snobs. Lydia was glad
to see that Mortimer's served a classical eggs Benedict—ham
and poached egg on an English muffin, smothered in hol-
landaise sauce. She dug in. "Speaking of Laura Haddon. Did
you ever find out why she didn't make it to the shoot?"

"Oh, God," Regina said, and set down her fork. "I forgot.
You've been away and haven't heard. It was really horrible."

"Horrible? What?"

"Two weeks ago. They found parts of her buried under the
George Washington Bridge. Or rather near it. They haven't
found the rest. The reports said she'd been dead for over a
month."

It took Lydia a while to absorb the horror of it. "God, that's
awful. I can't believe it." She sat stunned, stupidly shaking her
head. "Things like this happen to people you read about, not
someone you know."

"It's given me nightmares ever since I heard about it,"
Regina said. "And I was so nasty to her after she didn't show
up for the shoot. I refused to sit at her table at an AIDS benefit
held at the Armory. Gillian took my place."

Lydia realized she was still shaking her head, as if denying
what had happened to Laura Haddon. "I've always admired
her. A free spirit. Someone who did as she pleased and got
away with it. Only it looks like she didn't this time. What happened? I mean, how was she killed; did they say?"

"That's just it. It was death by brain embolism, but her head
was smashed in. And her fingers cut off."

"To hide fingerprints," Lydia said, paused, and thought it
over. "But then why would they leave her head? They must

have known she could be identified from her teeth. And if she died from a brain embolism, why hack her up?"

Regina pushed her plate away. "Please."

Lydia had long since stopped eating.

The waiter came over. "Is something wrong?"

"It's not the food," Regina said. "It's just something that happened to a dear acquaintance of ours." She proceeded to tell him all about it while Lydia wondered how an acquaintance could be dear. But in Laura's case, the description was apt. Laura was a dear, and Lydia thought of her as more than just an acquaintance after the surprisingly personal confidences Laura often made when they'd sat at the same table at some fancy do's, where Laura sometimes showed up in jeans and a white shirt, looking far more spectacular than anyone else there, despite her age and outfit.

"Oh, God, yes," the waiter was saying to Regina. "You're talking about Laura Haddon! Wasn't that shocking? It rocked the world."

Lydia thought that was a slight exaggeration since she'd neither heard nor read about it when she was home in Ohio, but then she'd been so busy getting reacquainted with her nieces and nephew that she hadn't kept up with the news.

"So have the cops found any suspects?" Lydia asked, after the waiter left.

"Nothing," Regina said. "It's strange. I mean, it's like the Mafia. Omertà. Suddenly no one in the fashion business knows anything. She was last seen dancing at a downtown club. Her cleaning lady reported her missing. It was a while before they found her—I mean found as much of her as they did."

"Are you saying people are afraid to say anything?"

"What do you think? I'm scared myself, and I don't even know what about. They questioned me, you know. The police. Remember when I called her after she didn't show up? I said, 'You're through, lady.' So naturally the cops interpret this to mean I intended to murder her. I'm still not sure I'm totally off their suspect list. Maybe they'll call you to verify it now that you're back. Back in town, that is. I sure as hell wish you were back at your job. I know we were never close friends, but I truly miss you."

Lydia said she missed Regina, too. They said emotional good-byes, drawn together by the horror of Laura Haddon's grisly death, and promised to keep in touch.

"If you hear anything more about Laura, let me know," Lydia said.

"Sorry to be so long," Lydia told Colombo. After putting his leash on, they walked the few blocks to Carolyn's on Seventy-eighth Street, Lydia still shaken by what she'd heard, taking the violation of Laura Haddon's beautiful body personally. The killers shouldn't be allowed to get away with it.

Lydia admired Laura's spirit. She'd always wanted to be like her—someone who could spit fashion in the eye and get away with it. Tugging at Colombo's leash to pull him away from the suspicious glop he was sniffing, she tried to dredge up Laura's confidences as if they might be clues to her murder. But all she could remember was Laura's admission to an affair with a married senator and some gossipy tidbits such as a designer who'd had his third face-lift. "Even men are doing it," Laura had said. "No one thinks anything of it, but just the thought terrifies me."

Lydia wondered what the police had come up with, if anything, and how long they'd pursue the case. Kramer had said the longer a murder went unsolved, the less chance there was of finding who'd done it. She rummaged through her mental file trying to think what friends she and Laura Haddon had in common, someone who might have known Laura well enough to suspect why she was murdered. She came up with Neil, who'd sometimes escorted Laura to some big event or other, where it was necessary for a model to wear a man on her arm. It had surprised Lydia that as beautiful as some models might be, they still had trouble finding a Saturday-night date. Maybe because men considered them unapproachable. She'd had the same trouble—not because she was a raving beauty, but rather because her snotty eyebrow scared them off.

Of course, it was five years ago when Neil had squired Laura around town. Back before he'd left *gazelle*. But it wouldn't hurt to call him and find out what he knew, if anything. Maybe he hadn't even heard of the murder. Sometimes Neil buried himself in his work to the exclusion of everything else.

She'd also call Kramer. He wouldn't know the details since he didn't work in the city, but he might know some cops who did. Of course, she intended to call him anyway, to let him know she was back.

Approaching Carolyn's town house, Lydia hoped she wasn't making a mistake by moving in with her. Still, it wouldn't be for more than a week and Carolyn could be delightful company when she wasn't being impossible. Actually, it was a pretty good deal. She'd have her own apartment on the top floor of a landmark house in a row of landmark town houses with age-softened brick and white-trimmed windows. And it was within walking distance of her new job.

Lydia climbed the stoop and pressed the bell set in a handsome door with a Palladian window. She waited. And waited some more. Maybe the doorbell wasn't working. She was raising a fist to knock when a voice called from below.

"We're down here getting ready for the grand opening."

Grand opening? We?

Carolyn stood in the small cement courtyard, smiling up at her. She wore a white pullover with a black yin-yang symbol and black corduroy jeans. She was thirty-three, two years younger than Lydia, and without makeup looked thirteen. People often took them for sisters—except Carolyn was prettier, Lydia thought, smaller-boned and neater-featured. Also, blonder now that Lydia had let her hair return to its original dirty blond after leaving *gazelle*.

Lydia retraced her steps to the sidewalk, lifted the latch of the iron gate, and stepped down into the courtyard. A boxed blue spruce strung with Christmas lights and popcorn nearly concealed the barred window on the ground floor. Most of the popcorn had been pecked off by the birds, leaving kernels.

Carolyn let out a small squeal and gave Lydia a big hug, greeting her as if they were twins separated since birth. "How were things in Ohio?"

"Great."

"I know what you mean. I couldn't stand it for long with my Boston Brahmin family either," Carolyn said.

Carolyn's cousin Frank, whom Lydia had met when she'd visited Carolyn at Oak Grove, had told Lydia that contrary to Carolyn's claims of an old Boston family background, her father was a fifth-generation Cape Cod fisherman, the last of a dying breed.

Lydia noticed a brass plaque on the door reading VASHTI'S ANIMAL SPA. "What exactly is an animal spa? And who is Vashti?"

"Vashti is me—the real me, that is. As you know, I've always adored animals, so I decided to open a spa for them. Come see how beautiful it looks," Carolyn said, opening the door and leading the way down the hall. Colombo trotted along behind them.

Lydia didn't remember Carolyn expressing an interest in animals before and wondered if this was an interest she'd developed after learning that Lydia was going to work at Nora's Ark. Neil claimed that Carolyn copied her, but Lydia had dismissed the idea. Maybe he was right, after all. The thought made her nervous, as if she should set a good example for Carolyn to follow. It also spooked her a little.

Carolyn came to a stop in front of an open door. "Recognize this? It used to be the dining room. Now it's the waiting room. As you can see, I've kept things simple."

Simple and expensive, Lydia bet. Walls done in a nubby beige linen matched the material covering built-in benches lining three sides of the room. In between stood low lacquered tables with exquisite Japanese flower arrangements. Only the tatamis on the parquet floor were inexpensive.

Carolyn slipped in a cassette that played a sitar instead of a samisen.

"Ravi Shankar. There were times at the funny farm when this was the only thing I could bear to hear. Isn't it heavenly?"

"You've done yourself proud. Is this where you preside?" Lydia nodded at the chair behind a desk.

"Heavens no, I have an office—where the kitchen used to be."

"Where are the kitchen and dining room now?"

"Upstairs in what was once the library. The music room is the living room, but the bedrooms are the same, still on the third floor. And you get the fourth floor to yourself. You'll love it. I started renovating last spring, before I was interrupted by that ugly episode."

Lydia didn't know whether Carolyn meant her ex-husband's death or nearly getting killed by her ex-lover. Probably both. Certainly both experiences had contributed to her breakdown.

"All this renovating must have cost a bundle."

"I'll make it back in my new business," Carolyn said confidently.

Lydia fervently hoped so. She also hoped Carolyn wouldn't become bored with the spa as quickly as she had with her other pursuits—be it lover or occupation. So far, Carolyn had been a sex therapist, part owner of an antique shop, past-life practitioner, and producer/director of what she called an exotic film, and others called porn, that she'd also starred in. These were just the undertakings that Lydia was aware of. There were periods in Carolyn's life that she referred to as her lost years and refused to talk about. Lydia wasn't sure whether Carolyn meant she'd spent them at the funny farm or doing something nefarious.

"Here's my office," Carolyn said. "Nothing special. Just an office office. The *pièce de résistance* is the Tranquility Room—come see it and meet my able assistant."

"You've hired an assistant?"

"Fate brought us together. He gives off positive energy like a human volcano. As soon as I saw him, I knew he'd be perfect."

"A real hunk, huh?" Lydia said.

"He's spiritual, not physical," Carolyn said loftily, placing a hand on a doorknob shaped like a ram's head. "I'm sorry. You can't come in here."

She was speaking to Colombo.

"Why not?" Lydia demanded. "I thought this place was for animals."

"First they have to undergo a purification ritual. And I hate to say it, but Colombo is as clumsy as his former master," Carolyn said, meaning Adam. "I don't want him breaking things and messing up the place before I open."

"That's okay, I'll clean up," a voice said, breaking in the middle like an adolescent's. But he *was* an adolescent, Lydia saw when he stepped out of the shadows of the Tranquility Room. Not a hunk but a lanky kid with a swoop of dark hair and inch-long lashes. He wore the same kind of pullover as Carolyn's but in reverse colors—black with a white yin-yang symbol.

The Tranquility Room was furnished somewhat like the waiting room, except in peach, with low benches, elegant lacquered tables and cabinets, and tacky pillows—embroidered, sequined, and tasseled. Tacky and elegant, just like Carolyn, Lydia thought, fingering one of the white stones on a shelf holding earthen ceremonial bowls and white candles.

The place was deadly quiet. No outside voices or traffic noises could be heard. The hush cast a spell over the three of them. For a minute no one spoke. Then Carolyn made the introductions.

"Lydia, this is my wonderful and able assistant, Amon."

Amon? Funny name for a kid. He blushed and eyed her shyly through fringed lashes. Lydia, who ordinarily couldn't abide teenagers, found this one adorable. She was sure that if Carolyn hadn't already seduced him, it was in the tarot cards. It upset her to think of it: sexy he might be, but he was still a kid. On the other hand, weren't teenage boys and women in their thirties supposed to be more sexually attuned?

"Show Lydia the waterfall," Carolyn instructed.

Amon fiddled with some buttons behind a Japanese print of peasants wending their way up Mount Fuji, and water began to trickle between two rollers above a slate wall. The water gained momentum as it increased in volume and ended in a merry splash in a pool at the toe of Lydia's ankle boots.

"It's meant to be hypnotic, but if that isn't enough, there's also the drum and this rain stick." Carolyn tilted a long, wooden pole toward the floor. The sound of rain accompanied the waterfall. Lydia closed her eyes and pictured herself in a rain forest.

"The Indians used it," Amon said.

"Amon means Native Americans," Carolyn said in a tone meant to admonish.

"Native South Americans," he pointed out.

Lydia decided this was one okay kid.

"You may as well get in practice and explain to Lydia what we do here," Carolyn told him.

Amon cleared his throat. "Uh, you've heard of reiki?"

"Lydia is among the unenlightened. You'll have to spell it out," Carolyn said, proceeding to do so herself. Literally, figuratively, and pedantically. "It's spelled r-e-i-k-i but pronounced RAY-kee—an ancient Tibetan healing technique that provides energy transference through the reiki master to where it's most needed for healing the body, mind, and spirit. Reiki translates into 'universal life force.' "

"How do you transfer energy to an animal?" Lydia asked.

"The usual way. With the laying on of hands or rubbing of crystals. Or I can use this." Carolyn handed her what looked like a small dark blue stone, surprisingly light.

"Plastic?" Lydia asked, bouncing it in her palm.

Carolyn grabbed it back. "It's a tachyon. And don't bounce it. It's very, very expensive."

"You mean you rub that thing on hairy little stomachs and they're miraculously transformed?" Lydia asked.

"Lydia is a negative force, a nonbeliever," Carolyn informed Amon. She turned to Lydia. "Come on, I'll show you your new home. We'll take the elevator."

"It's only temporary," Lydia reminded Carolyn, who sometimes believed what she wanted to, then accused others of going back on their word. The elevator was across the narrow hall from the waiting room. Carolyn pressed a button. "This will be your own private entrance. You won't have to traipse through my part of the house. And we'll keep the waiting-room door closed so you won't have people peering out at you. Anyway, you'll be gone during the day when my clients are around."

There was quaking and groaning in the elevator shaft, but no sign of an elevator.

Carolyn sighed. "Creaky, but it works. Installed for my invalid grandmother."

The part about installing an elevator for an invalid grandmother might be true, but the grandmother wasn't hers. Carolyn's ex-husband, Adam, had bought her the house—after their divorce. Lydia wasn't surprised that Carolyn had moved her allegedly Boston Brahmin family to New York since she moved them about frequently to suit her convenience.

Joints creaking and groaning in various areas, the arthritic elevator arrived with a jolt. The wait was worth it. An accordion door folded open to reveal handsome mahogany paneling etched in an Art Nouveau gold floral design.

There was just room for two adults and one big dog. The elevator shuddered. So did Lydia. "You're sure it's safe?"

"It's fine. Amon fixed it. He's wonderfully clever with his hands."

Un-huh. "Carolyn, that kid is a child," Lydia reminded her.

"He's seventeen. He told me," Carolyn said indignantly, as if that wasn't almost half her age.

"He has to be lying. He can't be more than fourteen, if that. And by the way, how did fate bring you two together?"

"I know you're a cynic, but it really was fate. He picked up a *Village Voice* left behind on the subway, saw my ad for an animal assistant, and called. Isn't that amazing?" Carolyn was looking Lydia straight in the eye, a trick she often used when lying. Lydia wasn't sure if she believed her.

"I assume he has parents somewhere," Lydia said.

"The poor child is an orphan, but I found him a place at Horizon House—that's an Episcopalian shelter for homeless children. Father Spence, the man who heads it, owed me one. He was a client."

"Client?"

"When I was a sex therapist. He was always very grateful to me for my help."

The elevator jolted to a stop, the door folded open, and Lydia, following Carolyn, stepped out into the nineteenth century.

"I furnished it with family heirlooms since I knew your stuff was in storage," Carolyn said.

The heirlooms—no doubt collected from Carolyn's antiquing days—included an honest-to-God Tiffany lamp, a grandfather clock, and a pie-crust table.

The kitchen was more up to date but equally impressive, with a black-and-white-tessellated floor, pine cupboards, dishwasher, washer, dryer, and a freezer big enough to stand in during a heat wave. Inside was a bottle of Dom Pérignon. "Thank you," Lydia said, remembering that Carolyn could be thoughtful.

"To celebrate our new life together," Carolyn said.

"But it will only be a week at the most."

Carolyn merely smiled.

The bathroom came with a Jacuzzi and heated towel racks, complete with initialed towels—a rather sloppy job, but the initials were Lydia's.

"I embroidered the initials myself," Carolyn said. "I'm trying to stop smoking. You can take them with you when you leave. If you can bring yourself to, that is."

The bedroom looked like something in a Bloomingdale's catalog with a bed smothered in decorator pillows and windows swathed in pink-and-green flowery curtains that matched the wallpaper. A white telephone and answering machine sat on the bed table.

"I had it hooked up with your old number," Carolyn said.

Lydia was beginning to feel trapped. She pulled back the curtains and looked out at leafless branches down to a garden with a winged-cherub fountain. Beyond the tree, the windows of an apartment building reflected the sun that had managed to break through the clouds after all.

"I hope you like it."

"It's terrific. There wasn't anything you didn't think of."

"Only the best for the best, and it's just a thousand a month."

"Except I won't be here that long."

"But it will be a month before I can get someone else. That's small potatoes with your kind of money."

Lydia didn't remind her that they both received the same amount from Adam, a multi-mixed-up multimillionaire, who'd left a trust to be shared by Carolyn, his first ex-wife; Vanessa, his second ex-wife; and to Lydia's amazement— her. Why, she still hadn't figured out, since she'd been neither wife nor lover. Either Adam had wanted to spite his former wives, or else he'd left the money out of sympathy for the mountain of hospital bills left behind after Mark's death.

Lydia wrote a check for a thousand dollars and handed it over.

"I won't ask for a security deposit since we're friends," Carolyn said.

And because she knows I'd leave and check into a hotel at such a display of chutzpah, Lydia thought. Still, listening to the creaking elevator returning Carolyn to Vashti's Spa to prepare for the grand opening, Lydia couldn't help but feel, along with Carolyn and Vanessa, that the money was rightfully theirs. Which didn't mean she was about to hand it back. It just meant that she felt responsible for caring for Adam's dog, Colombo, and his ex-wife Carolyn. Which might have been what Adam had intended.

Lydia went over to the window and looked down on her new neighborhood. Actually, it wasn't a new neighborhood since she'd lived just a block away. But there was still a big difference. This block contained no commercial buildings except for an upscale antique shop and an architect's studio. Her old block had tacky little stores—dry cleaners, shoe repair, a locksmith, and a pretty pink brick house, bought by the city from a Johnson's baby products heiress, that served as a drop-in homeless shelter where people got deloused and fed a good hot meal before being sent on their way.

The phone rang, interrupting her thoughts. Lydia let the machine answer for her. After driving all night, she was too wiped out to talk to someone she'd rather not. It could be Regina calling to complain some more about Gillian, or Gillian calling to complain about Regina. But the call came from someone at her new job, not the old one. It was Richard Coates, head of Nora's Ark. "Are you there?" he asked, then, "I guess not," he answered as if talking to himself. "Please call me when you get in." He left three phone numbers where he could be reached. Why did he want her to call him? Maybe because volunteers weren't exactly dependable, and he just wanted to be sure she'd be in tomorrow.

She'd call him later, Lydia decided, kicked off her shoes, and after pushing aside the decorator pillows, flung herself on the bed for a good long nap. But sleep didn't come. The thought of Laura Haddon's mutilated body intruded. Neil must have heard about it. What did he think? She needed to discuss it with someone. She reached for the phone and started to punch out his number, then stopped. Neil wrote until four in the afternoon and refused to answer the phone while he worked.

She phoned Kramer at the station house. No need to look up his phone number since she knew it by heart. All they seemed to do these days was communicate by NYNEX.

Instead of Kramer, she got Barolini, the man who'd tried to nail her for killing Adam. "He's off duty today. Who's calling?"

She hung up rather than listen to Barolini complain about the rotten hand life had dealt him. She called Kramer at home. He wasn't there either. "I'm back," she told the answering machine. Kramer called a half hour later. He'd been out getting groceries. They exchanged news about what each had been doing during the other's absence.

"I wish I could come in and see you tonight," Kramer said, "but Andy's playing in *Snow White* at school." He lowered his voice. "Damn, it makes me mad. You'd think her teacher would know better than to put on something where being pretty is such a big deal. But Andy says the kids chose it. She's crushed because she got the part of the Wicked Witch. I told her she didn't have to take it, but she did."

"Tell her the Wicked Witch is a juicier role. That Snow White is insipid. All she does is stand around and smile."

"Would you please tell her that yourself?"

"Put her on."

Andy answered shyly, although she wasn't a particularly shy child. Lydia told Andy what she'd told her father.

"What does insipid mean?"

"Blah. Like white bread."

"I like white bread," Andy said.

In fact, Andy liked everything Lydia trotted out as an example of insipid. Lydia decided she wasn't mother material and was relieved when Kramer returned to the phone. She asked him about Laura Haddon. He'd heard the gruesome details but was unfamiliar with the facts.

"She was a fantastic person. And for someone who might do crazy things, very wary. Any chance you can find something out?"

Kramer promised to get in touch with a former pal of his at the Nineteenth Precinct. "I'll see if he knows anything."

"Call me when you find out."

"I'll let you know in person tomorrow night. That is, if you're free."

"Sounds good to me."

Lydia hung up feeling considerably cheered by the prospect of seeing Kramer and somewhat hopeful about learning what had happened to Laura Haddon. "We'll get to the bottom of this yet," she told Colombo after she hung up. Colombo looked optimistic, and brought her his leash as if he were ready to get on the trail immediately.

CHAPTER 3

Returning from her walk with Colombo, Lydia stopped by Vashti's Animal Spa to see how preparations were going. Carolyn was drinking green tea and ordering Amon around. Lydia was sure Amon wasn't his real name, and wondered if Carolyn had named him after an Egyptian slave.

Back upstairs, she remembered Richard's call. She'd decided to phone him and set his mind at ease. She'd liked him immediately when he'd interviewed her at the shelter over a month ago. He looked like a blond Woody Allen with thinning hair, horn-rim glasses, an anxious manner, and a jacket that gave the impression of being two sizes too big for him, even if it wasn't.

She'd wanted to meet her future coworkers when he showed her around the shelter, but the interview had taken place after her workday at *gazelle*, and only a skeleton staff was on hand. "But we always have someone here with the animals," Richard assured her. "I made it a rule after some kids broke in, tortured the animals, and nearly destroyed the place."

Lydia called all three numbers. Richard wasn't at his home or the animal shelter, but she found him at the last number she called, a research lab at Rockefeller University. "My day job," he explained. "I usually only get to the shelter evenings and weekends."

He cleared his throat and coughed. She'd told him during the interview that she was going home to Ohio before she started working. Now he asked if she'd enjoyed her trip, how her family was, and if she was glad to be back. Next he'd ask about the weather. Stalling. She guessed he wanted to ask a favor and wasn't sure how to go about it.

Colombo, who had been standing nearby—he often hung around to listen in when she was on the phone—wandered out of the room.

"I hope everything's okay," she prompted.

"Oh, yeah, except for one small thing. I hate to ask you this since you're a volunteer, and I know we agreed that you'd put together a newsletter beginning the first of the year, but something has come up, or rather someone hasn't shown up. I was hoping maybe you wouldn't mind filling in for a day or two. Unfortunately, a lot of our volunteers have taken off for the holidays."

"Fill in as what?"

"Heidi, our assistant office manager, went out for lunch the other day and didn't come back. She's a flake, but basically a nice lady. P.S. is going crazy."

"P.S.?"

"Oh, yeah, sorry. She's the office manager. The initials sometimes confuse people. She calls herself P.S. and tends to get testy if you call her anything else. Then she won't answer."

Great. Just the sort of prima donna Lydia would adore working with. "I wouldn't know how to begin managing an office."

"You really don't have to do much—just keep an eye on things."

"What things?"

"Office things," Richard said cryptically.

"What happened to Heidi? Was she hurt?"

"She quit a week early. We knew she was leaving. But we didn't expect it to be today. She's going on an around-the-world cruise. Spur-of-the-moment decision. That's Heidi for you."

"That's hardly the kind of thing you'd do spur of the moment. She'd have to book in advance."

"Well, that was what she told us, anyway. Maybe she lied. I've been interviewing like crazy but haven't come up with anyone."

"I'm sorry, I'd like to help, but I've just moved into my new apartment," she said, stretching the truth a little, wishing it was true. "I'm in the midst of unpacking and hanging pictures and stuff," she added for good measure.

Richard apologized profusely and said he understood. "I tend to be inconsiderate when it comes to the animals."

"This has nothing to do with the animals. It's office work."

"It has everything to do with the animals—ordering food and medical supplies, sending out the rescue squad, follow-up calls on adopted animals—a million little details."

Just a minute ago he'd said that all she'd have to do was keep an eye on things.

"P.S. is swamped. Practically lives at the shelter. No telling how long she'll be able to keep it up. In fact, I don't know how long we can keep Nora's Ark afloat. Or what happens if we can't."

"You'd place the animals in other shelters."

"I've already looked into that. They're overcrowded as it is. The ugly truth is that hundreds of loving, trusting animals, including puppies and kittens, would have to be p.t.d."

"What does that mean?"

"Put to death," he said.

"What time should I be there?" she asked with a sigh.

The sun streamed in through the stained-glass windows, casting rainbow colors on the cement floor. Entering the shelter was like entering a church, except for the smell of antiseptic. Light laddered down from the domed glass skylight onto puppies and kittens as it might have on the infant Jesus. Actually, the shelter had been a church in its past life. Richard had told her this during the interview, adding that he didn't know the denomination. "The other part, the holding rooms and hospital, is a former warehouse. Mother added the offices when she took over."

According to Richard, putting the puppies and kittens in the reception area lured people in. "Later we show them the other guys in back. You'd be surprised at the times someone spots an animal in back they're sure is meant only for them and forgets all about the cute ones in the showcase cages. Kind of like choosing a mate in marriage," he added.

Lydia refrained from asking if that was how he'd chosen his. Anyway, he might not be married. He wasn't wearing a wedding band.

She'd arrived at the shelter a half hour late, due to the excitement of opening day at Vashti's Animal Spa. Carolyn had a near-hysterical fit after discovering that the waterfall in the Tranquility Room didn't work. Amon fixed it with some flicks of the right switches. He managed it very diplomatically.

Seated at the reception desk of Nora's Ark was a pretty young girl in a T-shirt reading CATS AGAINST ANIMAL EXPERIMENTS. A nameplaque identified her as SHANTEL WILLIAMS. She had uptilted green eyes and pecan-colored skin.

Lydia introduced herself. "I'm a volunteer, filling in for Heidi, the assistant office manager."

"Oh, yeah, she was kind of ditsy but a lot of fun. I'll miss her," Shantel said. Her green eyes inspected Lydia's blazer, long skirt, and ankle boots every bit as critically as Milke used to. And it looked like she didn't approve of what she saw any more than Milke had. "That's a neat pin," she said. Lydia supposed she passed muster, after all.

The pin was a black-and-white cat with movable parts that she'd bought at Mable's on Madison Avenue, named after the original Mable who'd long ago gone to cat heaven.

"I'm supposed to be helping P.S."

"Lucky you," Shantel said, rolling her eyes toward the ceiling.

"Is she difficult to get along with?"

Shantel smiled, and nodded toward a door with a frosted-glass window. "She's in there."

The door was closed. Lydia heard angry voices behind it, but couldn't make out what was being said. "It doesn't sound as if I should interrupt."

"You got it," Shantel replied.

A number of people carrying coffee cups went back and forth past the frosted-glass door, while a few boldly lingered nearby, listening and whispering to one another. When the door opened suddenly, everyone scattered, but not so far away that they couldn't see or hear what was going on.

A stocky man with long dark hair and a short bull neck came storming out of the office. "You can't fire me, man, I quit," he shouted at Richard, who stood in the doorway.

"Have it your way," Richard said.

"If I had it my way, you'd be dead." The man's eyes lit on Lydia. "He's evil, man, evil. He works for the devil." He sprinted down the hall to the reception room and grabbed at a black leather jacket on a nearby coatrack. The jacket got caught on a hook, and the back of his bull neck reddened as he jerked it free, nearly knocking over the coatrack in the effort. Jacket in hand, he made a dash to the door. "You're going to regret this," he called to Richard before slamming out.

A tall woman with a mass of caramel-colored curls and a long horsey face appeared at Richard's side. "You've just lost us the best vet we've ever had," she said.

Lydia was surprised to hear that the bull-necked man was a vet. Veterinarians didn't ordinarily go around calling people "man." Especially women.

Richard stood in the doorway looking donnishly appealing and prim in his elbow-patched jacket and horn-rims, not evil or inept as accused.

Even so, Lydia was beginning to wonder if she hadn't made a horrible mistake coming to work here. Maybe she should make an unobtrusive exit. Too late. Richard spied her. "You made it," he called, coming over and shaking her hand. "I really appreciate this. We all do. Sorry about the fireworks."

He turned to the tall woman with the curly hair. "P.S. this is your new assistant, Lydia Miller."

"You hired my assistant without consulting me?"

"Temporary only. Lydia's a volunteer. She's going to start that newsletter we've been talking about for so long. But for now, she graciously agreed to pitch in while we're short-handed. I thought you'd be glad to have her help."

"Actually, I don't know much about managing an office," Lydia said, hoping she could escape her new responsibilities.

"I'll switch jobs with you," a voice called from behind

Lydia. "You can take my place in surgery. I can't stand the sight of blood."

A brunette with flawless skin and froggy eyes stepped into view. She wore a white lab coat over a nifty pin-striped Donna Karan suit, and white sneakers and socks. The sneakers explained why she'd come up from behind so quietly. "Look," she said, pointing to a red splotch on a sneaker. "Blood!"

"I'd think you'd be used to a little blood now and then," Richard said. "A dermatologist is better qualified to serve in surgery than a fashion editor. They need you down there." He turned to Lydia. "Sorry, I've got to run. I'm already late to work."

He snagged a blue parka from the same coatrack that the bull-necked man had nearly knocked over and started off for what Lydia guessed was his day job.

P.S. blocked his path before he reached the door. "We haven't finished our conversation yet," she said, and led Richard to the showcase cages, where no one but the animals could hear their conversation. Judging from her excited gestures, P.S. had a lot to say. So did Richard. Both were apparently arguing over how to run the animal shelter while ignoring the kittens and puppies clamoring for their attention in the cages behind them.

Richard had sounded somewhat sympathetic toward P.S. when she'd talked to him on the phone yesterday, but today it looked like major warfare. And what about that switch in his behavior from a nervous, genial guy to someone pretty much in command? Which was the real Richard?

"Is it always like this?" Lydia asked, turning to the dermatologist in the Donna Karan suit.

"I don't know, I'm new here, too. A volunteer. I gave up precious weeks of my Christmas vacation to work here, and *he* doesn't appreciate it."

"Maybe we should just leave," Lydia suggested.

"I would if it weren't for the animals. I can't bear to leave now that I've seen them." The dermatologist extended a well-manicured hand. "I'm Allegra St. John. My parents are musicians. My mother is a pianist and my father plays a violin."

Lydia wondered why Allegra gave her parents' occupations, then figured out she was explaining how she came by her musical name.

Out of the corner of her eye, Lydia saw Richard head for the door and P.S. striding toward her, caramel-colored curls bouncing atop the long horsey face, which looked longer now than before.

"Do I have to return to surgery?" Allegra asked P.S. when she reached them.

"Guess so. I don't make the rules around here." P.S. sounded bitter. "This way," she said to Lydia, and headed toward the office. "That's where you sit," P.S. added, pointing to a desk. I'm in here." She headed for an adjoining office and closed the door behind her.

I'll leave at the end of the day, Lydia told herself. She said the same thing to Shantel Williams who came in to see how things were going.

"Oh, you can't leave," Shantel said. "The animals need us, and we need someone here who knows what they're doing."

"But that's just it. I don't know."

"First, you go through the in-box. If you don't know how to handle what's there come out and ask me. If I can't help, just toss it in file thirteen."

"File thirteen?" Lydia asked.

"That," Shantel said, nodding toward the wastepaper basket.

By the end of the day file thirteen was almost full—a long day as it turned out. At home, Lydia had no sooner showered, dressed, and ordered takeout from William Poll, when Kramer arrived looking handsome and teddy-bear cuddly. He presented her with her favorite flowers—velvety purple and red anemones.

While Lydia searched for something suitable to use as a vase, Kramer told her he'd called his pal at the Nineteenth Precinct about Laura Haddon. "It's not their case, but he's looking into it."

"I called Neil last night," she said, arranging the anemones in a tall frosted glass. "He said he'd received calls from her friends who claimed to be mystified as to how such a thing could happen. Oh hell, let's change the subject. This is a celebration. We haven't seen each other in eons. How did it go with Andy last night?"

"I don't want to brag, but she stopped the show. Kid's a born mugger."

"So she wasn't upset about not being Snow White, after all?"

"Called her insipid. Wonder who she got that word from," Kramer said with a grin.

They dined by candlelight, sipping Carolyn's Dom Pérignon and feasting on William Poll's seafood dinner—clam bisque, shrimp salad, and poached salmon. Lydia had deliberately ordered takeout so they could be alone instead of eating out as usual.

But alone was not in the cards. Carolyn arrived on the creaking elevator to entertain them with stories of opening day at Vashti's Animal Spa. "You must be exhausted and ready for bed," Lydia hinted several times, reworded in several different ways.

By the time Carolyn took the hint and left, Kramer had to leave, too, since he was on midnight duty and it took him over two hours to get back to Southampton.

"You never got a chance to tell me how you like your job," Kramer said.

"I don't like the people, so I'm leaving," Lydia told him. And told herself that every day. And was still there at the end of the week. She agreed with Shantel and Allegra. Now that she'd seen the animals, she couldn't bear to leave them.

CHAPTER 4

It was the morning of New Year's Eve. The sky was gray and spitting snow, but the snow melted as soon as it hit the ground. Gary Grillo, aka Amon, wearing plastic gloves, picked up the litter in the courtyard outside the animal spa.

Today his find consisted of a crushed Dannon yogurt cup, a pocket comb, chewing-gum wrapper, and scraps of a torn letter in the wooden plant box with the dead geraniums—trash blown in from the sidewalk or tossed over the iron fence by passersby.

Gary dumped the trash into a garbage can at the curb, then looked up and down the street hoping to see Tiffany and Lucky. Although Tiffany lived west of Carolyn's, he never knew which direction she and her greyhound might come from.

The first time he'd seen her was the day after they opened, when this beautiful redhead around his age had brought in her iguana, Iggy Pop. With her was a pretty, older woman, who wasn't her mother but never said who she was.

"Iggy Pop hides behind a cactus plant in his terrarium and won't eat anything," Tiffany told Carolyn.

Carolyn said that iguanas were uncommonly shy and, after treating Iggy Pop with a tachyon and talking to him for a half hour, sent him on his way with Tiffany and the woman. Gary figured out later, after he got to know Tiffany better, that the older woman was Melissa Starr, the romance writer.

The next day Tiffany dropped by while she was out walking Lucky and told Carolyn that Iggy Pop was eating and crawling around the greenhouse. "He's back to normal," she said.

After that Tiffany stopped by often when she was out walking her dog. "It's not me she comes to see," Carolyn said in a teasing way, but he could tell she didn't like it. Especially when he started hanging around outside so he'd be sure not to miss Tiffany if she passed by. Besides being so beautiful, she liked animals. She was tall—a good five-eleven. She'd be great practicing slam dunks with like he used to do with Kathy.

Tiffany said she called her greyhound Lucky because he was lucky to be alive. "I rescued him from a dog-track owner up in Boston who was going to kill him. That's what those owners do when a dog loses races, they kill it! I'd like to kill them! Make them run and run and run around the track until they drop dead. Boy, would I love that!" She laughed.

Gary couldn't figure Tiffany out. She sounded like she went to some private school, like those snotty girls whose parents had vacation houses up home in Vermont, but she wasn't snotty at all. She told him she wrote romance novels for Melissa Starr, whose books were so popular that writers had to be hired to keep up with the demand. She looked too young to be a writer—like she should be in school. She said Melissa Starr said young girls were more romantic and therefore better at writing romance novels. "Anyway, I go to school. This is just part-time work. How about you? Why aren't you in school?"

"I'm part-time, too." If she knew he was lying, she didn't mention it. She didn't like questions, and neither did he. They'd silently agreed not to ask about parents or their past.

The snow had begun to stick and he was getting cold without a jacket. He gave up looking for Tiffany and went back inside to clean his room before Carolyn looked in and scolded him for being so messy. She was worse than Mom about picking up after himself. He missed Mom. He missed his kid brothers and sisters. Christmas Eve he'd called home and listened while Mom said hello, hello, hello. Her voice had sounded hopeful, almost as if she knew who it was. He hadn't trusted himself not to answer, and hung up.

Carolyn didn't like to be called Carolyn anymore—only

Vashti. But her reason for changing her name was different from his—she wasn't a fugitive from the law.

He always watched *Unsolved Mysteries* on the old TV set Carolyn had given him, afraid they'd do a story on how he'd killed Dad and disappeared. The only person who knew he hadn't done it was Tanner, the man who had, and who was out to kill him. Gary hoped Tanner would be looking for him in Boston, where people living in his area went instead of New York.

He destroyed a cobweb in the corner with a poke of his finger. He hated to do it. Spiders ate pests and were necessary to the ecosystem, but Vashti considered them creepy.

Gary got the janitor's broom from the closet and started sweeping up, moving around the white wicker chairs that Vashti stored in his room during the winter. She'd bought a cot for him to sleep on and warned him not to let the woman upstairs know he was staying in the storage room.

"I've told her you're staying at an Episcopalian boys' shelter," Vashti said. "It's called Horizon House and is run by Father Spence. Don't forget to say that if she starts questioning you. Especially now that she knows."

"Knows what?" Gary asked.

"How we became acquainted."

"You mean you told her I snatched your purse?" he cried.

"*Tried* to snatch it," Vashti pointed out.

"But I'm good at picking pockets," he said defensively. "That's where the money is—men's wallets. Women mostly carry credit cards."

"Picking pockets is nothing to brag about. I hope you've given that up. I didn't tell Lydia intentionally. She wormed it out of me. I thought she believed me when I told her I found you through a *Village Voice* ad, but I was wrong. She kept bombarding me with questions. I hate to lie, you know." He'd caught Vashti telling a couple of whoppers, but he didn't correct her.

After he finished cleaning his room, Gary hurried to the Tranquility Room, anxious to put things in order before Vashti appeared. He checked the candle supply, set the earthenware ceremonial bowls back on the shelves, and lined up the blue tachyons and white stones on the lacquer tray.

Vashti had said that in ancient times the white stones were given to released prisoners to show they were free. "They symbolize release from old ways of thinking," she'd explained.

The ceremonial bowls were used in the Burning Bowl Ceremony, a way of purifying people's lives and getting rid of the past. He'd read about it in a book on transformation rituals that Vashti had given him. He'd tried it—drawn a picture of the quarry and Dad floating dead in the water. It hadn't worked. His hand had become sweaty, the pencil slippery, and even he couldn't tell what the picture was about. But that didn't matter, the book said. The important thing was to draw it, burn it, and get rid of the memory.

But drawing the picture just drove the memory deeper. He couldn't get rid of it. Something always reminded him of that day. Like when the subway screeched to a stop, he'd hear the animals screeching in pain.

"Amon, it's after ten. You should be at your desk."

He turned to see Vashti standing in the doorway. She had a way of coming up from behind and surprising him. She wore her dancing-angels dress and the guardian-angel pendant that he'd given her for Christmas. It embarrassed him that the pendant was so cheap compared with what she'd given him—a parka, moccasins, T-shirts, and a smudge pot for getting rid of negative attitudes, although she'd said he didn't have any. But if he'd given her anything more expensive than the pendant, he'd have had to revert to picking pockets. Vashti didn't pay him much, but he got his room free.

Vashti came over and stood close to him, straightening the stones he'd lined up. She smelled mysterious, a smell that sort of made him think of secret rooms. When she put her hand on his arm, he jumped. "My goodness, do I scare you?" she asked, and smiled. He felt his face grow red. She often touched him, sometimes standing so close that no matter which way he moved, he'd touch her. Being close to her felt good, but made him nervous. He wasn't sure what he was supposed to do. Was he supposed to touch her, too? But what if she got mad? What if she ordered him to leave? Then what would he do?

"Gee, I didn't realize it was opening time. I better get a move on," he said, and almost ran from the room.

In the waiting room, he put the yin-yang robe on over his jeans and Om T-shirt. He sat down at the reception desk and tried to think of something to do. Vashti said it was good business to look busy. But why look busy if no one was around to see you? Just as he was asking himself this the buzzer sounded. A client, after all! He pressed the release button, pushed his hair out of his eyes, and switched on Ravi Shankar.

A woman in a green coat came in. She'd been in before with an Afghan. Today it was a cavalier King Charles. Her coat was buttoned up wrong and her hair went every which way. "I want to speak to Vashti," she said, approaching his desk. *"Now."*

"Wait here. I'll see if she's free."

She didn't wait, but followed him to the door of Vashti's office, shoved past him, and tossed the dog's leash his way. "Take care of him," she called, shutting the door in his face.

Gary expected Vashti to throw the woman out, but it was a good half hour before she reappeared. Vashti was with her, looking pale and all shook up. She wore her long black cape. "We're going out," she said. "Write Ms. H. Exner in the appointment book along with her dog's name." Vashti turned to the woman. "In case anyone checks. What is the name of your dog?"

"Reggie. And he's not mine. I borrowed him so no one would guess."

Guess what? Gary wondered. Why would she borrow someone's dog when she already had one? And why would anyone check the appointment book?

Vashti slipped the black hood over her blond hair. "Tell my clients that Vashti will return in an hour."

As soon as they left, Gary raced to the window, raised the bamboo blind a millimeter, and peered through the lacy ironwork to see what direction they'd gone in. He was just in time to see Reggie scramble into a cab after Ms. Exner. Then Vashti got in and the cab drove east, but that told him nothing since it was a one-way street. What had the woman said to make Vashti look so shaken?

It was snowing harder now. The doorman in the apartment building next door scattered salt on the sidewalk. Vashti didn't have any salt, but she had a shovel. Later, when more snow accumulated on the sidewalk, he'd go out and shovel it off. It would give him an excuse to see Tiffany if she came this way.

He was at his desk reading the book on transformation rituals when Vashti came back about an hour later. Snowflakes melted on the hood and shoulders of her cape. "Did anyone come in while I was gone?" she asked, her voice more breathless than usual. Her cheeks were pink from either cold or excitement. He wondered where she'd been.

Gary shook his head.

"No phone calls?"

He shook his head again.

"Well, if anyone comes in, let me know immediately."

"Yeah, okay. Are you expecting someone?"

"Anything can happen. You can pick up something from the health-food store for lunch. I'll have an alfalfa-sprout sandwich with lentil soup. You get what you like. Take some money from the cash drawer. And don't forget to lock up when you go out."

She disappeared behind her office door, closing it all the way—something she'd never done before. He heard her talking on the phone, but couldn't tell what she was saying.

When Gary came back with the food from the health-food store, Vashti was still making phone calls. She took her soup and sandwich without inviting him in to join her for lunch, as she usually did.

An hour or so later, when the buzzer sounded, Vashti was out in a flash, standing in the doorway. "See who that is before you let them in."

Gary lifted the bamboo blind and peeked out. "It's a man carrying a pug in a plaid coat."

"Let him in, then," Vashti said, and disappeared again. Gary pushed his hair out of his eyes, switched on Ravi Shankar, and pressed the release button.

"It's really snowing out there," the man said, stamping his boots before coming into the waiting room. All the same he left tracks on the tatami as he crossed to Gary's desk. He still held the pug in his arms. They looked alike, wrinkled foreheads and chubby. "Leo's depressed. He's got the holiday blues."

Vashti appeared in the doorway again. Gary had the feeling she'd been hiding behind the door listening. "We don't take anyone without an appointment," she said.

"This is an emergency. Leo's suicidal. I thought he'd be okay once he got through Christmas, but the nearer it gets to New Year's the more miserable he is."

Leo gazed unhappily up at Vashti and whimpered, his furrowed brow becoming more so.

Gary knew she'd take care of Leo. Vashti couldn't bear to see an animal suffer.

"Come along," she said.

The man stepped forward.

"I meant Amon, my assistant," Vashti told him.

Leo's owner frowned. "Strangers make him nervous."

"You're the one who's making him nervous. He catches your negative energy. Stay here, please." Vashti spoke firmly.

"If *he* goes with you, why can't I?" the man said, nodding at Gary.

Vashti smiled sweetly. "Amon's energy is positive."

Before entering the Tranquility Room, Gary performed the purification ritual in accordance with Vashti's instructions, squirting water from a plant mister onto Leo's forehead. Leo blinked and whimpered. Inside, Gary switched on the waterfall. Leo ignored the water trickling happily over stones and whimpered longer and louder.

Vashti patted him on the head. "There, there, you'll be fine. We'll nourish your body as well as your spirit."

Gary's cue. He got a box of Heavenly Canine Cuisine from the lacquered cabinet and poured some into a porcelain bowl decorated with dancing Kalis. Leo sniffed, gulped it down, and looked up hopefully for more.

"Feeling better?" Vashti asked. She placed him on a bench

and rolled a crystal over his already bulging stomach, all the while chanting softly.

Before Vashti, Gary had ceased to believe in spirits—occult or holy. He'd upset Mom and made Dad mad by leaving the Catholic Church in the fifth grade when Sister Anna Marie, his teacher, insisted the earth was larger than the sun. Since meeting Vashti, he wondered if there wasn't some mysterious spirit after all. The fact that certain things she tried didn't always work wasn't entirely in her disfavor. After all, prayers weren't always answered either. In fact, Vashti had a better batting average than God. Her effect on Leo was like magic. By the time they returned him to his master, Leo looked like a happy sultan, his jaw relaxed like he was smiling. Gary wondered if the Heavenly Canine Cuisine was doped. The box didn't list its ingredients.

"Well, look at this. He's a new man," Leo's owner said, beaming. "Thank you, thank you, thank you. I can't thank you enough."

Vashti smiled sweetly. "You can pay my assistant. A hundred fifty." Fifty more than usual.

Leo's owner didn't seem to mind. He counted out seven twenties and a ten, snapped Leo into his plaid coat, and donned a cap and earmuffs. "You're going to make a wonderful healer under your mentor's tutelage, Amon," he said. "You've got the golden touch."

"Poor man," Vashti said as Leo's owner bowed himself out. "Some people just can't connect with animals. You either have it or you don't."

She disappeared into her office again, but a few minutes later she appeared in her cape and boots.

"I'll take that hundred, sweetie. Keep the fifty as a holiday bonus," she told him, holding out her palm. "Leo's owner is right. You're going to make a wonderful, wonderful healer."

"That's because of my teacher," he said, and felt his face burn.

Vashti kissed him on the cheek. "I'm a very good teacher, you'll see. I have to meet someone. I'll stop off at the supermarket for groceries on my way back. If I get back."

"If?"

"I was joking," she said, but she didn't look it. Her face was pinched, like she was scared or mad at someone or both.

"You can put the 'Closed' sign out. I don't know how long I'll be gone. Wish me luck," she said, and left.

Gary went outside to hang up the sign. The snow was coming down hard, the branches of the blue spruce covered in white. Cars drove by with their lights on. He glanced up and down the block but couldn't see much in the snowy mist. Maybe Tiffany had decided to stick close to home in this weather. She might just take Lucky to Central Park, which was closer to where she lived between Madison and Fifth. Once he'd walked her and Lucky home. She lived in a big old mansion like the kind used as foreign embassies. He wouldn't have been surprised to see a plaque outside and cars with diplomats' license plates illegally parked nearby.

The snow was thick and heavy like back in Vermont. It made him homesick. He thought again of Mom and his kid brothers and sisters, of Kathy and Coach Kline, and basketball practice. He could even hear the voices echoing in the gym. He thought of all the things he was missing. He thought of Dad buried in the cemetery, the snow silently falling on tombstones around him. He thought of how everyone in town considered him a murderer—even Mom.

It looked like Tiffany wasn't coming today. Maybe he wouldn't see her for the whole weekend. He went inside and picked up the book on transformation rituals.

It was almost an hour later when he heard someone banging at the door. He put the book down and went out into the hall. Carolyn might have forgotten her keys. She'd been very upset when she left.

He'd barely opened the door when Lucky came flying through the air, nearly knocking him down.

"Quick! Lock the door!" Tiffany said, stepping in behind the dog. Her cheeks were flushed beneath a pair of big black sunglasses, her hair wild.

"What happened?"

"Lock the door, please. He'll be looking for me!"

Gary locked the door wondering who *he* was.

"I couldn't find Iggy Pop. I had to leave him behind. I know he hid him somewhere."

"Who's he?"

"Melissa Starr."

"I thought you said 'he.'"

"Melissa Starr *is* a man. That's his nom de plume. That's French for pen name."

"I know that, but you never said Melissa Starr was a man before. I thought he was that woman who came here with you."

"Oh, *her*. She's pathetic."

They stood out in the hall, just inside the door. Lucky leaped up and licked his face, barking, adding to the confusion. Gary wondered if he should ask her in, but where would they go? She might think he intended to hit on her if he invited her to his room. Beautiful girls like Tiffany must have men hitting on them all the time. She was wearing a black leather jacket with lots of hardware. With her long red hair falling around her face and those big black sunglasses, she looked like that biker chick he'd seen in the TV movie the other night. Like a girl who'd kiss and kill, and you'd die happy. Then he saw she wasn't tough—she was scared.

"He locked me in my room, but I got Sierra to let me out." Gary figured Sierra wasn't a mountain but another romance writer. "If I don't get Iggy Pop, he'll kill him," Tiffany said. "You have to help me get him."

"How do we do that?"

"I don't know, but I'll think of something."

"Why did he lock you in the room?"

"Because I found out what he's up to. I told Jamie and Heather. I thought I could trust them, but they blabbed."

"Are they romance writers, too?"

"Yeah," Tiffany said. She reached into her leather jacket pocket and pulled out a gun. "I got this before I left. It's a thirty-eight. He keeps it under his pillow."

Gary wondered how she knew he kept it under his pillow. Did she have to make his bed or what? She was twirling the gun by the trigger. "Is that loaded?" he asked.

"What good would it be if it wasn't?" She slipped the gun back in her pocket. "Aren't you going to invite me in?"

"Oh, well, sure, but I, uh, just have a room. Is that okay?"

"Why not?"

He led the way down the hall, embarrassed to have her see a room full of summer furniture with chairs stacked up. He took a deep breath and opened the door.

"Oh, isn't this cute, just like a little summerhouse," Tiffany said. "It's small, though. That cot looks too narrow for two."

His heart stopped until it occurred to him that she must mean Lucky.

"Listen, Tiffany, I don't think Vashti will like it if you stay."

"You don't want me," Tiffany said, and started crying.

"Yes, I do, I'd really like it, but—"

When she took her sunglasses off to wipe at her tears, he saw why she'd worn them—for the same reason Mom wore them after Dad knocked her around. One eye was nearly swollen shut, the other purple, yellow, and green.

"Did Melissa Starr do that to you?"

"I'm afraid of him. I don't have anywhere else to go."

"How about your parents?"

"You mean Mom and my stepdad? Never! Vashti won't object if she doesn't know I'm here. I won't stay long. Just until after the blizzard. Lucky doesn't have any fur. He wouldn't be able to stand the cold."

The phone started ringing. Gary ignored it. Tiffany needed him. "Yeah, sure," he said, wondering how he was going to manage this.

"I knew you'd help me," Tiffany said, and planted a kiss on his lips, right there in the doorway. A spot that would be forever sacred.

Suddenly a light was shining on the stairs. "Amon, will you answer the phone, please?"

He looked up to see Vashti standing at the top of the landing. "What are *you* doing here?" she demanded. She sounded mad. Lucky began barking wildly and raced up the stairs. Gary reached for the ringing phone just as Tiffany reached into her leather jacket pocket.

CHAPTER 5

Outside, the wind pasted fat snowflakes against the office window and bent the skinny branches of a young tree. It was four o'clock in the afternoon and already dark. Lydia's desk lamp cast a small circle of light in the twilight office, but shed no light on Form CS4251-87b. Across the top someone had written *Top Priority—See to immediately*.

Lydia and P.S. were the only humans present. The animal shelter had become eerily quiet now that the others had gone home early to get ready for New Year's Eve. The only sounds were an occasional yip, the crow of a rooster recently rescued from a cockfight, and whispered phone conversations behind the closed door of P.S.'s office. This morning P.S. had come in looking mad, lips set tight. Her caramel-colored curls bobbed angrily with each step. No one crossed her, including Lydia.

Lydia took a sip of English Breakfast tea—the only tea available in the closet cum kitchen—ran her fingers through her hair, and frowned at Form CS4251-87b. She'd found it at the bottom of the in-box. Maybe Heidi had buried it there in an act of defiance. The word was that Heidi hadn't even come back to pick up her paycheck. She must have hated this place, Lydia thought. Or hated P.S. She was beginning to see why.

The form looked like the kind you filled out when you went to a new doctor for treatment. Besides asking age, sex, and breed, there were also inquiries about numerous kinds of illnesses, some she didn't even know animals were prey to. But what struck her as strange was the query about degree of sexual activity with three blanks to check off for normal, unusually active, or hyperactive. At least they hadn't gotten around to asking that in doctor's offices—yet.

Lydia had learned a lot of things in the few days she'd been at the shelter, but very little pertaining to work. The staff was like a big, dysfunctional family, with a lot of whispering, raised eyebrows, and conspiratorial and murderous looks exchanged among the vets, assistants, adoption and grief counselors, clerical workers, animal trainers, and groomers—even the rescue squad, who wasn't around that much. Of course, she was still too new to be trusted with the real dirt, but she'd caught onto the basics. There was a war going on between the Richard and the P.S. factions.

Office politics were nothing new to Lydia. It was one of the many reasons she'd quit work at *gazelle*. But political infighting was only to be expected on a fashion magazine. What she hadn't expected to find were such bitter feelings at a nonprofit animal shelter, where people were united by a common cause. Depressing.

The P.S. faction claimed that P.S., the protégée of the founder, Nora Coates, should rightfully be head of the shelter instead of her son Richard, who didn't, they said, give a damn about animals. They claimed that Nora hadn't trusted him and cut him out of her will, leaving everything to the shelter— which was the real reason Richard had taken over, so he could get his hands on the money left to the animals.

The more radical hinted of darker things, implying that Richard hadn't been, as he claimed, in Cambridge when Nora died, but right here in New York, lacing strychnine into his mother's English Breakfast tea. Nora had died of poisoning, never mind what it said on the death certificate.

The Richard faction claimed that P.S. had brought on the heart attack Nora had really died of during a heated argument over P.S.'s flagrant disregard for the animals' welfare. Subsequently, Richard had sacrificed a brilliant career as a biochemist at Harvard to come charging down from Cambridge on his white horse and rescue the animals from starvation and neglect—taking a second-rate job at Rockefeller University to keep the shelter going and giving up his life's work.

Lydia sighed. It almost made her nostalgic for her days at *gazelle*.

P.S. came striding out of the office, a coffee mug in one hand and cigarette in the other. Lydia inhaled deeply, enjoying secondhand smoke now that she'd stopped smoking again.

"P.S., is this important?" She held out the form.

P.S. leaned forward to get a good look, and snatched it from Lydia's hand. "Where did you get that?"

"It was in my in-box."

"I'll take care of it."

Lydia wondered if there was something she'd missed.

"Why are you still here?" P.S. asked.

Lydia had stayed on thinking she might be helpful. An admittedly silly thought, considering she didn't know what she was doing.

"I'm in no hurry to leave. I'm not going anywhere special."

"On New Year's Eve?"

Lydia shook her head. She remembered sitting at Mark's bedside at St. Vincent's Hospital this time last year, both knowing he wouldn't see the new year through. New Year's Eve was scarcely something she felt like celebrating.

"How about you?" Lydia asked.

P.S., suddenly friendly, plopped down on Lydia's desk, dumped the paper clips from the glass ashtray, and flicked in ashes. "Geoffrey is taking me to the Rainbow Room. He's hiring a limo with a bar and TV in back. Geoffrey does things in style. A real dreamboat. Eleven years younger than he thinks I am. My God, you're just a kid. Go out and live."

Lydia assumed Geoffrey was P.S.'s boyfriend. She didn't tell P.S. that her husband had died of AIDS in August and her good friend **Adam** had drowned a month later. It sounded too much like a soap opera. Also, she didn't want to think about it, much less discuss it. She focused her attention on P.S. When she'd heard P.S. was in her fifties, she'd thought it was just another malicious rumor spread by the Richard faction. But like poor Laura Haddon, P.S. was well preserved. Lydia tried to figure out how she did it. Mostly it was her great body—long legs and a long waist that made you forget about that long horsey face. P.S. capitalized on her assets, wearing black leggings and oversize sweaters that struck sexily at the curve of her behind. Today's sweater was caramel-colored to match her hair.

"Why aren't you going out tonight?" P.S. persisted. "You're not a bad-looking kid."

"I'm not exactly staying in. I'm going out for dinner," Lydia said, omitting to mention that the person who'd invited her was Carolyn, and dinner was downstairs in the town house. Lydia had no compunctions about lying to nosy people. She was also prepared to lie about who and where and what she was wearing, but P.S. merely said she was glad to hear it and let the subject drop.

"I'm getting some coffee, want some?" P.S. asked.

"Thanks, I'll stay with tea."

P.S. bounded up from the desk with an alacrity that made Lydia feel as ancient as Mother Teresa.

"P.S., may I ask you a question?" Lydia said, deciding that as long as P.S. was being almost friendly, she might try asking the question that no one answered.

"Shoot."

"What was that fight about between Richard and the vet?"

"Dr. Boyd? I told you, ask Richard."

"I did. He said it was a matter of shelter policy, but he didn't say what the policy was."

"There's your answer," P.S. said, and bopped out of the office.

Which was no answer at all. Lydia gave up and tried Carolyn's number again to see if there was anything she could contribute to dinner. Still no answer. Probably Carolyn had given Amon the afternoon off and was out grocery shopping.

P.S. had left Form CS4251-87b on Lydia's desk. She looked it over, trying to figure out why P.S. had snatched it away from her. It was then that she saw that the form was from the Société chimique and had nothing to do with Nora's Ark. But if it was from a French society, why wasn't the form in French and why was it from a place called Woodboro, Vermont? Richard was a biochemist. Was that the connection? She didn't get it, but then she didn't get a lot of things that went on here.

When P.S. returned with her coffee, Lydia handed her the form. "You forgot this."

"Oh yeah, thanks. This isn't ours, you know."

"I noticed. So what is it doing here?"

"Beats me," P.S. said.

Lydia had an idea that she was lying.

A few minutes later Lydia heard the murmur of P.S.'s voice in another closed-door phone session.

"Anyone home?" a cheerful voice called out, and a smiling face peeked around the door. All that good cheer depressed Lydia.

"Hi," Allegra said. She wore hot-pink ski pants, jacket, and Gucci boots, which were wet from the snow. Her creamy complexion was rosy from the cold air. Lydia wondered which came first. Had Allegra become a dermatologist because of her flawless complexion, or had being a dermatologist given her the know-how to keep it that way? Allegra's short, dark hair was as beautifully cut as her Donna Karan suits. Milke would love her.

Although the perfect grooming gave an illusion of beauty, closer inspection showed that Allegra wasn't really pretty. She had a short neck, protruding eyes, and a low forehead that the blue-black bangs didn't quite conceal.

"You came back?" Lydia asked.

"I felt guilty. I thought I could help you guys out in the office."

"Thanks. There isn't a lot to do. That is, there probably is, but I don't know enough to know what. Maybe you can tell me something, though. What was that fight about between Dr. Boyd and Richard?"

"Oh, well, I must say I'm on Orin's side."

"Orin? You know him?" Lydia assumed Orin was Dr. Boyd's first name.

"I came in before you, remember?"

Only one day before, but unlike her, Allegra was one of

those perky people who made friends quickly. "Why are you on his side instead of Richard's?"

"Well," Allegra said, wheeling up to Lydia's desk in a vintage typing chair. "After he went to all the trouble to find someone to donate property for keeping surplus animals, Richard rejected the offer."

"What are surplus animals?"

"You know, the old and sick and just plain mean, that no one wants. Richard insists on keeping them here. It's ridiculous, really. They'd be so much happier where they could have space to run."

"You mean like an animal farm?" Lydia asked, naming something dear to her heart.

"Exactly," Allegra said.

"Why won't Richard do it?"

"Because it wasn't his idea."

"But surely he wouldn't up and fire someone for making the offer."

"He didn't fire him, Orin quit." Allegra sniffed the air and waved a hand in front of her face. "You smoke?" she said, accusingly.

"Not lately."

"Well, someone's been smoking in here," she said, and spying the light under P.S.'s door, rose abruptly and headed for her office. But instead of complaining as Lydia expected, Allegra called out a friendly "Hi, may I come in?" and closed the door behind her.

Fifteen minutes later Allegra and P.S. emerged from the office, P.S. looking like a mattress in a puffy coat. "Come on, we're leaving," she called to Lydia. "Bud's holding down the fort."

"No, he isn't. He sneaked out with the others earlier on." Lydia didn't like to snitch, but Bud was the security guard and should stay on duty, after all.

"Not to worry. Richard's due in any minute. Let's go."

"Thanks. I'll just hang around until he gets here. He said someone should be here at all times."

As soon as she said it, Lydia knew she shouldn't have. It was a mistake to quote Richard to P.S.

"In case you haven't noticed, Richard Coates is an asshole," P.S. said. "Are you coming with us or staying? It won't be easy to get a cab now, and it will be impossible later."

Lydia was torn. She didn't want to stay and incur P.S.'s wrath now that P.S. had become almost friendly, but she didn't want to leave the animals unattended either.

"Come on," Allegra coaxed. "There's a blizzard out there. If you don't leave now, you'll never get home."

Why were they making such a big deal about her staying on? You'd think they'd be grateful. Didn't they worry about the animals? Lydia dug in her heels and turned stubborn. "I only live a few blocks away. I can walk."

"Suit yourself," P.S. said. She and Allegra left the office arm in arm, as if to emphasize what good friends they were, reminding Lydia of her grade-school days.

"I'll lock you in," Allegra called from the reception area.

Lydia wondered why Allegra had bothered to come back in rotten weather only to leave a half hour later.

The door slammed, and the shelter was quiet except for the crowing of the fighting cock, who didn't seem to know roosters crowed only at dawn.

To kill time, Lydia straightened out the desk drawers. She was separating adoption applications from follow-up forms and shelter stationery when she came across a sheet of paper with the beginnings of a letter.

Dear Miriam,
You said to write if the situation became desperate

The letter broke off. Desperate? Did that mean a desperate situation here or something connected with the writer's love life? Or both? Who'd written it, and when, and why had the writer stopped so abruptly? Had Heidi written this letter before the lunch she hadn't come back from—even to pick up her paycheck? What if something had happened to her? Richard had said P.S. had talked to Heidi later. But he only had P.S.'s word for it. Or for that matter, Richard could have been lying about P.S.'s calling her.

Lydia became aware of barking and yipping out in the reception area. Richard, finally! Now she could take off. But the barking had turned to growls, and the dogs wouldn't growl at Richard.

CHAPTER 6

Lydia tiptoed to the doorway and peeked out into the high-ceilinged room dimmed by the snow piled up on the glass dome. A pigtailed man with a beer gut and a bushy red beard sauntered about in snakeskin boots, carefully looking over the reception area. With him was a dark-haired girl of about seven who peered in the cages at the animals. She wore only a thin blue nylon jacket that looked inadequate for the weather, while the man was dressed warmly in a knit cap, muffler, and a plaid lumber jacket. How had they gotten in? Lydia wondered. Allegra had said she'd lock up.

The man joined the little girl at the cages. Pointing a finger at Emil, a German shepherd, he made a clicking sound as if he were pulling a trigger. Emil leaped against the cage.

Undaunted by Emil's snarls and leaps, the man started fiddling with the door of his cage.

"Open that cage, cowboy, and he'll take your head off," Lydia said, stepping out of the doorway. She had no idea if this were true. Judy, the animal trainer, claimed Emil was docile and lovable and insisted that all he needed was a good home.

"Greetings and salutations," the man said, stripping Lydia with his eyes. Not easy that, since she was covered from turtle-necked chin to ankle boots. "You the person I'm supposed to see?" He spoke in a hoarse voice as if he had a cold.

"See?" she asked. "About what?"

The man looked her over again, but this time seemed to be sizing her up. "About getting my girl a dog for Christmas."

"That doesn't mean you can reach in and grab one," Lydia said. "Christmas was a week ago. Aren't you kind of late?"

"You know how kids are. She wasn't happy with what she got. Said she wanted a dog."

Lydia stooped to make eye contact with the child. "Do you want a pet? It's a big responsibility."

"Sure she wants one."

"I asked her."

"She's shy."

"Why do you want a pet?" she asked the little girl.

To divert her attention, the man pointed to a mixed-breed puppy. "How about him?" he asked the girl. "Ain't he cute?" He turned to Lydia. "She wants that one."

"You didn't ask, you told her."

"I know what she wants. She's my kid."

Lydia wasn't so sure. She was a beautiful little girl who didn't look at all like the bearded man. The child could have been bribed to come along as a cover-up. Bunchers sometimes did that. She'd read an article about them in a fact sheet published by PETA, the People for the Ethical Treatment of Animals. Bunchers were the dregs of humanity, just a few notches above child molesters, people who preyed on helpless, trusting animals. They grabbed pets from backyards, cars in parking lots, or tied to a parking meter while their owners were on errands. They even ran fake ads in the newspapers claiming they wanted to adopt a pet. When they got a bunch of animals together, they sold them to a dealer, often one with a license, who conveniently pretended he didn't know that the animals were cherished pets and sold them to hospitals or university research labs for experimentation. Or the animals might be sold illegally, and for far larger sums of money, to commercial laboratories that were part of such companies as cosmetic manufacturers. There were even cases in which animals had been sold to religious cults for bloody sacrifices.

"I'll get you an application to fill out. You can bring it in Monday after New Year's," Lydia said. She felt a flash of hatred so intense that she involuntarily stepped back.

"Forget it. I'm not filling out any fucking form. I'll get you for this," the man said, and yanked the child out the door.

Lydia locked up after them and returned to her office feeling shaken. After closing the venetian blind so that no one could see she was alone, she sat at her desk and worried about the little girl, sure that she was unrelated to the man. Maybe the man was screwing the kid's mother, who was too high on crack to care what happened to her child.

She checked her watch. Not quite five, but it felt like midnight. Where was Richard? To pass the time, she wandered into P.S.'s inner sanctum and snooped around. No one went into P.S.'s office unless they were invited, and few were.

The wall was covered with various posters featuring William Wegman's weimaraners in different costumes and poses. Also a calorie chart. The desk held a small copper kettle of dried blue wildflowers, a wicked-looking dagger letter opener, and a pile of newspapers and magazine clippings.

Flicking idly through the clippings, Lydia came to a highlighted magazine item and began reading about the prevalence of women with a "poker-faced look." It reminded her of something, but she couldn't think what.

"At first, I thought this look was endemic to New York City women," said William Walsh of Thorne & Rudman, "but my job calls for a lot of traveling, and I've been seeing that look in every city of any size, from Albuquerque to Atlanta. Women with power jobs. Smiles that never go beyond their lips. Makes you wonder if it isn't an occupational hazard, if these women wouldn't be happier doing what comes naturally—tending to home, husband, and children."

The article went on to say that the others hadn't gone so far as to ascribe the look to unhappiness in the workplace but to an unlucky choice of plastic surgeon.

Then she remembered Milke's cigarette holder tapping on

an item in a newsmagazine on the very same subject. Funny that it had caught both Milke's and P.S.'s attention. Written in the margins of various articles were the names of the magazines (mostly *Newsweek* and *Time*) and newspapers (*The Washington Post*, Cleveland *Plain Dealer*, *Chicago Tribune*, and *The New York Times*), along with the dates that covered the period of April to December. The pieces all repeated essentially the same thing. Besides Poker Face, the expressions were alternately described as Frozen Face, Stone Face, The Trance, PopEyes, and the Bug-Eyed Look.

Lydia was wondering why P.S. was so intrigued by these items when she heard the phone ring in her office. She rushed to answer it, hoping it would be Richard saying he was on his way. It was Kramer. The third time today. He was still lamenting the fact that his mother had broken her word. She'd volunteered to sit with Andy so that they could see each other on New Year's Eve, then changed her mind, saying she was going out. "She didn't even say with whom. I mean who with," Kramer amended. He thought he wouldn't sound like a real cop if he spoke correct English.

"Look, it's okay. Carolyn has invited me to dinner. Your mother has a right to go out and enjoy herself," Lydia said, feeling generous. She wasn't as sorry about not seeing him tonight as he was about not seeing her. "After all, she's what? In her sixties?"

"She's seventy-one."

"Well, that's scarcely doddering. She might even be going out with some man."

"Do you think so?" Kramer sounded worried.

"I intend to be going out with men in my nineties," said Lydia, ignoring the fact that she scarcely dated now.

"Yeah, you're right. I'm being selfish."

"You're not the least bit selfish. You're one of the nicest people I know. If I were celebrating New Year's Eve, I'd like it to be with you. Only I really don't feel much like celebrating."

"Tuesday I'm driving Andy to Montreal to visit a few days with my former in-laws—Laura's family," Kramer said. Laura was his dead wife. "Andy's way ahead in her class so they don't mind if I keep her out an extra week."

Lydia suspected Kramer was leading up to something, and she was right.

"I have an idea, but I'm not sure you'd go for it."

"Try me," she said.

"If you came along, we could stop at a ski resort after I dropped Andy off. I know a couple of great places where the slopes aren't so mobbed."

Lydia twirled a paper clip on the end of her pencil. "Tuesday is short notice. And how will Laura's parents feel when they see us together?"

"Hey, Lydia, it's been seven years."

"All the same, it must be wrenching. Let me think about it, okay?"

After wishing each other a sad Happy New Year, they hung up.

She went on twirling the paper clip, wondering if she wanted to spend a few days—or nights, which is what the trip was really about—with Kramer. She didn't want to get into anything serious. After Mark had died, she'd sworn she'd never get involved with another man, and here she was heading in that direction with Kramer in less than six months. It had taken Kramer seven years to recover from his wife's death. He was sweet and thoughtful and they shared a certain chemistry. But Mark had had the same attributes, besides being beautiful, talented, intelligent, and charming. If Mark, who had everything, had failed her, what could she expect of an ordinary mortal?

A door slammed somewhere in back. Lydia paused in her paperclip twirling and listened. In the sudden stillness, she heard the paper clip drop on her desk. Richard never came in the back way. But how could she be sure? She'd been here for less than a week. Bud, the security guard, should have locked up in back, but he was drunk most of the time and might have forgotten. What if the man with the bushy beard had dropped off the little girl and come back to steal the animals? Or the teenage animal torturers returned? That part of the shelter spooked her, with its maze of hallways and numerous rooms. Goddammit, where was Richard anyway?

Lydia walked out into the reception area. She wasn't about to risk an encounter with Bushy Beard by going into the bowels of the shelter alone. She'd take Emil along for protection. But looking at him—ears up, body tense—she wondered if she should risk opening the cage. Despite Judy's claim that Emil was now tractable and adoptable, he looked fierce, ready to take her head off.

"Yo, Emil baby, how we doing?" she asked, speaking the kind of language she imagined a tough dog like Emil would better understand.

Emil's ears twitched and his eyes rolled white. The rescue squad had had to tranquilize him when they'd brought him in. Still, Judy knew how to deal with hard cases. She called it tough love. Lydia let Emil sniff her hand, and when he didn't bite it off, she opened the cage door.

Emil bounded out, then waited patiently while she attached the leash. Mental note: Tough love works. Remember that the next time you're fool enough to fall in love, she told herself.

Emil preceded her along the main corridor, ears up, on the alert. Did he know something she didn't? The corridor was bright with fluorescent lights and white-painted walls. Shadowless. Hallways veered off in various directions. Lydia gingerly tried the doors to various rooms—grooming, examining, surgery, and recovery. The holding rooms, where the animals were kept, locked automatically. She always had to remember to take her keys along if she wanted to get out. Screaming and banging on doors wouldn't help since the walls were soundproofed to prevent the animals from hearing noises in the hall and starting a ruckus inside, overexciting themselves, and setting one another off.

Emil took the ramp to the storeroom in the back of the building leading to the outside run. Lydia followed, giving him his lead. He sensed things better than she did. They walked in shadows now. No more fluorescent lights, just plain lightbulbs, some of which had burned out and had yet to be replaced by the maintenance crew.

Emil growled.

"What is it, boy?" she asked.

Almost at the same moment a trolley loaded with heavy equipment rolled down the ramp toward them, speeding up with momentum. Lydia dived out of the way. So did Emil.

"Watch out!" a cheerful voice called—after the trolley smashed into the wall. The sound of equipment falling from the trolley echoed down the halls, followed by a maniacal laugh like the Joker's in *Batman*. Bud, the security guard, stepped out of the shadows. He was tieless and not wearing his uniform jacket. "Scared ya, huh?" he asked, a sloppy grin on his face.

Lydia tried to make allowances for the fact that Bud wasn't too bright. Gorilla shoulders and a dinosaur brain. And drank on the job. He should have been fired long ago. But she'd been told that Richard wouldn't fire him out of regard for his dead mother, Nora, who'd had a sentimental attachment to Bud since he'd come with the building, so to speak—not the church part, but the warehouse, where he'd worked as a guard before she had bought it and converted it into the shelter.

"How come you're still here?" Bud asked.

"Because I thought you weren't. I saw you leave with the others."

"That was for coffee."

He'd probably gone out for a drink. "We have coffee here," she said, and headed back.

Bud was still laughing about scaring her half to death.

Lydia couldn't bring herself to put Emil back into a cage. If he'd whined or given her pleading looks, she could have handled it. Instead he ran to the door as if to say, Let's go home. Lydia lured him into her office with some dog biscuits. She put on her Garbo hat and long black coat, wishing she could take Emil with her. But Colombo's feelings would be hurt. He hadn't yet recovered from the death of his master. For weeks he'd waited at the door for Adam to come and claim him. Lydia had fruitlessly hoped that either Carolyn, or his other ex-wife, Vanessa, would take him. Then she'd become hooked. Colombo and she belonged together. But what to do with brave, sweet Emil longing for a home?

It could break your heart working here.

She was psyching herself up for caging Emil when the dogs in the reception area began barking. This time they sounded friendly. Even the crow of the fighting cock had a welcome note to it. A minute later Richard appeared in her office doorway. He wore an anorak and trousers tucked into his boots, looking like he'd come from the north woods instead of the East Sixties.

"Rotten night," he said. "It was murder out there. Cars skidding all over the street and into each other, tying up traffic. Sorry it took me so long to get here."

"You could have saved time by walking."

"Yeah, but I had my car." He wiped off his foggy horn-rims with a linen handkerchief initialed RC, and set the glasses back on a long, lonely nose.

Lydia stood with her coat on ready to leave, but it seemed rude to take off the moment he arrived. After hanging his anorak on the coatrack, Richard came and stood by her desk, straightened the desk pad, and toyed with some pens in a mug as if he were working up to saying something.

"Coming down with a cold," he said, and sneezed as if to prove it. Which wasn't, she guessed, what he wanted to say. He looked around. She shifted from one foot to the other.

"Awfully quiet here," he said. "Where is everyone?"

The wall clock said 5:37. "They left early to prepare for their big night out on the town."

"A good reason to stay in and avoid the mob."

"Agreed."

"Why are you still here?"

"Busy," she said, not wanting to explain about how she'd thought Bud had sneaked out. She was more concerned about leaving, but first had to ask her question. "What's the real reason you didn't accept Dr. Boyd's offer?"

Richard pushed his glasses up on his nose and sighed. "The offer is as phony as he is. If this place actually exists, which I doubt, we'd have to build a shelter and find people to staff it.

And although Mother and I disagreed on a lot of things, there was one thing we did agree on, which is that just because an animal is aging and ill doesn't mean it hasn't a chance of finding a home. You'd be surprised at how many people want to adopt them. Why be so quick to put them out to pasture?

"Furthermore, Dr. Boyd isn't a doctor of veterinary medicine. He faked it. I checked with Cornell. They'd never heard of the guy. Of course, P.S. doesn't believe me."

"Why not?"

"She likes him. A lot of people do. Anything else you want to know? Any problems?"

"A buncher came in. I think that's what he was. He had a little kid with him as a decoy."

"Big guy? Red beard? Pigtail?"

"How did you know?"

"A Vermont shelter faxed an alert. I should have warned you."

"Well, someone should have." She was getting overheated in her coat. "Okay, I'm leaving now. Would you mind putting Emil back? I took him out of the cage for company."

"He can keep me company, too."

But when she headed for the door, Emil trotted after her, apparently preferring her to Richard. She gave him a good-bye kiss between the ears.

"See you tomorrow," Richard called, appearing in the office doorway.

"Tomorrow? Don't tell me you expect me to be here on a holiday!"

"I meant for open house. No one mentioned it? You might want to come and get acquainted with your fellow workers." He was interrupted by a coughing spell. "It starts at two-thirty. It's a tradition. People who used to work here come, too. They bring their spouses and kids or"—he paused—"whatevers."

"Yes, okay. Maybe."

"Is there anyone you might like to bring?" he asked.

"I don't have any whatevers."

Richard smiled. "Neither do I," he said. "Happy New Year," he called as she went out the door.

CHAPTER 7

Lydia plunged through the snow, glad to get away from the shelter with all its problems and out into an uncomplicated blizzard. The night sky cast an eerie, whitish light. The air was crisp. Clean. She stuck out her tongue to taste the snowflakes, recalling childhood winters, belly flopping onto a sled, hurtling down a hill and out onto the frozen Great Miami River. Her sister, Chots, had stood by clutching her sled to her chest and crying, afraid to try the hill and jealous of Lydia's enjoyment, which Lydia enjoyed all the more because of her little sister's tears.

She passed few people on her way home. The snow leaked into her ankle boots, and by the time she reached Second Avenue, her feet were icy chunks. A sneaky wind caught her unaware, whipping her hair across her face. Second Avenue had been cleared by a snowplow—fine for drivers, but pedestrians had to climb mountainous snowdrifts at crosswalks. Traffic moved at a fairly good clip, snow swirling in car headlights. Except for an ecstatic husky rolling in the snow, everyone plodded along, head down, shoulders hunched. She wanted to tell them to look at the jazzy neon signs throwing pink, green, and blue shadows on the snowy streets, at the tops of skyscrapers floating above the clouds. See how beautiful the city could be.

Of course, tomorrow would be one big, sloppy mess.

She remembered a snowy afternoon in Central Park with Mark and his Leica. Sun splintered by the bare branches of trees, an ice-blue sky above creamy hills, backed by West Side apartment buildings. An afternoon like a surrealist movie. She saw it all in slow motion. A snowball leaving Mark's gloved hand, taking forever to sail toward her. His head thrown back, hair tousled, smiling, laughing. Beautiful beautiful Mark.

Beautiful and dangerous. Reckless. How reckless she hadn't guessed. He'd hidden it from her and continued playing Russian roulette with his beautiful body. Maybe that's what attracted her to Kramer. Kramer was safe. But a cop's life could be dangerous. Was she attracted to the wrong man again? Why not fall for someone like Richard Coates, nice and bland? He'd be good for her. But so was bean curd. On the other hand, Richard might be as evil as Boyd had claimed. Which did not increase his appeal. Danger was one thing, evil another.

She turned onto Seventy-eighth and followed tire tracks down the middle of the street. The only cars around were small white hills strung along the curb. The harsh sound of metal scraping cement carried to her ears in the pillowed stillness. Across the street and up ahead, Amon, wearing only black jeans and his yin-yang sweatshirt, shoveled snow off an already snow-cleared sidewalk, stopping occasionally to look in her direction.

Why was the kid working so late anyway? Especially on New Year's Eve. Carolyn worked him too hard. What he needed was to play a little. Lydia packed a snowball and lobbed it his way. The snowball clipped his ear.

"Gotcha," she said, pleased with herself. But before she could take aim with another snowball, a high-speed missile whizzed by. "Hey! That came too close for comfort."

He grinned at her under the streetlight. Another snowball whizzed by. She hadn't even seen it leave his hand. She'd hate to think what would have happened if he'd hit her. He packed a lot of power into that throw.

"Hey, kid, you've got a killer's eye."

Amon stopped in his tracks. Blood drained from his face. Even in the dim light, she could see his pallor. Lydia heard a car coming up from behind and jumped to the sidewalk. The car window rolled down and a cop stuck his head out. "Watch it, lady, or I'll run you in."

Haggerty was driving. DiFilippi rolled up the window on

the passenger side before she could take aim. She smashed a snowball against the back window.

"That could get you in trouble," Amon said. "They're cops."

"Also friends." At least DiFilippi was. Lydia had met them back when Adam's killer had been out to get her.

"Excuse me, got to get back to work," Amon said, his voice as icy as the air, and resumed shoveling away nothing.

Obviously a friend of the law was no friend of his. But they'd been in a plainclothes car, an ordinary Toyota, identifiable only to other cops—or criminals. Lydia remembered how pale Amon had become when he spied the car. Or was that because she'd said he had a killer's eye? Whichever it was, she didn't like it.

She'd become suspicious of Amon ever since she'd gotten Carolyn to admit that she hadn't met him through a *Village Voice* ad but when he'd tried to snatch her purse. "He's a mere child," Carolyn had said, excusing him. "And he was far more frightened than I was."

Lydia didn't consider purse snatching as trivial as Carolyn obviously did, and had been surprised and disappointed to hear that the kid was a thief, however unsuccessful. It had been Carolyn's lying she'd suspected, not Amon. But now that she thought of it, the kid was too sweet, too quiet, too polite—the kind the neighbors always expressed surprise about when the bodies turned up in the backyard.

"You'll have to go in through Carolyn's part of the house," Amon said just behind her as she lifted the latch on the iron gate. She hadn't known he was following her.

"Why?"

"The elevator broke down," he said, suddenly appearing in front of her like Aladdin's genie, and blocking her way to the downstairs door.

"Not again," she said.

"Carolyn couldn't get a repairman on New Year's Eve. I tried to fix it, but I didn't do any good."

"Yeah, okay. Thanks for telling me. You're working late. Doesn't Father Whatsis set a curfew?"

"Father Spence. He said we could stay out later on New

Year's Eve," Amon said, and watched until she reached the stoop steps, then disappeared into the house.

Lydia ran up the steps, keeping to the area he'd shoveled clear. It was already covered with a sprinkling of snow.

Carolyn had grossly misled her when she'd said the elevator would be her own private entrance, Lydia thought, unlocking the door. Also, she'd had to have a special lock installed on the elevator door after a dejected dalmation had suddenly appeared in her living room, along with its owner. Considering that she was only staying for a week, Lydia was annoyed at having to shell out extra money for the special lock. At this rate, she'd have saved money by staying at the Plaza.

The house was quiet. No sign of Carolyn.

Lydia headed up the two flights of stairs to her apartment. The minute she entered, a giant whirl of orange fur greeted her. She gave Colombo a hug. He danced his dog dance around her as she put on his leash. "You're not going to like that snow," she told him. Wrong. He loved it.

A half hour later she was back in her apartment with a happy dog and frozen toes. Lydia dropped her Greta Garbo hat on the pie-crust table, hung up her coat, and kicked off her boots. She dried her nearly frostbitten feet with a fluffy towel, then dried Colombo's paws. After that, she put on a pair of warm white socks and poured herself a glass of strega. She'd already been coffee-and-tea'd to death at the shelter.

Seated on the couch, inhaling the liqueur and listening to the mellow tick of the grandfather clock, she absorbed the soothing effect of a room bathed in the violet glow of the grape-etched Tiffany lamp—all, excluding the liqueur, compliments of Carolyn. That was just the trouble. It was impossible to stay mad at the woman.

Lydia thought again of Amon and wondered if he'd been waiting for her when he was outside shoveling snow. He must have been since he'd gone in right after he'd announced that the elevator was broken. He wouldn't have been waiting around to tell her that, would he? Still he was a conscientious kid, and it was difficult figuring out what went on in the mind of a fourteen-year-old boy, although Carolyn still insisted he was seventeen—probably so she could calm her conscience if and when she seduced him.

Lydia became aware of the winking answering machine. Maybe Kramer had left a welcome-home message as he sometimes did—something funny, or just plain sweet, or telling her the kind of dumb joke he knew would make her laugh.

"It's tough returning to an empty place when you're used to finding someone there," he'd said, speaking from experience. But at least he'd had Andy to come home to after Laura died. Well, she had Colombo. But lovable as he might be, Colombo still left certain things to be desired. She pressed playback. "Happy New Year," a perky female voice said. "This is to remind you that you are due for your annual dental checkup with Dr. Greenberg on Tuesday, January fourth, at two-thirty." Obviously, a woman lacking in sensitivity if she thought the prospect of seeing a dentist was something to look forward to.

Two hang-ups followed. Wrong numbers or someone selling something. Lydia polished off her strega and flopped down on the couch. She wasn't due downstairs at Carolyn's until eight. She looked forward to a nice uneventful supper and a quiet New Year's Eve watching one of Carolyn's collection of Disney animal movies or her own current favorite, *Babe*— unlike life, something with a guaranteed happy ending.

CHAPTER 8

Promptly at eight o'clock, wearing blue jeans and a "Support the Right to Arm Bears" T-shirt, Lydia took the stairs down to Carolyn's, carrying her contributions of vegetable couscous and Moët.

The hall on the bedroom floor was dark. Usually Carolyn kept the light on, since it never occurred to her to turn it off.

The living room was also dark, except for a pair of glowing, copper, Orphan Annie eyes. Juggling bowl and bottle, Lydia flicked on the switch. An empty Shaker rocker pitched back and forth. Alf was here. She'd glimpsed Carolyn's cat before, a beautiful tawny-haired, baby-faced Persian. Glimpses were all she ever got. Alf ran from everyone but Carolyn, who'd used the acronym of the Animal Liberation Front, the animal activist group that had rescued him, for his name. They'd found him with electrons implanted in his head when they'd raided a research lab. He was one of the few animals who'd survived the experiments performed on them, and Carolyn had volunteered to take him.

After calling Carolyn's name and getting no answer, Lydia walked from dark living room to dark dining room and into the kitchen, where a light shone on a grocery bag slumped on the counter.

The kitchen wasn't like most narrow New York kitchens, but large and old-fashioned, with wooden cupboards and an informal grouping of table and chairs by a window. Snow piled high on the outside window ledges. The night appeared a ghostly white against a backdrop of blurred lights from tall buildings.

The grocery bag was half-unpacked. Wilting vegetables, cartons, cans, and a container of melted ice cream sat haphazardly out on the counter. The ice cream had dripped into a beige puddle on the linoleum floor. Remembering the melting ice cream at that famous double murder in Los Angeles, Lydia felt a sudden chill. Absurd. Nothing had happened to Carolyn. No doubt she'd been interrupted by a phone call while unpacking the groceries. Or perhaps she'd forgotten some important ingredient and run out to Gristede's to get it. But would she be likely to do that in a blizzard? And would Gristede's be open after eight on New Year's Eve? Maybe Carolyn remembered something that needed tending to downstairs at the spa. And left the ice cream to melt?

Lydia punched the animal spa number and got a busy signal.

She sighed. That explained it. Carolyn had dashed downstairs for some trivial reason, the phone had rung, and she'd started talking. Carolyn could outtalk any teenager on the phone. She was probably chatting away down there, unmindful of a hungry dinner guest. Or she might be deliberately prolonging the call so her guest would prepare dinner.

After mopping up the ice-cream puddle, Lydia searched the refrigerator for inspiration on what to eat. Not much in the way of nourishment—Perrier, Dom Pérignon, two eggs, and some yellowing cottage cheese. A box of Kron chocolates resided in an otherwise empty crisper. Lydia helped herself to several pieces, half expecting her mother to scold her for spoiling her supper.

Back at the counter, she inspected the cans, cartons, and wilting vegetables: tofu, bean sprouts, scallions, ginger root, water chestnuts, sesame-seed oil, and a box of tapioca. Obviously Carolyn planned something Chinese. But what Chinese recipe called for tapioca pudding?

It suddenly occurred to Lydia that the spa phone might be on the blink, downed by the blizzard, which would explain the busy signal. At any rate, it wouldn't hurt to check. She took the stairs two at a time, calling Carolyn's name as she descended. Only an echo answered. She paused at the landing. Down below, the hall light, which she'd thought of as bright, looked dim, leaving the hallway in shadows. A thin yellow line showed under the office door. Lydia descended the rest of the steps noisily to scare away any possible intruders. But all the ground-floor windows were barred, and Amon wasn't the kind of kid to forget to lock up so someone could walk in. Still, he was a kid, and kids forgot.

She checked the door leading to the courtyard. Triple-locked. She walked back to the office, opened the door, and looked in. A light shone on a desk littered with papers and a coffee mug with the PETA logo of a running rabbit. Among the papers was a copy of the list of nationwide animal shelters stamped PROPERTY OF NORA'S ARK, above it the name "H. Exner" written in ink. Who was H. Exner and how had Carolyn come by Nora's Ark property? Shelter names in the eastern states had been checked off. Had Carolyn been calling them? What about?

Lydia headed for the Tranquility Room, still troubled by the cluttered desk. Carolyn was a neatness freak—she wouldn't have left such a mess. Just outside the Tranquility Room, Lydia saw the reason for the busy signal—the phone dangled off the hook. After restoring the phone to its proper place, she tried the ram's-head doorknob. The knob didn't give. Locked. Lydia had never known Carolyn to lock the door before.

Maybe Amon could tell her where Carolyn had gone. He must have returned to the Episcopalian shelter by now. She'd give him a call. Back in Carolyn's office, she got the Horizon House number from the operator and punched it in. A kid answered.

"Could I speak to Amon?" she asked.

"Amon who?"

"I don't know his last name. Ask around. Someone there must know him."

"I know everyone here, and there's no such person, first or last name," the kid said, and hung up.

Well, of course. She'd known all along that Carolyn had given him that name.

Lydia glanced at Carolyn's appointment calendar, even though she didn't expect to find anything, since Amon kept track of what few appointments there were. Besides, if Carolyn had left in a hurry, she'd scarcely make a note of it. The December 31 page was blank, except for the formula $A = Y + B^2$. Some animal-food formula for special treats during treatment?

Lydia was starting to get seriously worried. Granted, Carolyn was an impulsive person, prone to doing things on whim, but she wouldn't have left the phone dangling off the hook, a littered desk, groceries half-unpacked, and ice cream out to melt. But then Carolyn might be upstairs right now, back from wherever she'd been and wondering what had happened to her.

Lydia hadn't taken more than three steps up when she heard a small thud in the vicinity of the storage room. She froze. Listened. Silence.

Probably a mouse or a squirrel. Some small animal that had

managed to get in from the garden. Was she going to begrudge
the poor little thing safe haven from a blizzard?

She started up the steps again, and had just arrived at the
landing when she heard another thud. Louder this time. Too
loud for a small animal. She wished she'd thought to bring
Colombo along and that she hadn't turned off the light, leaving
the hall in darkness. She told herself she was being needlessly
edgy. The outside door was locked and the windows were
barred. It had to be an animal. Maybe something bigger than a
squirrel. Hadn't a coyote been spotted in Brooklyn a while
back?

Unbidden, a picture came to her of Carolyn gagged and tied
to a chair, desperately throwing things at the door to get her attention. Idiotic. But if it was so idiotic, why not check and
prove to herself how idiotic it was? Put her mind at rest.

Lydia tiptoed back down the stairs. Standing in the hallway,
listening, she became aware of an unfamiliar scent, something
like cinnamon sprinkled on a tropical flower. The scent wasn't
Carolyn's, whose perfume smelled of musk and money.

Lydia wondered if it was her imagination, or if someone
stood on the other side of the storage-room door.

DiFilippi had told her to call the precinct whenever she suspected anything, but that was back when terrible things were
happening. No one was after her now. He was probably off
duty anyway. Even if he wasn't, he'd come with his sidekick,
Haggerty, an obnoxious type who'd smirked when she'd said
she was being stalked.

Lydia waited, straining her ears in the silence. Nothing. She
stepped forward, turned the doorknob, and entered. Fumbling
for the wall switch, she heard the rain just before night crashed
down.

CHAPTER 9

Cold hard cement.

She opened her eyes.

Amon crouched over her, swabbing her forehead with a damp towel.

"You okay?" he asked.

"What happened? Why are you here? Where's Carolyn?"

His eyes strayed toward the storage-room door. "She isn't here," he said. His voice cracked.

"Obviously."

Had his voice cracked because he was lying or because he was an adolescent? Again she thought of Carolyn in the storage room, trussed up, with a handkerchief stuffed in her mouth. But that was crazy. Amon adored Carolyn. It suddenly occurred to Lydia that she might have interrupted a seduction in progress. Carolyn had finally gotten Amon where she wanted him—in bed, or in this case, on a wicker sofa—and she wasn't about to let something like dinner interrupt.

But there was a wild, cornered look in Amon's eyes—like the look she'd seen in animals ready to fight to their death—that she doubted he'd have if nothing but some hanky-panky was going on. Lydia tried to recall if she'd actually been inside the storage room when she was hit. She remembered opening the door. She remembered the sound of rain. Rain? Now the door was closed, and she lay out in the hall, flat on her back. How did that happen?

She sat up and, feeling dizzy, lay back again. She fingered her head for lumps. Nothing noticeable, but there was a very tender spot at the crown. "Who zapped me?"

Amon's eyes opened wide in feigned innocence. "Vashti said to put the rain stick over the storage-room door so it would bonk anyone who broke in. Guess it worked."

Especially with someone wielding it, Lydia didn't say. "I thought you kept the rain stick in the Tranquility Room."

"We have two." His eyes darted nervously toward the storage room again. The door was open a quarter of an inch. Lydia could have sworn it had been closed a minute ago. Was someone standing behind it, listening?

"Maybe you should get checked out in Emergency at Lenox Hill Hospital. It's just a few blocks away. If you want, I'll go with you," Amon said.

Nice of him to offer to help after he'd whacked her.

"I'm okay."

She tried sitting up again. Not so bad this time. Amon gave her a hand, and she got shakily to her feet. Without saying a word, she headed toward the storage room.

He stepped in front of her, blocking the way. "You shouldn't move around too much in your condition."

"Just wanted to see how that thing managed to fall on me."

"I told you. The rain stick was positioned over the door so it would fall the minute anyone opened it." He remained unmoving. She was five-nine, but he already had an inch or two on her. His eyes said back off. She hadn't known brown eyes could be so cold. Someone had to hit hard to knock her out like that. Amon was shaky—jittery. Was he harboring a little thug friend in there? She'd like to ask him what his real name was and where he was staying if not Horizon House, but now was not the time. Still, she might be able to find out something without danger of bodily harm.

"I thought you had a curfew at Horizon House," she said.

"I thought I told you they let us stay out later tonight."

Little smart-ass. He knew enough to keep his lie consistent, at least. "You've been hanging around down here all this time?" she asked.

"I came back to give you Vashti's message. I forgot to tell you before I left."

"What message? You could have called me on the phone."

"I did. I got your machine. Vashti said to tell you she might be late. She had to look in on Iggy Pop."

"Iggy Pop? That obscene rock star?"

"It's an iguana."

"Whose? And why is Carolyn looking in on it? She isn't a vet."

"She's better than a vet. She cures without pills. And tends to the spirit as well as the body."

"And could get sued for practicing medicine without a license. You didn't say who owned Iggy Pop."

"He's residing at the home of a romance writer."

"Residing?"

"Yeah. He doesn't belong there."

"You mean the romance writer doesn't own him? What's her name?"

He hesitated. "Why do you want to know?"

"Just curious."

For a minute she thought he wouldn't tell her. "Melissa Starr," he said, as reluctant as if he were the CIA disclosing a secret.

"How long ago did Carolyn leave?"

"Gee, I dunno. A little after you came in."

"That was hours ago. She should have called me instead of leaving it to you."

"It's my fault. She didn't know I'd forget. She'll be back any minute," he said, clearly anxious to get rid of her. He twisted the terrycloth towel around his arm as he'd have liked to twist it around her neck. Terrycloth? Then it dawned on her.

"Does Carolyn know you're camping out in there?" Lydia asked, nodding toward the storage room.

"What makes you think I am?"

"I called Horizon House. They've never heard of an Amon anyone. And the washroom has paper towels, not terrycloth."

"Carolyn said I could."

"She didn't tell me."

"She said you think I'm a career criminal because I snatched her pocketbook."

"You mean tried to. A career criminal would have done better."

"Am I supposed to thank you for that?" he asked.

She laughed. He smiled a smile that would have left her weak in the knees if she was a kid his age, and left her none too steady now. She wondered if he and his little thug friend—if that was who hid behind the door—had contraband stashed in the storage room. She'd love to have a look in there, but she wouldn't have the chance tonight. He'd be sure to stick around now that he knew she was onto him.

"Okay, see you later," she said, and started up the stairs, aware that her exposed back made a nice target for a knife or a bullet. She stopped and quickly turned around. He was standing, hands in pockets, looking harmless enough. "By the way, where does this Melissa Starr live?" She deliberately sprang it on him, not giving him time to lie. It worked.

"One of those big old mansions on Seventieth Street near Fifth Avenue. Why?"

"Just curious." It sounded like he'd been there, or been by at least, which made her more curious.

Back upstairs, Lydia rummaged around the kitchen and found a giant bag of Wisconsin-cheddar popcorn to assuage her hunger until Carolyn got back. Since that could be any minute, there was no point in returning to her apartment. She went into Carolyn's living room to keep watch. Two copper eyes glowed in the dark.

"It's okay, Alf, I'm a friend."

Alf didn't believe it. He was gone.

Lydia left the lights off and parked herself on the sofa by the window, reminding herself to keep her popcorn-greasy hands off Carolyn's Florentine watered silk.

She could imagine what Melissa Starr looked like—a blond Jackie Collins decked out in false eyelashes, clothes that fit like panty hose, and the kind of strained face and tendoned neck that came from strenuous workouts to keep in shape.

A car passed by, driving as slowly as if it were in a funeral cortege. Apparently, the blizzard was too much for the Sanitation Department to deal with—most of the side streets were nearly impassable. At least muggings and rapes would be down. Not that the muggers and rapists weren't out there. Like the proverbial postman, neither rain, heat, nor gloom of night stayed them from the completion of their appointed rounds. Especially the gloom of night. There were just fewer potential victims abroad on a night like tonight. Bad weather had its plus side.

A limo drove up in front of the town house across the street and a few minutes later a couple came out, dressed to the nines, the woman bundled up in what looked like ermine, the man in a chesterfield coat and tuxedo. Lydia remembered how gorgeous Mark had looked in his tuxedo. They'd been seeing each other for a little over a month when they'd gone to Milke's New Year's Eve party, and had slipped away just after midnight to go to his loft and make love. She remembered the rain on the skylight above them, and thinking nothing could be better. Nothing had been. She doubted it ever would be.

Lydia tore herself away from her memories to keep street watch. Gaslights in front of her favorite store, the Antique Mystique, flickered shadows on the snow. She could hear carriages clip-clop by in the snow and imagined that Jack the Ripper, in top hat and opera cape, lurked in the darkness.

Lydia checked her watch. A quarter to ten. Hard to believe that Carolyn would stay away so long without calling. Had Amon lied? Were he and his little thug friend holding her prisoner down in the storage room? She couldn't very well conduct a search of his living quarters, but she just might drop in on Melissa Starr and see if Carolyn was really there. Drop in? Melissa Starr lived some ten blocks away. Besides, she didn't know her address. All she knew was that the lady lived on Seventieth near Fifth. But Amon had said it was an old mansion. There couldn't be many of those around. Anyway, she was too edgy just to sit and wait. And the exercise would be good for her.

Lydia ran up the stairs to her place. She put on her Garbo hat and ankle-length coat. Colombo thumped his tail eagerly, assuming he was going for his walk.

"Later," she said. But why not now? It wasn't as if she were paying a social visit. If she found Melissa Starr's place she'd merely ring the bell and ask for Carolyn. If Carolyn was there, to hell with her. Lydia would come back home and order take-out. But if she wasn't, then what? Lydia told herself she'd figure that out later.

CHAPTER 10

Colombo tugged at his leash. Lydia skidded behind him down the icy steps to the sidewalk, where he stopped, sniffed out the right snowdrift, and peed. On Third Avenue, the snow was packed down by foot traffic, and he happily trotted alongside her.

Considering how hard the snow was falling, a surprising number of people were out, mostly New Year's celebrants tooting horns and shouting. Colors seemed brighter, sounds louder, and spirits higher. Including hers. Lydia was glad she'd come out. She crossed from Third Avenue to Lexington and on over to Park, heading downtown.

The farther west she went, the quieter. The night became hushed and obscurely eerie. By the time she reached Madison and Seventieth Street, traffic was light and she passed only one person—an earmuffed jogger, exhaling frosty breath, running in the opposite direction. She found no mansion to match Amon's description on either side of the block between Madison and Fifth Avenue. Maybe she'd missed it, although that didn't seem easy since Central Park bordered the west side of Fifth Avenue. She retraced her steps, wondering if Amon had lied or simply gotten the address wrong.

Her failure to find the mansion merely spurred her on. She backtracked five blocks, searching up and down each street between Madison and Fifth from Seventy-fifth to Seventieth. She found few mansions but several stately town houses that Amon might have thought of as mansions. She checked the names in the slots next to the doorbells and found no one named Starr.

After reaching Seventieth again, she proceeded to Sixty-ninth and on to Sixty-eighth, where she found the name Starr in the vestibule of a brick town house. There were only two doorbells, and the second slot was empty. Did that mean Melissa Starr had the town house to herself or that one of the apartments was vacant?

Lydia pressed the black button. "Who is it?" a man said—or that's what she guessed—the callbox was so staticky she couldn't quite hear.

How to answer and be admitted? "A friend of Vashti's," Lydia said, since that was what Carolyn called herself professionally.

The buzzer sounded. Lydia pushed open a heavy wrought-iron and glass door and entered an enormous mirrored and chandelier-lit marble hall. The antique mirrors looked filmy, the hall dusty, and the chandelier dim. The place had a faintly neglected and vaguely menacing look to it, like an Edward Gorey drawing. But the man in blue jeans and V-neck sweater, rounding the graceful curve of a stairway, looked wholesome enough in an aging boy-next-door sort of way—a swoop of light brown hair, blue eyes, average height. He must be Melissa Starr's husband or boyfriend, Lydia thought.

When he reached the bottom of the stairs, she noticed that his sweater was cashmere, his jeans custom-made, and his loafers a beat-up pair of Guccis. No socks. She couldn't be sure the light was so dim, but she thought the casual swoop of hair might be an intricately woven, expensive toupee. There was nothing aging about his boy-next-door smile since his teeth were capped.

"You're a friend of Tiffany's? Where is she?" he asked anxiously.

"I said Vashti, I don't know any Tiffany."

"Then why are you here?" The man frowned. He looked ready to show her to the door.

"I'm looking for someone who was here earlier."

Something dark flickered in his eye. "In that case come in. I'd like to hear more about it."

Lydia hesitated. Despite his wholesome appearance, she didn't quite trust this man. He was like a miscast actor, someone who wasn't what he pretended to be. Maybe he was the man whose name wasn't in the slot. "I guess if Vashti isn't here, I'd better be on my way," she said, edging toward the door, tugging at Colombo's leash.

"Vashti? Come to think of it, the name sounds familiar," he said. Was he lying? Lydia remembered the flicker in his eye when she'd said Vashti was here earlier. Something had clicked.

"That's her professional name. Her real name is Carolyn Auerbach." Lydia took another step back.

"An alias? How intriguing! You look like one of my heroines. Especially in that hat."

"You're Melissa Starr?"

He bowed and smiled, appearing to get a big kick out of her surprise. "Stuart Starr in real life," he said, extending a hand.

"Lydia Miller."

"Darling, is that Vashti's friend?" a woman with an actressy voice called down. "I have a message for her."

Lydia wondered how Carolyn had known she was coming here.

"Who is this Vashti?" Stuart asked. "I know I've heard that name. My wife has a way of not explaining things."

A few seconds later a drop-dead-gorgeous blond around Lydia's age came clicking down the stairs in feathery, high-heeled mules and white silk lounging pajamas—the kind of outfit women wore in thirties movies. Her platinum hair was marcelled à la Jean Harlow. Lydia wondered if fashion had reverted to the thirties when she wasn't looking. Milke would be ecstatic. Maybe Milke, with her love of thirties style in general and of Chanel in particular, had something to do with it.

"How in the world did you find us?" the woman asked before she reached the bottom of the stairs.

"I found your address on Vashti's appointment calendar," she lied. "What was her message?"

"Diandre Denvers Starr," the blond said, holding out a hand with dragon-lady nails and an Elizabeth Taylor–sized diamond. "Call me Di. I'm awfully sorry."

"Sorry?" Lydia asked.

"I'm so terribly forgetful."

Colombo sat down as if he expected the conversation to take a while.

Di sighed. "Vashti asked me to call and tell you she was going out to dinner with a friend, but I forgot."

She was the second person who'd forgotten to pass on Carolyn's message, but what bothered Lydia was that Carolyn was too cowardly to deliver the messages herself or else she was in some kind of trouble and didn't have the time.

"That's just nifty," Lydia said. "She invites me for dinner and doesn't show up."

"Maybe it was a drink she went out for," Di amended. "She'll be back later with Iggy Pop, so you might as well stay."

"What's this about Iggy Pop?" Stuart asked.

"Oh, goodness, I forgot you didn't know." Di frowned prettily, then brightened. Although her voice sounded theatrical, a good actress she wasn't. It was obvious she was lying. "Tiffany must have told you about the woman who worked such wonders with Iggy Pop when he hid in the terrarium and refused to eat."

"Tiffany didn't tell me a goddamned thing. She got lucky and left."

Lydia wondered if Tiffany was their daughter.

"Well, anyway, when Vashti came over this evening and told me that Iggy Pop might be carrying this horrible disease, I became frightened. We took him to Noah's Ark immediately to have him examined."

"Nora's Ark," Lydia corrected. "It's an animal shelter, not an animal hospital. Why would you take him there?"

"You shouldn't have let him out of the house," Stuart said. His face had taken on an ugly purplish hue. He seemed disproportionately upset over an iguana, that according to Amon, wasn't even his. "And there of all places."

"I didn't know so many people knew about Nora's Ark," Lydia said.

Stuart Starr said he'd never heard of it, but that wasn't how it sounded.

"She didn't tell *me* it wasn't an animal hospital," Diandre complained.

Stuart Starr looked about to strangle her.

"Well, I'm *sorry*, but I didn't want us to get that horrible salmenolla poisoning. Vashti said iguanas are especially susceptible to it. Humans catch it from them and die. They're running tests on him, and if he's okay, she's bringing him back, so we don't have to worry."

"It's salmonella *not* salmenolla," Stuart said angrily. Di looked close to tears.

"A not uncommon mispronunciation," Lydia said, coming to Diandre's defense.

Diandre took her hand. "Come have a drink. Vashti will be back any minute."

Maybe Diandre hoped to escape Stuart's wrath by keeping her there.

"Yes, do stay. I'm forgetting my manners," Stuart said, recovering his regular-guy smile.

"Thanks, but I have my dog with me."

"That's all right, he's invited, too. Hi there, pooch, what's your name?" Di asked. Colombo ignored her. Maybe he thought "pooch" was an ethnic slur.

Lydia decided to stay. Besides feeling sorry for Di, she'd like to see the surprise on Carolyn's face when she returned and found her here. "Yes, okay."

Di brightened. "Come on, let's get out of this drafty hall," she said, and walking toe-heel, toe-heel, one foot in front of the other like a runway model, led the way across the mirrored hall to a door. When she opened it, Lydia smelled furniture polish and floor wax and heard the sound of girlish voices.

"It embarrasses me to ask, but would you mind taking off

your boots?" Stuart said. "We've just had the floors done, and the kids worked so hard at it."

"How about Colombo's paws? What's he supposed to do?"

"Paws won't hurt. Animals are light on their feet."

He didn't know Colombo.

Lydia kicked off her boots. A big toe with the remains of fuchsia nail polish had nudged its way through her black pantyhose.

Stuart hung her coat in the closet but insisted she keep her hat on. "Do you mind?" he asked, and tilted the brim over one eye. "There. You should always wear it that way." He placed his hands on her shoulders and guided her to a full-length mirror, posing himself just behind her, the way designers stood behind models wearing their creations. Lydia wondered if he was one of those regular-guy gays that people often assumed were straight. The fact that he was married didn't mean anything, since marriage wasn't that uncommon among gay men his age.

"See? You look like a thirties movie star," he said.

"You mean like Norma Desmond in *Sunset Boulevard*?" Lydia said, shrugging off the compliment, which seemed to have upset Diandre.

"I'd say more a combination of Garbo and Dietrich," Stuart said. Lydia wondered if the reason Diandre had adopted the Jean Harlow look was to please Stuart, who, like her, spent his down time watching old movies on TV.

"Stuart? Di? Come look," a girlish voice piped up, and a young girl stepped out into the hall. Despite the fact that she wore a shapeless, gray jogging suit and a red western bandanna, Lydia saw that she was quite pretty, with large gray eyes and a heart-shaped face. Lydia wondered if she was Stuart's daughter by a previous marriage. She looked too old to be Diandre's, but Stuart could be anywhere from his late forties to a well-preserved sixty.

"Where do you want the Baccarat?" the girl asked, holding up a stemmed glass.

"On a top shelf, sweetheart. It's not for everyday use," Stuart said. He put an arm around the girl's thin shoulder. "This is Heather. One of my genius writers. And these are Jamie,

Sierra, and Shannon, the other three little geniuses who help me keep up the demand for Melissa Starrs."

Three leggy young things in jeans and oversize T-shirts had joined Heather. Jamie was waiflike with huge brown eyes and dark hair cut English schoolboy style. Sierra was tall and willowy, with golden eyes and golden skin, straight, shiny black hair, and high forehead and cheekbones. She wasn't just the most beautiful black girl Lydia had ever seen, but the most beautiful girl she'd ever seen, period—and she'd seen a lot of pretty women in her modeling and magazine-editing days. Shannon had black curly hair and eyes as green as the river Liffey. Or as green as Lydia imagined it to be.

The girls made a big fuss over Colombo, who basked in their attention.

Stuart stepped into the kitchen. "You're doing a terrific job cleaning, kids. Great! Come and see what they've done, Di. Isn't this terrific?"

"Terrific. You've done yourselves proud," Di said, smiled at them, then headed down the hall. Lydia assumed she was supposed to follow.

"You girls might start on the entrance hall after you've finished in the kitchen," Stuart suggested.

"I could start on it now," Heather said eagerly.

Lydia found their volunteer slave labor depressing. Pretty young girls that age should be out having a good time on New Year's Eve.

Under track lighting, satyrs lasciviously cavorted with nymphs in ornate gilt-framed paintings. In keeping with the romance-novel theme, Lydia supposed.

She caught up with Diandre. "How old are those kids? They look too young to be writers."

"Stuart says younger is better. Don't you, dear?" Di said, turning and looking behind Lydia. Sure enough, Stuart had followed.

"The younger the more romantic," Stuart said, an obvious leer in his voice, probably meant to needle Di.

Warring couples annoyed Lydia. Let them fight it out in private. "Who did Vashti go out with at Nora's Ark for a drink?" she asked.

Di's white silk shoulders shrugged. "Some sexy guy."

"Sexy?" She couldn't mean Richard. "Was he wearing glasses?"

"I didn't get up as far as his face. What a bod!" Di winked at Lydia. It was her turn to get back at Stuart.

"That must be Hank the Hunk. He's a vet who works nights in surgery. I've heard he only talks to animals or pretty women."

"He must love Jessica Rabbit," Stuart said.

Di had already started down a black wrought-iron stairway circling what looked like a fireman's pole. It was completely different from the graceful staircase in the hall and completely out of place in the town house. "Careful you don't break your neck," Diandre called up cheerfully, expertly navigating the dizzily winding stairs in her high-heeled mules.

"Maybe it would be easier to slide down the pole," Lydia said, glad she was in her stocking feet. Colombo flopped down at the top of the steps, refusing to go any farther.

Instead of leading to something modern, as a wrought-iron stairway might suggest, the steps opened onto a miniature palace of Versailles—marble, mirrors, and chandeliers, lots of antiques, and windows draped in crimson velvet.

Other than the rolltop desk, there was no sign that anyone wrote in the room. No word processors, computers, or even typewriters. Maybe they wrote historical romances dipping quill pens into inkwells, with the room providing the atmosphere. Or maybe they worked elsewhere.

"Where are your working quarters?" she asked.

"They're on the upper floors," Di said. "Each girl has a writing room."

"Do you write, too?"

"I'm the story creator."

"Where are your books?"

Stuart nodded at a closed door. "In my study."

"I'd like to see them."

Di picked up a paperback from the coffee table next to a

white phone with a speaker. "Here's one." She handed it to Lydia.

The cover showed a picture of a woman in a hoop skirt and windblown hair kissing a bare-chested black man under a tree dripping moss. Titled *Forbidden*. Above it was written *Like* Gone With the Wind *with an even more daring Scarlett and dashing Rhett*.

At the far end of the room, French doors opened onto a greenhouse, eerily lit by blue lights.

"What's out there?" Lydia asked, peering through the glass. She supposed she was being a bore, nosy and rude, with all her questions, but she found the setup bizarre. Why would four pretty young girls choose to stay in and clean house on New Year's Eve?

"Oh, that's Stuart's little hobby," Di said dismissively.

"Nothing special," he agreed.

Lydia looked out at the blue lights shining on rows of white flowers and some strange looking mushrooms. Beyond the snowy outside ledges the scene reflected into the night. "I've never seen red mushrooms before."

"Red with white flecks. You see them in old German still lifes," Stuart said.

"I'd love to get a closer look."

"You don't want to see any boring mushrooms. Besides it's chilly out there," Stuart protested.

She'd thought a greenhouse was supposed to be kept warm. "I don't mind," she said, slid the French doors open, and went out into a sweltering climate.

Despite his apparent reluctance to show her the greenhouse, Stuart was obviously enthusiastic about his gardening. It didn't take much encouragement for him to explain such factors as the right temperature and soil for growing conditions.

"What are those white flowers?" Lydia asked. "I've never seen those before either."

"Orchids. They may not look so spectacular, but they're extremely rare. They were once used as an aphrodisiac," Stuart said, leering. "They're a bitch to grow in captivity. These are commonly known as ladies tresses and grow in dry open areas.

In this country their Latin name is *Spiranthes cernua*. In Europe, it's *Spiranthes autumnalis*. Stop me if I'm boring you."

"You're not. What are the mushrooms called?"

"*Amanita muscaria*. Very tasty. Also very poisonous."

"How would you know what they tasted like if they're so poisonous? Who would live to tell?" she asked.

"Some of the European varieties are safe."

"How did you come to grow them?"

"I was a botanist in my other life. I wear a lot of hats."

"Such as?" Lydia picked up an opaque bottle half-hidden between the orchids and mushrooms. He snatched the bottle away. "Plant food. You shouldn't leave it out to litter up the place," he scolded Di, and shoved the bottle into a drawer below the shelf.

"Let's go back in and have some brandy," Di said, taking Lydia firmly by the elbow and steering her toward the French door. "Brandy is just the thing for a night like this."

"In a flask brought by a sled dog," Stuart said, with a too hearty laugh, stepping up on the other side of Lydia. She felt as if she were a prisoner on a forced march between them.

Inside, she sat down on a maroon velvet couch that Colette would have coveted, while Di gracefully settled herself on its twin across from her.

Stuart poured brandy into snifters over by the antique rolltop desk that served as a bar. After handing her and Di a glass, he got one for himself, and settled on the couch close to Lydia. She scooted over to leave room, sure he'd deliberately sat close to her just to make Di jealous. It must be a little game they played to spark their love life. Apparently writing romances wasn't enough.

Stuart raised his glass. *"Bonne année."* Just then the phone rang. He made no move to answer it, although it sat less than a foot away on the coffee table. Neither did Di.

"Stuart, it's that call you were expecting from St. Moritz," a girlish voice called from the speaker.

"Excuse me," Stuart said, and sprinted across the room to take the call in his study.

"I'm supposed to be in on this," Di said, and signaling Lydia to be quiet with her finger to her lips, stealthily lifted the receiver from the phone on the coffee table.

Lydia picked up *Forbidden*, pretending to be interested in the book while straining her ears to listen in. All she heard was a man speaking in a faint foreign accent. Di lolled across the Colette couch on the back cover of the book, dressed in silk and feathers à la Barbara Cartland and billed as Melissa Starr. The publisher was Quicksilver Press. But Quicksilver Press was a vanity publisher. What about Stuart's claim that his books were so much in demand he had to hire writers? If he paid to have the books published, that didn't make sense.

Ten minutes passed. Di still held the phone to her ear, listening raptly. Brandy in hand, Lydia wandered out to the greenhouse to take another look at the red mushrooms. Things were getting curiouser and curiouser. Something strange was going on in this house. Why would anyone want to grow something poisonous? Or orchids that didn't look like orchids and weren't even pretty? Remembering the bottle Stuart had snatched from her hand, she decided to risk another look. Di sat with her back to Lydia, listening in.

Lydia tiptoed over to the drawer. After a quick glance to make sure Di wasn't looking, she opened it. She saw dozens of opaque white bottles. No identifying label. And in the drawer with them a copy of *gazelle*. The most recent issue, which was being put together when Lydia had left. Why keep it stuck away in a drawer?

Lydia was about to reach for it when she heard footsteps behind her and looked up to see Di, as white as her white silk pajamas, tight-lipped and furious. "Just why are you snooping around out here?"

"For the same reason you were eavesdropping. Curious."

"For God's sake, don't tell him I was listening. Quick, get back in here before he sees you." Di grabbed Lydia's arm, with what Lydia suddenly realized was not so much force as fear. Di was afraid of Stuart Starr with his genial, regular-guy smile.

And suddenly she realized something else. The Starr residence wasn't just a stable for romance writers. It didn't so much resemble a miniature Versailles as it did a French bordello. The paintings upstairs with the cavorting nymphs and satyrs. The four beautiful young girls. They didn't write romance novels here. *Forbidden* was a plant.

Footsteps rattled on the iron stairs. Stuart wore a belted polo coat, thirties style, a match for Di in her Jean Harlow lounging pajamas. But how about her in her Garbo hat? And still wearing it, just to please a pimp.

"I have to go out for a while," he said, taking Lydia's hand and kissing it before she could grab it back. "Till we meet again."

"Just what the hell are you up to at this hour of the night?" Di demanded, her voice trembling with anger.

"Business. Don't worry, sweetheart. I won't be long."

"Maybe I should leave while you settle this between yourselves," Lydia said.

Di grabbed her arm again. "No, stay," she said, hanging on. "I know what you're up to," she told Stuart.

"Fine. Then it doesn't require any explanation. Good-bye again," he told Lydia, and hurried up the stairs.

"Fine with me if you never come back," Di shouted after him, and headed for the brandy bottle on the rolltop desk. She held the bottle out to Lydia. "More?" she asked brightly.

"No thanks. I'd better be on my way."

"You're not waiting for Vashti? I wish you'd stay. That bastard upsets me. He's up to something. I can't trust him."

"Writing romances isn't what you're about, is it?"

"What do you think this is?" Di asked, picking up *Forbidden*.

"Quicksilver Press? A vanity book. A plant. Something to allay your neighbors' suspicions."

"Our only neighbor is an old lady who lives next door and is never around. She summers in Newport and winters in Palm Beach. Almost everything else on the block is either some foreign embassy or business. Anyway, you don't have to worry. No one is here tonight. New Year's Eve is always a bust. They're all with their wives and girlfriends."

"Still, I'm surprised no one's noticed."

"Oh, we're very careful of our image, and naturally, we give protection money to the cops. Plus we're always discreet. And very particular about our clientele. I make it a point to see that my young ladies adhere to house rules. I'm an ace disciplinarian."

"By young ladies, do you mean those babies upstairs?"

"Stuart and I look out for those kids far better than their parents. You saw how happy they are here. They ran away from their parents, but they don't run away from us.

"Mother love is a myth. I know from experience," Diandre continued, sounding bitter. "I try to do for those girls what wasn't done for me. If it weren't for Stuart and me, those kids could be dead by now. Or out on the streets, catering to the worst kind of diseased deviant. They have no marketable skills. No way of making a living. Kids come to us. We don't go to them. You saw for yourself how devoted they are. Grateful. It hurts to turn so many away."

"Regular house parents."

"You've got it," Diandre said, missing the sarcasm and tearing at her cuticles with an obviously nervous gesture. "And they obey house rules. I charge them a dollar for each swear word or ungrammatical expression—'like' for 'as if,' 'goes' for 'says.' And any 'you knows.' They must be meticulous in their dress and cleanliness. The only sexy clothes they wear don't show." She'd torn off her cuticle, leaving blood. "Plus they're applying their earnings toward a higher education."

"First they have to finish high school," Lydia said, setting her brandy glass on the table so hard it nearly broke. She was feeling ill from the brandy, or maybe from her surroundings.

"They'll finish their senior year this spring. All except Tiffany. She has two years to go."

"Tiffany? I don't remember meeting any Tiffany."

"She's away right now. But she'll be back. Unfortunately. Heather is interested in epidemiology, Sierra wants to be a linguist, Jamie a lawyer, Shannon a child psychiatrist, and Tiffany a vet. Or so she says. She's a shallow young lady with no interest other than clothes, her looks, that damn dog, and that stupid Iggy Pop, who could very well give us all some fatal disease. Between you and me, I hope Vashti doesn't bring him back. He's icky. I hope they say he's contagious and has to be quarantined. Or put to sleep.

"I hope Tiffany doesn't come back either," she continued. "I'm glad she left. I just hope she stays wherever she went. But I bet he's out there right now tracking her down. Or maybe he doesn't have to. Maybe they're in this deal together."

"What deal?"

"The deal he was discussing in that call from St. Moritz. Don't ask me what it's about. I don't want to know."

"Then why were you eavesdropping on the phone?"

"Because I think it could get us in trouble. If he's as involved as I think he is, I'm taking the girls and leaving. We're not really married, you know. He won't marry me, but he's happy enough to lie about it. Wants everything to appear so proper and aboveboard."

Lydia was growing weary of Di. And of waiting for Carolyn to return with the iguana. It occurred to her that Diandre's wish might be granted. The iguana might be contagious, and Carolyn had no more intention of coming back here than she had of keeping their dinner date. Carolyn always found convenient rationalizations if there was something else she preferred to do. She might very well have met up with Hank the Hunk, who knows?

Lydia stood up. "I'm feeling sick from the brandy." Sick from the brandy and from the thought of the children upstairs being manipulated by Diandre and Stuart.

"You didn't have that much."

"I've had enough," she said.

Ignoring Diandre's protests, she hurried up the iron stairs, grabbed Colombo, and made a fast getaway. She'd hoped to have a private word with Heather when she was out cleaning the hall, but Heather hadn't yet gotten around to it. Besides Kramer, Lydia decided to speak to DiFilippi, who was in the Starrs' precinct. She'd get those two brought up on morals charges.

CHAPTER 11

Returning home, Lydia walked along Fifth Avenue, passing bundled-up groups of people, plowing through snow, headed for Central Park, where the end of the annual New Year's Eve run was celebrated with a display of fireworks. The revelers' high spirits contrasted with her dark mood.

The mantel clock chimed the half hour when she and Colombo entered the apartment. It was only eleven-thirty, but it seemed closer to midnight. She still felt depressed from her encounter with Di and company, sorry for the young girls whose lives Di and Stuart Starr controlled.

Deciding that a shower might lighten her mood, she lathered up with Calm Down, donned an oversize PETA T-shirt saying RESPECT YOUR FELLOW EARTHLINGS, and crawled into bed feeling clean and sleepy.

But the minute she hit the sheets, she was wide-awake. She thought of Kramer again. Even though she didn't see him often, she missed him—his solidity, his self-deprecating humor, and the way he looked at her as if she were the only woman in creation. Nights with Kramer at a not-too-rustic ski lodge, drinking mulled wine and making love in front of a roaring fire sounded like a peachy way to begin the new year. Tomorrow she'd call him and accept his invitation.

The thought put her in such a good mood that she decided to spread some cheer. Her parents had always stayed up to watch the ball drop on Times Square, but now her mother watched it alone. Lydia punched out the familiar eleven-digit number on the phone and waited for her mother to answer. As she listened to the ringing phone she pictured her mother sitting with

Chots's kids while Chots was out partying, making up for two lost years waiting for her deadbeat husband to return.

The phone went on ringing. Maybe her mother had given up waiting for the ball to drop, turned off the TV, and gone to bed. Just as Lydia was about to hang up, her mother answered.

"Why, Lydia honey, how are you?" She sounded so pathetically cheerful to hear from her that Lydia suffered pangs of remorse for not calling sooner.

In the background, a recording of Guy Lombardo played "Auld Lang Syne." Another New Year's Eve ritual her parents had observed for as far back as she could remember. Hearing ice tinkling in a glass, Lydia became worried. Had Mom become a solitary drinker?

"Honey, could I call you tomorrow?" her mother asked. "It's midnight and I've got company."

"Sure, Ma, who?" Another widow no doubt, both reminiscing about the good old days when their husbands were alive and the children home.

"Russ Milhauser."

"Russ who?

"Russ Milhauser. You remember him. He owns that grain-and-feed store over near Little Creek. It's my oldest—Lydia," her mother said in an aside.

"Happy New Year," a man called into the phone, tooting a horn in her ear.

"Same to you," Lydia said, and hung up, wondering what on earth possessed her mother to take up with someone like Russ Milhauser. For that matter, why had her mother taken up with anyone? She was almost at retirement age. But retiring from work didn't mean retiring from life, Lydia realized. Besides, her mother had done just the opposite from most people. She'd gone to work, taking over the family moving business that Lydia's great-grandfather had started in the early 1900s. A picture in the family album showed him standing proudly in front of a big truck that her father had told her was a Biederman. The truck was lettered MILLER MOVING & STORAGE. Now that Chots had joined her mother in the business, it was fourth generation. Maybe the fifth would continue the tradition if one of Chots's kids decided to take over after winning an Olympic gold in gymnastics, as all three expected to do when they grew up.

Lydia turned off the lights and closed her eyes. But sleep still eluded her. She couldn't find the right position. She tossed and turned, upsetting Colombo, who liked to lie on her feet, which upset her, since she felt trapped with his inert body imprisoning them.

No point in turning the TV on. The focus would be on celebrating New Year's, increasing her feeling of loneliness and isolation from humanity. She suspected that there were thousands like her out there who found holidays depressing. Witness the sharp jump in suicide rates during Christmas and New Year's. T. S. Eliot was wrong—December was the cruelest month, not April. She was sure that any TV station brave enough to ignore holidays would have a sky-high Nielson rating. Not everyone in the world had families to be with, or, for that matter, families they wanted to be with.

Lydia felt a sudden twinge of hunger and remembered that she'd forgotten about ordering takeout when she'd returned from her dismal visit to Melissa Starr. She got up and went to the kitchen, but the only food in the refrigerator was the leftover poached salmon that she'd ordered for dinner from William Poll when Kramer came to see her. She'd had to order an entrée for four people in order to get them to deliver it, and she'd been eating poached salmon ever since. She was sick of it. Other than the couscous ingredients, she hadn't shopped for food. She decided to go down to Carolyn's and get the couscous.

Carolyn's kitchen was dark. Funny, she could have sworn she'd left the counter light on. Lydia opened the refrigerator door. No couscous. And the champagne had disappeared. Both the Moët and the Dom Pérignon. Carolyn must have come back while Lydia was out, polished off everything in sight, and gone straight up to bed. But the two missing bottles of champagne puzzled her. Carolyn scarcely drank.

Lydia found a loaf of French bread in the freezer, defrosted it in the microwave, snatched a bottle of valpolicella from the wine rack, and started back upstairs. A loaf of bread, a jug of wine, but no thou.

On the third floor she paused outside Carolyn's bedroom door, debating the pros and cons of waking her up to tell her what a shit she was. She suddenly became aware of whispers and muffled giggles. This explained the disappearance of the champagne and couscous, but not who Carolyn had shared it with. The noises followed Lydia upstairs, quickly escalating to sighs and cries, moans and groans. By the time she reached the top, she heard a shriek on a descending scale.

And a Happy New Year to you, too, Lydia silently called.

Back in bed alone, she poured herself a healthy glass of wine while Colombo eyed the bread. "You had your dinner," she reminded him, and wondered if Carolyn had brought home her drink date, Hank the Hunk. She had yet to meet him since he arrived late at the shelter after a long day's stint at the Cat and Dog Hospital, apparently as dedicated to animals as he was to his pursuit of women.

Lydia refilled her wineglass and thought again of Kramer, who didn't have to prove himself by chasing after women. It wouldn't be a dereliction of duty at the shelter to spend a few days with him. After all, she was a volunteer. She pictured après-ski drinks and cross-country skiing under a Vermont moon.

She decided to call him and tell him she'd go. Andy would be in bed and Kramer would be watching a video or maybe reading Parini's biography of his favorite author, John Steinbeck, that she'd given him for Christmas. Even if Kramer was asleep, he wouldn't mind her waking him with this kind of news.

Lydia put the half-eaten bread on the paper napkin on top of the night table and punched out Kramer's number. She got a jolt when a female voice answered the phone—a voice sounding too old for Andy and too young for Kramer.

"Could I speak to Kramer?"

"He's not here."

"On duty?" she asked. Something must have come up.

"I dunno."

"Are you Andy's sitter?"

"Yeah, who are you?"

"A friend," Lydia said, and hung up, feeling decidedly unfriendly. Betrayed. When his mother had backed out, Kramer had said he couldn't get a sitter at the last minute. It looked like he'd found one easily enough in order to go out with someone else. She reminded herself that just because she lived like a nun didn't mean he had to live like a monk. Still, the feeling of betrayal persisted. He had lied.

Lydia noticed Colombo licking his chops, and looked for the bread on the night table. Gone. "Bad," she said. "Shame. I can't trust you either."

The phone rang, and she made a dive for it. She knew it would be Kramer calling to apologize for missing her call and to explain everything.

First heavy breathing. Then: "You're gonna be in for a surprise, cunt," a man said in a hoarse voice, and hung up.

Lydia shivered and reached for the valpolicella. Who? The voice wasn't the least bit familiar, and yet there was something about the hoarse voice that made her think she'd heard it recently. It wasn't Stuart Starr's. That she was sure of. Then she remembered the red-bearded man who'd threatened to get even with her. He'd spoken in the same hoarse voice, as if he had a cold. This was probably his idea of a joke.

When the phone rang again she waited, body tensed, for another venomous message. She let her machine answer the call.

"Happy New Year," Neil said, and started crying.

She picked up. "I'm here. What's wrong?"

"Sorry for the outburst. I've been watching a replay of Tennessee Williams's biography and it always makes me so unhappy. He was such a sweet, gentle man. A genius. And the critics tore him apart in his later years, like the vultures in *Suddenly Last Summer*. No wonder the poor man turned to drugs."

Unlike Tennessee, Neil had yet to have a play put on Broadway, off Broadway, or even off off Broadway. The one play he'd had produced was by a regional theater in his home state of Michigan. "Maybe I should have stayed put," he'd said. "They appreciate me there, after all." That was before he'd seen the production.

"How's Steve?" she asked.

"That slut. He went out. God knows where and with whom. I'm throwing him out tomorrow."

She'd heard that before, and wondered if Neil worried that Steve might get AIDS in his reckless rovings and bring it home. But it wasn't the sort of thing she could mention.

"So what are you doing, sweetcakes?" he asked.

"Feeling weepy and sorry for myself."

"Ah, what's wrong?" Neil was immediately sympathetic. "I expected you to be out with Kramer."

"That's what's wrong," Lydia said, and told him about her phone calls—first the threatening one, which worried Neil more than it did her, and then the one to Kramer.

"No one can be trusted anymore except me and thee. Come visit me in your place and we can be unhappy together."

Lydia said maybe and hung up. After talking to Neil, she felt better about feeling bad. That's what friends are for, she told herself, and closed her eyes. She was almost asleep when the phone rang. Neil again.

"I forgot to tell you about what I heard from Gabriella. I'm sure this doesn't mean anything, but you said to tell you everything I heard about Laura Haddon. Gabriella was over the other night for dinner—we're friends again now that she's forgiven me for cleaning out her cellar while she was away. She was so sure I'd tossed out something highly valuable, but of course nothing was missing. It was only trash, after all. Which was why I cleaned it out. You'd think she'd thank me.

"But I digress. Gabriella told me that when she returned from Milan she'd had lunch with Laura. This was around the end of November, shortly before Laura turned up missing. She said Laura had been quite cheerful and told her that she was taking the plunge and having something done to counteract time's ravages."

"You mean plastic surgery?" Lydia asked.

"That was Gabriella's interpretation."

"But she was terrified of that sort of thing. She certainly wouldn't have been cheerful about it."

"I know," Neil said, "but maybe she was putting up a brave

front. It makes me wonder if she hadn't met some guy she was wild about."

"Well, Regina Fellows did say they had to do a lot of touch-ups on her recent photos. Maybe she did decide to go under the knife, but I still can't see her being cavalier about it."

"Maybe just fatalistic, who knows? Anyway, you wanted to know. I hope I didn't wake you."

Lydia denied it. Mention of Regina Fellows reminded her of *gazelle*, which in turned reminded her of the copy in the green-house drawer. Besides being curious as to why the magazine was kept there, Lydia was eager to see the new issue. It would be the first in four years without her name on the masthead. She wished Milke, Gillian, and the rest of the staff well, but she rather hoped that this issue wouldn't be as good without her.

Carolyn subscribed to it, and probably had a copy downstairs. Lydia hurried past Carolyn's bedroom, trying to ignore the noise on her way down. It wasn't easy. She had to admit that whoever it was with Carolyn had staying power. She found the magazine under a pile of other fashion magazines and rushed back upstairs again and got into bed.

Suzannah was on the cover. Like Madonna and Neil's friend Gabriella, Suzannah went by her first name only. Lydia did a double take. The cover line to the left of Suzannah's youthful, slightly bony shoulder, read $A = Y + B^2$, MIRACLE OR MYTH? — the same formula that was written on Carolyn's desk calendar. She was sure *gazelle* wasn't writing about dog food.

Lydia flipped through a lot of ads until she came to the article. The writer, Trish Ackers, was someone she'd never heard of. On the opposite page, Suzannah held a dewy white flower to her dewy white cheek. Lydia saw with surprise that it was identical to the orchids in Stuart Starr's greenhouse. What was going on here?

First came a definition of the formula: *A* stood for Anima, *Y* for Youth, and B^2 for Beauty squared, whatever that meant. Just a gimmick, she supposed. Next came an abbreviated dictionary definition: "*anima n* (L animate, NL, fr. L, soul) 1 a: soul, life: *specif.* the passive or animal soul."

"You know how it goes," Trish Ackers began.

*You wake up in the morning dreading to face yourself—
not because of what you've done the night before. What you
can't face is your face—those little wrinkles and fine lines
hinting of horrors to come.*

*You brace yourself and look into the mirror. And what do
you see? It can't be! But it is! A miracle—you in your youth.
That girl is back. The real you. The one you thought you'd
lost after your nineteenth birthday, before that impostor
took over. But this you is even better—smarter and more
confident, and younger and prettier—the way that great designer up there should have done it in the first place. Life
will open up again.*

*And it was all so simple, so painless. So quick! A simple
injection that hurt no more than a bee sting. Without the
bruises and discomforts, the expense and suspense of cosmetic surgery. And you didn't waste weeks hiding out until
the bruises had gone.*

Cleopatra would have killed for this!

The article gave Suzannah's age as "going on thirty-seven"
crediting her youthful appearance to Anima. Trish was stretching the truth a bit. Suzannah was thirty-five, an advanced age,
as models go. Aside from Laura Haddon, Cheryl Tiegs, and the
legendary beauty Carmen, who was in her sixties, thirty-five
was considered next door to senior citizen, ready for permanent retirement. Lydia wondered how Suzannah felt about this,
not only giving her real age, but adding two years.

Lydia read on. Anima was currently utilized in exclusive
European spas but unavailable in the United States, where it
awaited FDA approval. Its producers claimed that since Anima
was a cosmetic and not a drug, it was not subject to govern-
ment approval, but the FDA disputed this claim, saying that
evidence indicated that Anima penetrated the skin and had an
effect below the surface. "Since the European users have only
praise for Anima and no ill effects have been reported, it's difficult to understand the FDA's bias against this product," Trish
continued. "I can only assume that it's controlled chiefly by
men, who don't understand women's urgent need for this

dream remedy. But maybe we'll get lucky and they'll see the light. Meanwhile rumor has it that certain dermatologists can be persuaded to give injections with or without FDA approval, if the price is right."

"Now wait a minute, Trish," Lydia said. She hadn't realized she'd spoken out loud until Colombo sat up and gave her a puzzled look. Lydia was just as puzzled by what she'd read. Trish Ackers was making some pretty reckless claims. There were no statistics given on how many European women had used this product, and for how long. And would she have heard of any complaints? Also, during her stint at *gazelle*, Lydia had often spoken to FDA people, a lot of them women. If the FDA was biased against Anima, Trish Ackers was even more biased in its favor. The article was clearly a publicity plant, whetting the consumer's appetite, priming her to shell out an astronomical sum on The Product the minute it appeared on the market. Publicity plants weren't rare in magazines. In fact, many magazines depended on them, but they were against Milke's principles. How had this slipped past Milke's gimlet eye? Gillian should know something about this. She'd call her tomorrow.

CHAPTER 12

The snow had stopped falling sometime during the night, and the sun shone brightly in the blue-white sky. Despite a night of fitful sleep, Lydia had awakened early, walked Colombo, and bought groceries from a nearby Korean market. After her errands she sat at the window sipping her after-breakfast coffee. Outside, a fat icicle reflected rainbow hues in the sun. Down below in the garden, pigeons pecked at bird feed in a snow-cleared area. Perched on the wing of the cherub fountain, a starling looked on.

Lydia wondered if Carolyn knew that her beloved assistant was feeding pigeons, encouraging them to hang out in her garden. Although Carolyn professed to love all animals, birds and insects, she hated pigeons with a passion. But maybe she forgave Amon all his trespasses. Who knows—he might have been in Carolyn's bed last night, not Hank the Hunk.

The house had been eerily quiet when Lydia had gone out and returned from her errands. Either Carolyn was catching up on her beauty sleep or she was avoiding any embarrassing encounters by steering clear of her.

The phone rang at her elbow. Lydia picked up.

"Happy New Year," Kramer said, sounding chipper. Because he'd had good sex last night? "I hope I didn't wake you."

"I'm just having my first cup of coffee," she lied. She wasn't sure why. Maybe because he'd lied to her.

"I could call back later."

"Now is okay. You talk, I'll listen."

"I know this is last minute, but Mom asked if Andy could spend the day with her. I guess she feels guilty about last night. Any chance we could get together?"

Maybe the sex hadn't been so good after all. "I've made other plans."

"You're not working today, are you? Aren't they expecting too much?"

"Actually, I'm going to an open house at the shelter. It's a tradition." She hadn't seriously considered going until she said it.

"Oh." Pause. "How late does it last? We could have dinner at least."

"Isn't that a long way for you to come just for dinner?"

"It's worth it. I went out last night, after all," he confessed. Probably he'd guessed she'd been the anonymous caller.

"Did you have a good time?"

"Drinking with Barolini isn't my idea of fun. But he was close to suicidal. He still hasn't been able to find a writer for his true-crime story. He thinks if he becomes famous his wife will come back to him. I feel sorry for the guy."

"I don't," she said. After all, Barolini had tried to nail her for the murder in his true-crime story.

"Anyway, I didn't get away with telling him I didn't have a sitter. He volunteered his kid. She's staying with him until his ex-wife and her husband get back from St. Martin. I didn't want to go out, but I was stuck."

"Poor you," Lydia said, suddenly feeling cheerful. She announced that maybe they could meet for dinner after all. "I'm not going to the open-house thing until late. You can pick me up at the shelter around six."

"Have you decided anything about the ski trip?" he asked, somewhat hesitantly.

"I'll let you know tonight."

Lydia waited until eleven to call Gillian about the Anima write-up. Gillian was a late riser and might be even later the morning after New Year's Eve. Neither Gillian nor the electronic Gillian on the answering machine answered the ringing phone. She gave up and called Milke.

Listening to Milke's ringing phone, Lydia decided she'd begin by wishing her a Happy New Year, then segue into the subject of Anima. But Milke beat her to it. Lydia got no further than "Hello."

"Don't tell me you want to know, too? You'll have to get in line, sweetie."

"You mean Anima?"

"What else? We've gotten calls about it from Thailand, Tel Aviv, Tibet, and Tabasco."

"Tabasco? Is that some red-hot South American country?"

"Don't be a smart aleck. That's what it sounded like. The sales have been phenomenal. We've sold out on the newsstands."

Lydia watched the sun glint on a fat icicle as Milke chattered on. She'd have to let her run down before she could start asking hard questions. It took about fifteen minutes of uninterpretable noises and exclamations. Except the longer Milke talked, the less enthusiastic she sounded.

"You don't sound very happy about it," Lydia said, when Milke had wound down.

There was a pause, another uninterpretable Milke noise, and something close to a wail. "Darling, can I trust you?" Milke asked, and didn't wait for an answer. "I have to tell someone. I'm terrified."

"You've always been able to take success in your stride."

"I'm afraid the magazine's reputation for credibility is about to be destroyed—not to mention mine. The only thing I can be thankful for is that I insisted on inserting a claim that there was no proof that Anima worked."

"A disclaimer? I didn't see any."

"Damn that little bitch. She must have deleted it. I could be in serious trouble."

The icicle had begun to drip. "Why did you go along with something so vague and carelessly written in the first place?"

"Gillian. I let that child talk me into it. She said she'd checked the facts and I believed her. I could wring that stupid little girl's stupid little neck," Milke said. "If I knew where to find her. I suppose she's hiding out on some tropical island with that awful boyfriend of hers, Nigel."

It came back to Lydia—that press release touting Anima. She'd hadn't believed its claims, but Gillian must have.

"I've run into a wall of silence," Milke wailed. "After we received all those pathetic phone calls from hopeful women begging to know where and when they could buy this magic potion—if there was any hope of its soon being on the market—I told Gillian to call the author to find out. After all, it had been at least five months since she'd written it.

"The only number Gillian had was the writer's agent, whose phone number had appeared in the press release and address on the cover letter of her manuscript—Munger & Miles. I've never heard of them, have you?"

The question was rhetorical. "They said Trish Ackers was a pen name, and refused to give Gillian her real name or phone number, so I got on the phone, and they told me the same damn thing. 'Don't call her, she'll call you.' Can you imagine someone from an upstart agency that no one has ever heard of saying that to *me*?" Milke asked indignantly.

"Did she call?" Lydia asked, eye on the dripping icicle.

"She talked to Gillian. With a cock-and-bull story that only an idiot like your former assistant would believe. Trish Ackers—whoever she may be—claimed that the lab in question didn't want its name revealed for security reasons. They'd already encountered spies planted by their competitors, and they couldn't risk making their name known for fear of more, she said."

"Then you don't know Trish Ackers's real name or the name of the lab?"

"Something even stranger. Trish Ackers hasn't cashed her paycheck. And Munger & Miles is no longer in business. What do you think of that?"

Lydia thought of Heidi, who hadn't come back to get her check, either.

"I'll be the laughingstock from Seventh Avenue to the Boul' Miche, if this turns out to be a hoax. And I have only myself to blame for believing that silly little twit who quit before I could fire her."

"I can't imagine her quitting; she was so excited about the promotion."

"If she hadn't quit, I'd have fired her," Milke repeated.

"I'd love to talk to her. Did Gillian know Laura Haddon?" Lydia asked, not knowing she was going to ask the question until it was out.

"Oh, wasn't that frightful? Poor Laura. One of the few people left with any sense of style—besides me, of course. Who'd expect such a brutal murder among civilized people? Semicivilized," Milke amended. "We were all cut up about it."

A poor choice of words considering the circumstances of Laura Haddon's death, Lydia thought.

"Now that you mention it," Milke continued. "I think Gillian and Laura sat at the same table at some AIDS benefit thing at the Armory. Regina had refused to sit with Laura, still furious with her for not showing up at her shoot at the Met. You remember that?" Lydia also remembered Regina telling her about it at Mortimer's. "It was the day you told me you were leaving," Milke was saying. "This terrible thing would never have happened if you'd been here. Have you thought of coming back? My offer still holds."

Lydia was familiar enough with Milke's non sequiturs to know that she was referring to the piece on Anima appearing in *gazelle* and not Laura Haddon's murder. "Give me until February. I'll let you know then."

After she hung up, Lydia tried to straighten the twisted phone cord. She wondered if Gillian had mentioned Anima to Laura Haddon the night of the AIDS benefit, which would have been before Laura had lunch with Gabriella and spoken of counteracting time's ravages with no mention of undergoing the knife. But what would that have to do with Laura's murder?

Still fiddling with the phone cord, she also wondered how long she could stick it out at the shelter. Other than Richard; Shantel; Judy, the animal trainer; and the animals themselves, she didn't particularly like anyone there. Of course, she'd be working on the newsletter as soon as Richard found someone to replace Heidi and could probably manage the newsletter in her spare time. Maybe she would go back to *gazelle*, provided she got Milke to agree to let her run the magazine her way.

The icicle fell from the window—what little there was left of it.

Around two-thirty Lydia got dressed for the open house— dressed but not dressed up, since she was sure no one else would be, with the exception of Allegra, who probably put on a Donna Karan to take out the garbage. Lydia topped her black corduroy jeans and T-shirt with an Ungaro jacket for her dinner with Kramer.

Carolyn still wasn't around when Lydia left. Maybe she'd gone out. Who knows, Lydia thought, I might even run into her at the open house in the company of Hank the Hunk.

CHAPTER 13

The party was well under way when Lydia entered the shelter. An old Beatles tune with Paul McCartney singing "Rocky Racoon" echoed under the domed ceiling strung with red balloons and silver streamers.

Lydia worried that the high-decibel level would disturb the animals in the display cages, but the cages had been moved. She'd find out where they'd gone and say hello to Emil later.

After hanging her coat over someone's jacket on the crowded coatrack, she walked to the fringe of the crowd and looked for Carolyn and Hank the Hunk. No hunks and no Carolyn. There were quite a few people with children, but few children with two parents, and the single parent was generally a mother. Almost everyone wore slogan T-shirts, including an infant whose T-shirt said BABIES FOR BEARS. An attractive couple wore Stop and Go sweatshirts like the kind modeled by Paul and Linda McCartney in the PETA catalog. The woman's was a green GO VEGGIE and the man's a red STOP EATING ANIMALS.

Despite the domestic appearance, an underlying feeling of animosity pervaded the room like the smell of antiseptic. A number of Richard people gathered around him at the buffet table while the P.S. people hung around her at a makeshift bar by the stained-glass windows.

Shantel Williams bopped up to Lydia and introduced her companion, a gray-haired woman some forty years older than Shantel, fifty pounds heavier, and several shades lighter. "Ilse is the animal groomer," Shantel said. "She clips and shampoos all that filthy fur, and underneath is like an apricot poodle or something."

"You should see those little things when they are brought in. They are shivering, you know," Ilse said in an accent Lydia couldn't place. She was probably German with a name like Ilse. Wasn't that Ingrid Bergman's name in *Casablanca*?

"—they are so scared, they are peeing, you know," Ilse said. "I tell them I love them in Spanish, German, French, and English. Never mind my English is not so hot."

"Theirs isn't so hot either," Shantel said.

"Toys the rich get tired of and throw away. It breaks your heart, you know?" Ilse asked.

Lydia knew.

The walrus had given way to "Rocky Raccoon," one of the many songs deemed appropriate for the occasion.

A chubby blond man in his forties focused a camera on Lydia. "Take off your jacket so I can get a good shot," he said.

"I'm not into cheesecake."

"Hey, don't be so touchy. I don't want your breasts, just your slogan."

"I'm not wearing one."

"Why not? Everyone else is."

"That's why not," she said, and elbowed her way past the Richard people to the buffet table, where she picked up a paper plate and filled it with two mini white pizzas, deep-fried tofu, and Chinese fried walnuts.

"Having a good time?" someone asked in a hoarse voice. Richard stood beside her, sporting a red nose and his usual tweed jacket. "Excuse me," he said, whipped out a handkerchief, and honked.

The music had shifted from the Beatles to Elvis singing "You Ain't Nothin' but a Hound Dog." A politically incorrect choice for an animal shelter, Lydia thought.

"Did two women and an iguana come in here last night?" Lydia asked Richard after he'd pocketed his handkerchief.

"I wouldn't know. I knocked off early. Not long after you went home. My cold got worse, and I was running a fever. So I called Hank to take over. I'm surprised he didn't have a date."

"Who's that?" a voice asked behind them.

Richard turned. "Oh, hey, we were just talking about you."

"*We?*" Lydia asked, wheeling around to see who she was supposedly discussing.

Richard introduced them. "This is Hank Levine, veterinarian extraordinaire, and this is Lydia Miller. Lydia's pinch-hitting for us until we get someone to replace Heidi."

If he was the guy Carolyn had taken to bed with her, Lydia could see why. He wasn't just good-looking, he also looked like Carolyn's cat, Alf—at least his hair and eyes were the same tawny color. He was also a hunk, but not the calculated kind who worked out; the broad shoulders and tight tush seemed to be something he was born with.

"Richard, I have a question," P.S. called imperiously. Richard reluctantly went over to join the enemy camp.

"Were you here last night when Carolyn and another woman brought in an iguana?" Lydia asked Hank as soon as Richard left.

"Oh, yeah, you know Carolyn? Nice lady."

And a good lay?

"Listen, I feel really rotten about what happened last night. If you see her, please tell her I'm sorry," Hank said.

"Sorry?"

"Yeah. I called to apologize, but she wasn't in. I expected Bud to keep watch, but he'd disappeared. Off on a toot, I bet. He hasn't shown up for the party either. I guess he knows I'll give him hell when I see him."

Lydia was confused. "What does Bud have to do with it?"

"Oh, there he is, my favorite veterinarian," Allegra interrupted, appearing out of nowhere and latching onto Hank's arm. "Isn't it a pity we don't work the same shift? The only way I get to see this guy is to stay late," she told Lydia.

Lydia wondered if that was why Allegra had returned to the shelter yesterday afternoon, leaving with P.S. when she found out Hank wasn't there.

Allegra wasn't wearing her usual Donna Karan but a nautical Ralph Lauren blazer with gold buttons, which looked ridiculous with her stiletto heels.

Come off it, Lydia, she told herself. You're no longer in the rag trade.

Hank disengaged himself from Allegra's clutches. "Would you like something to drink with that?" he asked Lydia.

She was surprised to see that she still held a paper plate with untouched food. "Yes, okay." Maybe if Allegra didn't stick around, Hank would explain what Bud had to do with him and Carolyn last night.

No such luck. Allegra followed them across the room to the bar by the stained-glass window. P.S. and her followers had moved on, while Richard seemed to have lost his followers along with his bearings. He fiddled with his glasses, a bewildered Woody Allen look on his face; but with Richard appearances could be deceiving. With Woody Allen, too, for that matter.

The bar consisted of bottles of red and white wine, designer water, and cans of caffeine-free and no-cal soda, with one bottle each of the hard stuff—all unopened.

"What's your pleasure?" Hank asked.

"I'll have Perrier, thanks," Allegra said.

Hank handed her a bottle.

"It isn't open and I need a glass."

"Help yourself," he said, and looked inquiringly at Lydia. She preferred good beer to cheap wine, and said she'd have a Heineken, which was the only kind of beer in the tub of what was now ice water. Hank got two bottles. Lydia didn't have a chance to ask him any more questions with Allegra hanging around.

"Wildfire" was playing, but not for long.

"Someone turn off that goddamn music," P.S. shouted. Someone did.

"I can see why she'd be sensitive about a song about horses with her face," the chubby, blond photographer said.

Allegra blew up. "Don't you just hate it when men criticize women's looks?" she asked angrily. "Especially when they're far from Adonises themselves and are considerably overweight."

The photographer hastily removed himself.

Lydia wondered if in defending P.S., Allegra was defending herself, sensitive about her bulging eyes. She might have been subject to a lot of teasing when she was a little kid. Children could be cruel. Suddenly Lydia remembered the descriptions in P.S.'s newspaper clippings of froggy eyes and frozen faces of women with high-visibility careers. Could the use of some magic remedy have backfired in her case, similar to the silicone breast implants? Allegra was a dermatologist who'd be aware of collagen and Botox injections, or anything else of that nature that came down the pipe. Such as Anima? Of course, it hadn't yet been approved by the FDA, but that didn't mean it wasn't being used illegally.

Lydia was debating if she should ask Allegra about Anima when she became aware of an altercation up on the makeshift podium, where P.S. and Judy, the animal trainer, struggled over the rights to the microphone. P.S. grabbed the mike from Judy and held it out of her reach. "I'm in charge, and I'm the one who speaks," she announced.

Judy made a flying leap and recovered the mike. "Richard is the head of this shelter, not you," Judy said.

For once P.S. didn't argue. Judy was shorter but built like a sumo wrestler. "Richard, come up here," Judy ordered.

Richard was pushed up on the podium by his fans. Judy shoved the mike in his face and stood by, arms across her chest, as if she were his personal bodyguard.

Richard straightened his horn-rims, blew his nose, and cleared his throat. "First, I want to thank you all for coming today. I consider this a tribute to Mother, who . . ."

Hank put a hand on Lydia's shoulder. "Come and see my patients," he whispered. "Richard has a tendency to be long-winded, once he gets started."

"He's going to be mad if he catches us walking out on his speech," Allegra said, tagging along. Her stiletto heels clicked loudly on the cement as she kept up a running commentary on what Richard was saying until his voice became too faint to hear.

At the door to the recovery room, Hank took out his keys.

"You keep it locked?" Lydia said.

"Since last night, when the iguana was stolen."

Stolen? Lydia was about to ask how it happened, but she realized her question would go unheard in the cacophony of animal noises that greeted Hank. A basset hound actually looked happy, while a wheatie too sick to raise its head raised its eyes hopefully.

"They're all here, thank God," Hank said. Reaching into a cage, he brought out a gray cat with white paws, wearing a lampshade collar around its neck. "This is Emily," he said.

"What's wrong with her?" Lydia asked.

"Kidney stones," Hank said in a low voice, as if it might disturb Emily to know.

"Why would someone with kidney stones wear a lampshade collar?"

"She licks herself in the wrong place. That's not good."

Hank peered into the cage at a hound dog. "Why, hey there, Bubba, how you doin'? You're lookin' mighty good today."

Lydia stood by as Hank went from cage to cage speaking to the animals. Allegra followed.

Hank proceeded to introduce all the animals, including Hamlet, the basset; Lion, a golden retriever; and a mixed breed called Bensonhurst. "That's where he was found," Hank explained, and gave a rundown of each animal's ailment and stage of recovery.

"What is this, Allegra?" he asked, pointing to a bare spot behind the ear of a Siamese kitten.

"I haven't the faintest."

"It's a parasite. You should know that, you're a dermatologist."

"My patients only wear fur, they don't grow it. Why did you ask if you knew?"

"You know what Toynbee said?" Hank asked. The question was rhetorical. "Toynbee said the first sign of the destruction of a civilization is cruelty to animals. Women tell themselves minks are mean, so it's okay if they're killed. But if they heard one scream, they'd think twice. Minks are skinned alive, you know. That way the fur is more lustrous."

"That's a lie put out by animal nuts," Allegra said.

"I'll take you for a visit to a mink farm, okay? Then we'll go to a cosmetic lab and see rabbits and cats blistered for shampoo and blinded for hair spray."

"Don't," Lydia said, clapping her hands over her ears. She couldn't bear to watch animals preying on one another in documentaries on PBS, much less hear what humans did.

"They don't test shampoos on animals anymore," Allegra said.

"I'll show you. And I'll show you a lab where brains are cut open without anesthesia to prove already proven theories."

Lydia ducked into another room to escape Hank's vivid descriptions, and found herself in the operating room, a place she detested. Sitcoms, soaps, or anything to do with hospitals were on her to-be-avoided list. She didn't get her kicks from seeing anyone suffer, animal or human, and had yet to see *E.R.* or a rerun of *M*A*S*H*.

Lydia remembered Allegra's saying she couldn't stand the sight of blood. Maybe Allegra was playing devil's advocate, taking the opposite side. Instinct told her Allegra was up to something, but what? Was Allegra a bad guy or a good guy?

Hank came in and picked up a scalpel. Lydia backed toward the door. "Before I operate, I always show the animal the instrument and explain what it's for," he said. "But that doesn't help much. In fact, sometimes it makes things worse."

"It's like having a sadist show you the instruments he intends to torture you with," Lydia said, making a hasty exit.

Hank followed her out. "Jesus, you're right. All along I've been scaring these poor guys to death. They see me as a male, white, middle-class, middle-aged monster."

In the recovery room, he said a long good-bye to his patients, winding up with "See you later, fellas," and turned to Lydia. "I hope I do," he whispered, nodding toward a small empty cage. "Iggy Pop's. Someone just walked in and grabbed him."

"Where were you?" she asked.

"Having a drink with Carolyn at Dresner's. Bud was supposed to be here, but he must have sneaked off. I think it was

Iggy's owner who stole him. The blond who came here with Carolyn."

Lydia laughed. "She was only too happy to get rid of him."

"Anyway, why couldn't she take him if he was hers?" Allegra put in.

"He wasn't," Lydia told Allegra.

"Because she was starving him, that's why," Hank said.

"Who told you that?"

"Carolyn. At first, I was pissed when she came in demanding I run tests for salmonella and what not. I told her this was a shelter not an animal hospital. All the while she was standing behind the blond, making frantic signals. Just a minute." Hank stopped and lit up a skinny brown cigarette, then leaned against the wall. "I'll smoke this back here so the secondhand prohibitionists don't call the Nineteenth Precinct, have me handcuffed, and thrown in jail."

"If P.S. gets away with it, why not you?" Lydia asked.

"They're scared of her," he said with a smile.

"Well, personally, I think it's very inconsiderate. It chokes me up," Allegra said, coughing to prove it.

"Feel free to leave," Hank told her.

Allegra didn't accept the invitation. Lydia borrowed a cigarette and lit up, too. Her first cigarette of the year, and it better be her last. Two years before she'd lit up on New Year's Eve and it had taken most of last year to break the habit.

Allegra stayed put but let them know she disapproved by coughing and waving away smoke. Hank winked at Lydia. "You were talking about Carolyn," she reminded him.

"Oh, yeah. Well, I agreed to do the tests since that's what she wanted. Or that's what I thought. She told me later she just wanted Diandre to think that so she could get the iguana away from her before it starved to death. After I agreed to the tests, she told the blond there was no need for her to stick around. She'd get back to her later with the tests results, but first we were going out for a drink so she could give me Iggy Pop's history."

"Did you ask her out for a drink?" Allegra said.

"That was the first I knew about it," Hank said.

"She must be pretty," Allegra said.

"She's a wonderful person. I wish she'd stayed, but she said it was an emergency."

"You mean you weren't with her later?" Lydia said.

"I wish. I'd no sooner ordered the drinks at Dresner's than she made this phone call and said she had to leave. The last I saw of her, she was standing in a snowdrift trying to wave down a cab. I guess she got one because she was long gone by the time I'd finished our drinks. Maybe I shouldn't have. When I got back I found the iguana stolen. I hope she forgives me."

"Are we going to stand here all night, or are we going back?" Allegra asked.

"No one's keeping you," Hank said rudely.

"It's spooky here. I don't want to go back by myself."

Hank stepped on his cigarette. "Through with that?" he asked Lydia. He took her cigarette butt along with his, doused both in a sink in the guard's room, and threw them into the trash can before they started back.

Lydia turned the doorknob on her right. The door was locked. She tried the one on the opposite side. Also locked.

"What are you doing?" Allegra asked.

"I want to see what's back here. I haven't explored this part of the shelter yet."

"There's nothing in these rooms. They're either empty or full of junk," Allegra informed her.

"Un-huh," Lydia said, trying another door.

"I told you there's nothing in there. Richard keeps them locked."

"If they're locked, how do you know what isn't in them?" Lydia asked, turning a knob and entering a room. It was dark, except for the light from the hallway, and smelled of antiseptic and alcohol. Little wonder. Bud lay sleeping on the couch.

"So this is where he disappears to," Hank said, looking in.

Allegra wrinkled her nose. "Ugh."

A bottle of Wild Turkey lay on the floor near the cracked leatherette couch where Bud lay sprawled.

"Out cold," Hank said. "That explains why he wasn't home when I called."

"And how that iguana was stolen," Allegra added.

"But that happened last night," Lydia pointed out. "He should have awakened long before now."

"Maybe he blacked out." Hank shook Bud's shoulder. "Hey, time to—" He broke off. Leaning forward, frowning, he felt the pulse on Bud's neck, then tried his wrist. "Shit."

"What's wrong?" Lydia said, afraid to ask.

"He's dead."

"Oh my God." Allegra stepped back from the couch as if death were contagious.

Lydia looked at Bud's face. He didn't look dead, but blissful. Serene. More peaceful than she'd ever seen him, the lines erased from his forehead. His mouth relaxed, not set in his usual mocking smile. Maybe Bud had been a tortured soul. She regretted not liking him.

"Look," Hank said, and pointed to a syringe that lay halfway under the couch. "It's one of ours."

"Drug overdose," Allegra said, reaching for the syringe.

"Don't touch it," Hank yelled. "Call 911. I know that peaceful look. It's not from dope. It's from what we give the animals when there's no hope of recovery—sodium pentobarbitol."

CHAPTER 14

Lydia was experiencing delayed reaction. Bud's death had suddenly hit her. She stood on the sidelines wondering who would want to murder him. Provided it was murder. Maybe he hadn't been dosed with sodium pentobarbitol as Hank thought.

It wouldn't be clear whether it was murder, suicide, or drug-overdose until the ME made his report, Detective Heller, the cop who'd questioned her, had said.

Under the red balloons and silver streamers that shimmered in the draft of the constantly opening and closing door, the Crime Scene Unit, carrying black bags and assorted paraphernalia, raced to and from the back room where Bud's body was found, now cordoned off with yellow tape and declared off limits. The police brushed off questions from the partygoers, speaking only to one another. Lydia supposed they wanted to avoid giving out information about a cause of death not yet determined, but the effect was that their time was too important to waste on lowly civilians.

The sound of sirens had penetrated the supposedly sound-proof holding rooms, frightening the animals. Or maybe it was the scent of fear leaking through the walls that alarmed them. Hank had rushed off to the infirmary to comfort his patients, while other shelter personnel had dispersed to the holding rooms to restore calm. But with everyone descending on them at once, the animals had only become more agitated. Lydia, who'd been among the would-be calmer-downers, had decided the animals would be better off with fewer people and left.

She, Hank, and Allegra had been questioned by Detective Heller the moment he arrived, and told to stick around. Lydia said a friend was picking her up at six.

"Call and tell him you'll be late," Heller said.

She wondered why he'd automatically assumed it was a man. "I can't. He's on the LIE coming in from Southampton. He's a homicide detective, too," she added. Which, as she suspected, made it okay to leave, as long as she left her name and phone number. In return, Detective Heller gave her his card.

Two detectives worked the reception area, asking questions. The one with the Rudolph the Reindeer nose was interviewing Judy, the animal trainer. He looked puny standing beside her. The other cop, a woman with an earth-mother figure and a master sergeant's demeanor, concentrated on Richard, who nervously fingered the bridge of his horn-rim glasses.

The parents with children had been allowed to leave. Apparently, having a child automatically disqualified partygoers from being considered a murderer. The shelter personnel who weren't with the animals or being questioned had gathered around the bar, hitting the hard stuff instead of sipping the Perrier or chardonnay they'd been drinking earlier.

Allegra St. John was the center of attention, her flawless complexion glowing, eyes popping, as she repeated the story of finding Bud's body. The listeners' faces turned red from excitement or liquor, or both.

"How you doing, kid?" a voice asked behind her. "Holding up?" Lydia turned. Hank.

"Okay, I guess. Everyone all right back there?"

"I dunno. They're in a highly excited state, and well-meaning people don't help. I threw them out. Animals are sensitive to humans' feelings. This is going to slow their recovery. I hope the cops leave soon and the place settles down," he said, more upset by the disruptive effect of Bud's death on his animals than by the death itself.

The red-nosed cop moved on from his interview with Judy to the chubby blond man with the camera, and the matronly figured master sergeant had left a nervous Richard and now talked to P.S. Richard stood by the bar.

"Why aren't you drinking and enjoying the excitement like Allegra?" Hank asked. "It's not every day you have a murder, you know."

No, just two last year. And this year was only beginning.

"How much sodium pentobarbitol would it take to kill a human?" Lydia asked.

"Depends on the weight. I'd say about seventeen cc for Bud. He must have weighed around a hundred seventy. One cc for every ten pounds."

"Do you really think it was murder?"

"I dunno. Maybe I'm old-fashioned, but I think you have to hate to kill. The strongest emotion Bud ever evoked was irritation, although I admit he could irritate the hell out of me. Now, if P.S. had been found dead, that would be a different story."

"I gather you're not a P.S. follower."

"I'm just talking about how a lot of people feel. The P.S.

people might not like Richard, but the Richard people hate P.S. Hell, I'd like to see them all kiss and make up. The shelter would run a lot more smoothly. The only advantage to their fight for power is when I want something for the animals. If Richard turns me down, all I have to do is go to P.S."

"Kind of like pitting your parents against one another."

"Yeah. Except mine divorced and remarried, so there was the complicating factor of stepparents and stepbrothers and -sisters. Mom's husband had three kids, and Dad's wife, two. We all grew up confused. This business about an unhappy marriage being worse than a divorce for kids is a crock. When I marry it's going to be permanent. That is, if I do. I'm getting a drink. Bring you something?"

"Thanks, I'll have a scotch. Lots of ice, light on the liquor."

He sauntered off, the fringes of his western jacket swaying slightly above that terrific tush. He cleared his way to the bar by lightly touching the shoulder of each woman in his vicinity. The women responded with a smile, moving into his way instead of out of it.

After exchanging a few words with Judy, Hank returned with two deep amber drinks, handing her one. It pinched her nose and burned her throat.

"She's making herself out a bloody heroine over there," Hank said.

"Allegra?"

"Yeah. The day vet tells me she's rough with the animals. I don't know why in the hell she's here."

"She said she wouldn't be if it weren't for the animals."

"She has an odd way of showing it. Maybe she's just clumsy." He gave a brief laugh and looked around. "Bud could have been killed by just about anyone here."

"But some of us don't know how much sodium whatsit to administer and how to use a syringe." Which you do, Lydia didn't add.

He checked his watch. "It's after six. And it's going to be a while before they finish up back there. What do you say we go out for dinner?"

"Thanks. I'd like to, but my dinner date is just coming in the door."

Lydia set her scotch on the counter and hurried off to Kramer, planting a big kiss on his cheek, and catching him by surprise. He smelled of the outside, cool and clean in the overheated shelter, like a breath of fresh air. Which was just what he was. And just what she needed.

CHAPTER 15

Throughout dinner, Lydia was aware that there was something different about Kramer, but she'd been too involved in telling him about finding Bud in the back room to analyze what it was—nothing as minor as a haircut or as major as losing a lot of weight, although she suspected he was on a diet. He'd eaten his salmon but left his bread and baked potato untouched.

They sat in the back overlooking the garden, where a spotlight shone on snow patterned by tiny bird tracks. Kramer listened intently. Light from the fireplace, guarded by a giant stuffed lion, flickered across his face. She felt his eyes searching for what she really thought. Kramer was like that, always delving beneath the surface.

They were sitting at what had become their table at Le Lionceau, a restaurant she and Kramer had decided his favorite writer, John Steinbeck, must have frequented. For one thing, the restaurant was near the house where Steinbeck had lived on East Seventy-eighth Street, and for another, it was one of the few restaurants in the neighborhood that dated back to the early fifties when Steinbeck lived there. Most East Side restaurants, Lydia told Kramer, lasted only as long as it took to get from the appetizer to dessert, which was what they were just about to have now, along with a brandy that Kramer insisted they both needed.

"Steinbeck would have had one," he said. "They lived a more civilized life back then." He had a way of attributing his preferences to Steinbeck.

"So what's convinced you it was murder and not a drug overdose?" Kramer asked, after a sip of brandy. He'd bypassed dessert. She'd asked for raspberries.

"He was an alcoholic, not a user. I don't know really, I just feel it. There's something going on at that place. I mean more than just those two warring factions I told you about. Heidi, the woman I replaced, was so desperate to leave she didn't even come back for her paycheck. But then Trish Ackers didn't cash hers in either."

"Trish Ackers. Is she someone new?"

"No, she's . . ." Lydia realized she hadn't mentioned her phone conversation with Milke or the puzzling business about Anima, the formula on Carolyn's desk calender, and the orchid in *gazelle* that resembled the one in Stuart Starr's garden, and the newspaper clippings about the frozen faces and froggy eyes—all the bits and pieces that she was trying to connect. Then there was Laura Haddon's fear of cosmetic surgery and her sudden—according to Gabriella, anyway—cheerful declaration that she was counteracting time's ravages. But even if she'd had Anima in mind, that wouldn't necessarily have any relation to her murder. Or would it? At any rate, it was all too nebulous to mention at the moment.

Out of the corner of her eye, Lydia saw that the woman in the sequined sweater at the next table was relating the details of a recent dream, and analyzing what it meant, unaware that she was putting her date to sleep. Am I being a bore, too? she asked herself. "Trish Ackers is another story," she told Kramer. "How was your day?"

"Exciting. I polished the silver while I watched the Rose Bowl."

"Why did you polish it? Are you planning to give a dinner party?"

"No reason. It just seems wrong to let it tarnish, that's all. Go on with what you were saying."

"Nothing really. Do you think I'm jumping to conclusions about thinking Bud was murdered?"

"He was murdered, all right," Kramer said.

"How can you be so sure? You didn't even know someone was dead until I told you."

"Yes, I did. A police car was pulling out when I drove up. I showed the cops my badge and asked what had happened."

"Detective Heller said he wouldn't know until the ME's report."

"Yeah, well, in the case of something like poisoning, there have to be tests. He couldn't tell you since it wasn't official," Kramer said, defending his brother in blue.

Lydia set her brandy glass down hard. "Dammit, that makes me mad."

"What?" Kramer asked in his mild-mannered way, which only irritated her all the more.

"*You.* You knew more than I did. You could have told me instead of letting me mouth off all through dinner."

She glared at her raspberries instead of him.

"Come on, Lydia, all I knew was some guy was murdered. I didn't know you'd found the body. I should have guessed, though. You have a knack for doing that."

Lydia focused on the outside garden, glad to see the pristine snow was now being pockmarked by rain. It had been all too beautiful out there, and life wasn't like that.

"Lydia, for God's sake, this is nothing to be angry about. What's really bothering you?"

"Nothing," she mumbled, aware that she was acting like a spoiled child. "What makes you think there is?"

"Hey, if you don't want to go on that trip, just say so, you don't have to pick a fight."

She pushed her raspberries away. "That isn't what it's about."

"Yeah," he said. "Okay."

But her sudden spoiling for a fight with someone as likable—well, even lovable—as Kramer, made her wonder if he wasn't right. She wasn't ready to sleep with anyone, and this was pushing things. She didn't even know how much she cared for Kramer, or, for that matter, how much he cared for her.

Intelligent brown eyes regarded her from behind horn-rim glasses rather like Richard's. Then she realized what it was that made him look so different.

"Since when did you start wearing glasses?" she asked.

Kramer sighed. "Last week. I've been putting it off for over a year. I knew something was wrong when I had trouble reading the phone book."

She smiled. She'd never thought of him as being particularly vain.

"My age is catching up with me. I'll soon be forty."

"How soon?"

"Too soon. January sixth."

"We'll celebrate your birthday in Vermont."

"We will?"

Their tender moment of mingling smiles and fingers was interrupted by the waiter clearing his throat. Behind him, the fire was burning low in the fireplace. Nobody had bothered to throw on another log. They'd probably hoped to close early. The woman in the sequined sweater and her sleepy date had already left. And there hadn't been many people to begin with. Around them were a lot of empty white tables with inverted glasses and peaked napkins; few people went out on New Year's night.

"Will there be anything else, sir?" the waiter asked.

Kramer sighed and glanced at his watch. "Just the check, thanks." He turned to Lydia. "He called me sir—that proves I'm getting old," he said when the waiter was out of hearing distance. "God, it's after ten and I was supposed to pick up Andy before midnight."

"It's been a short night," she said.

"Short, but worth every minute."

"All I've done is talk murder."

"Hey, murder is my business," he said. The waiter overheard and gave him a leather folder and a quizzical look.

Kramer opened the folder, looked the check over, and

slipped some bills inside. It seemed strange to Lydia, who always used her American Express card, that some people still paid in cash. The waiter ignored the folder, although he'd seemed to be in a hurry to get rid of them earlier.

"Is Andy going to mind my going along?" Lydia said.

"To be honest, I'm not sure. She's not used to sharing me with anyone. It's time she learned, though."

Lydia asked herself if she was going to enjoy a trip with a resentful child. And no doubt Andy's Montreal aunt would resent Lydia, too. Never mind that her sister had died years ago—Lydia knew that her very presence would be a reminder of what things might have been. She was already beginning to regret her decision.

The waiter finally picked up the folder, and shortly afterward brought the change.

They got their own coats from the check room, since the coat-check woman had already left. Outside, rain bubbled on the sidewalk and pelted the snow at the curb. They ran to the car.

"I'll make reservations at a lodge tomorrow," Kramer said, before starting the car. He traced her chin with a finger. "The one I have in mind looks great. Of course, Vermont isn't as fashionable as Vail or Aspen."

"Or Gstaad or St. Moritz," she didn't say. Places she'd gone in her *gazelle* days. She didn't miss any of them particularly, but Kramer might think so. "Vail or Aspen is where people go to be seen, not for serious skiers," she said instead.

There was scarcely any traffic, so they made it to her place in about five minutes. The house was totally dark when they drove up. "Either Carolyn is still out," Lydia said, "or she went to bed early, which isn't like her. It will be so nice when I have my own place. Then I won't have to feel like her guardian. Also, we'll have some privacy, instead of having her drop in on us like the last time."

"What's the latest on your moving date?"

"If those two aren't out by next week, I'm moving in with them."

After a long good-bye kiss in the car, they hurried up the

slippery stoop steps, clinging to one another like drunks. Kramer insisted on seeing her inside the door and turning on all the lights.

"Maybe I should check out the house," he said.

"No need to."

Kramer was overly concerned for her safety, which sometimes annoyed her, but he was a born worrier besides being a cop—who saw all the horrible things that happened to people—so she forgave him. Good thing she hadn't told him about being bonked over the head last night.

They kissed good night again, and then it was her turn to worry about him, driving on a slippery LIE back to Southampton.

CHAPTER 16

She found Colombo waiting just inside her door, eager for his walk. Damn. "There are times I wish you were a cat and used kitty litter."

Colombo wagged his shaggy tail, happy with things the way they were.

She attached his leash and hurried him down the stairs, eager to get the walk over and done with. But once out in the sleety world, pelted by icy raindrops, Colombo balked.

"The quicker you go, the quicker you get back," she told him.

He gave her an accusing look, as if she'd ordered the lousy weather just to inconvenience him, and stepped forward gingerly. Luckily, he was in as much of a hurry to return to the house as she was, and didn't futz around.

Back in her apartment, Lydia doffed her dripping Garbo hat,

wet coat, and boots. She gave Colombo a rubdown with a big fluffy towel and made herself some tea. The wind had picked up. It whistled around the corners, hurling sleet against the window. Good thing she'd taken Colombo out when she did.

She was pacing the room in her stocking feet, puzzling over the pieces of the day, when she heard mewing outside her door. Mewing? That couldn't be Alf. It was. He ran down the hall, paused at the top of the stairs, and looked back at her. Was he trying to get her to follow him?

Colombo joined her at the door, which sent Alf scurrying down the steps, but not so far that she couldn't see him. He let out another meow, talking to her. Recalling the night Colombo had led her to Adam's dead body in the swimming pool out at Southampton, Lydia's heart began to pound. But a cat was not a dog. Cats did not lead people to scenes of disaster; a cat led them only as far as an empty food dish—unless Alf was inhabited by Vashti's spirit, guiding her to some mysterious destination. God, she hoped she wasn't picking up Carolyn's crazy beliefs.

After closing the door to keep Colombo in, she followed Alf down the stairs in her stocking feet. He scampered ahead, furry red-gold tail sticking straight up, never getting so far in front that she would lose sight of him. She couldn't believe this. Was he actually leading her somewhere? No, that was absurd. Still . . .

Reaching Carolyn's bedroom door, Alf paused again. Lydia heard strange sounds inside. The noises were different from those she'd heard last night. A lot of slamming and banging. If it was sex, it was rough stuff. Something kinky? Carolyn playing the role of dominatrix, beating up her mystery lover, slamming him around? Or she might be fighting someone off. Maybe she should make a quick exit and call 911. Wouldn't Carolyn love it if DiFilippi and Haggerty burst through the door and found her in flagrante delicto?

"Carolyn, are you okay in there?"

No answer, but the whacking and bumping went on.

"Carolyn? Answer me, dammit."

Remembering the bop on the head she'd gotten the night

before, Lydia hesitated, listening. The noises were monotonous. Almost rhythmical. She threw the door open, prepared to run. And gave a relieved laugh. God, she was really coming unglued.

White-dotted Swiss curtains ballooned out from an open window, where the wind slapped around the venetian blind. A pool of water stood on the parquet floor. Lydia slammed down the window and, after peeking into the bathroom to make sure no one was hiding, snatched a towel from the clothes hamper and sopped up the water.

Alf stood in the doorway watching.

"You," she said. "You're worse than I am. Imagining things. Except where in the hell is she?"

Hank had said Carolyn had been trying to flag down a cab when he'd last seen her. But Carolyn wouldn't take a cab to come back here. It would have been quicker to walk than to find a cab during a blizzard. Despite Carolyn's fragile appearance and her claims of suffering from Epstein-Barr and any other trendy disease that came along, she was actually strong and healthy.

Where had Carolyn gone? And who had shared the couscous and champagne—not to mention her bed?

Alf was mewing again, trying to lead her on. He'd misled her once; she wasn't falling for that trick again. A musky pungent smell of incense overpowered the smell of Carolyn's perfume. Lydia plunked down on Carolyn's bed, wishing that Vashti, or the current spirit of Carolyn's choice, would whisper in her ear where her ex-friend had gone. The bed was haphazardly made, which wasn't at all like Carolyn, who was neat to the point of obsession.

A glance around the room showed that the person who inhabited it had a contradictory character—the delicate, dotted Swiss curtains in direct conflict with the wicked collection of African spears and the Samurai sword, all dangerously suspended on the wall above the bed. Noticing three empty leather loops, Lydia realized that one of the weapons was missing, but couldn't think what it was. Something small and portable.

In a corner by the window, mounted on a pedestal, was the

sculpted head of a priestess with long coiled tresses, high cheekbones, and half-closed eyes. The priestess bore an uncanny resemblance to Carolyn, which explained why Carolyn had bought the piece. Lydia wondered if the priestess was Vashti, whose origin she'd been unable to track down. Carolyn's answer had been vague when Lydia asked her, saying only that Vashti assumed various forms.

Lydia found Vashti's spirit stubbornly silent and left the room. Alf was still waiting in the hall. The moment he saw her, he scurried down another flight of stairs. Lydia followed to see what he had in mind.

What he had in mind, of course, was food. He led her into the kitchen. The poor little guy was not only out of food but also water. No wonder he'd been so eager for her to follow him. He hid under the kitchen table, watching while she replenished his water supply and spooned Science Diet into his dish. After she moved away, he crept forward, ears up, keeping a wary eye out for any suspicious movement from the enemy. Her.

She kept Alf company while he ate, standing statue still, not wanting to frighten him away. Carolyn might be absentminded when it came to people, but it was totally unlike her to let an animal go hungry. Lydia was trying to figure out what was so important to Carolyn that she'd forget to feed Alf when she heard the barking.

Alf disappeared. The barking came from below. Down in the basement. Clever Colombo might be, but he had yet to repair and master running an elevator. And she'd left him locked in the apartment. Besides, the bark sounded nervous and high-strung, unlike Colombo's macho woofs.

Lydia opened the basement door and peered down. Dark. Carolyn always left the hall light on. Maybe Amon was in his room with the door closed.

"Amon, do you have a dog down there?"

The barking became wild, but welcoming. She proceeded down the stairs. The farther down the steps she got, the more frenzied the barks became. She'd nearly reached the last step when it occurred to her that she was making a mistake. The dog could be mad, or rabid, and about to attack. Safer to go back upstairs.

She'd no sooner thought this than a light flashed on and she found herself staring into the muzzle of a shaky gun.

"Hands up or I shoot." The voice was young, edgy, and deadly.

Lydia wasn't familiar with firearms, but whatever this kid had in her hands didn't look like a water pistol.

CHAPTER 17

"Stay where you are if you don't want to get plugged," a tall redhead said. She wore movie-star sunglasses, black leather, and blue denim. And looked to be about fifteen years old.

Lydia would have laughed at the cliché warning, except it wasn't a laughing matter. The voice was as high and excitable as the greyhound's bark, while the wobbling gun pointed at various parts of Lydia's anatomy, all, to her way of thinking, equally precious and vulnerable.

"Would you please put that damn thing down and tell me what you're doing here?"

The redhead smirked. "I'm not talking. None of your business."

"It is when you're holding a gun on me."

Lydia had a sudden flash. "You're the one who banged me over the head last night, aren't you?"

The kid smiled a dangerous, dimpled smile of acknowledgment. She was having a hard time focusing the gun on Lydia and restraining the dancing dog at the same time. She needed her pal Amon's assistance. Where was he? Lydia wondered. More important, where was Carolyn?

Carolyn might put up with a lot of funny stuff from Amon, but she'd draw the line at his bringing home a beautiful little girlfriend. Or would she? Carolyn might not object to a ménage à trois. She liked her fun and games.

The redhead was hanging on to the dog's collar, pulling him back while he tugged toward Lydia, prancing up and down, slavering, eager that they become friends. It seemed improper for a dog as beautiful and graceful as a greyhound to behave in such an undignified manner, but Lydia was glad. It kept the girl's mind off shooting her.

The greyhound bounded up and delivered a slobbery kiss on Lydia's cheek, then leaped up and kissed the girl, knocking off her sunglasses and sending them clinking on the cement floor.

The kid had an ugly black eye, puffy, surrounded by bruised and yellow skin.

"Who gave you that?" Lydia asked.

"I'm not talking." Then: "Lucky, sit!" she ordered.

Lucky? Something clicked. *She got Lucky,* Stuart Starr had said last night. Or something to that effect. At first, Lydia had interpreted the remark to mean that a kid named Tiffany had lucked out in some way, but he'd meant the dog. Lydia remembered his fury when he'd found out that Diandre had taken the iguana out of the house. "You're Tiffany, aren't you?"

The kid had tightened her finger on the trigger, still refusing to say anything.

"Did Carolyn lure Hank out of the shelter so you could sneak in and snatch your iguana?"

"I don't know any Hank."

"The guy on duty last night at Nora's Ark. That's when you got Iggy Pop. Where is he?"

The kid stepped closer, but still stayed out of reach. "You're not getting your filthy hands on him," she said, and tossed a quick glance over her shoulder toward the Tranquility Room, a dead giveaway.

"So you and Lucky ran away?"

The kid's face remained impassive, but at the sound of his name, Lucky's ears perked up.

"How you doing, Lucky?" Lydia asked. The dog nearly went berserk at the sound of his name, trying to break away from Tiffany and run to her. "Are you the Lucky I've heard so much about? Glad to meet you, Lucky."

The greyhound danced a frenzied dance toward her again, his nails scratching the cement. Tiffany yanked on his leash, but not hard. The one thing in her favor was that she clearly loved her dog.

"You're lucky to be here, aren't you, Lucky?" Lydia went on.

Just as she'd guessed, hearing his name so often was too much for the dog to resist. He broke loose and ran over and kissed her. Lydia could have kissed him back in gratitude. She grabbed his collar to keep him beside her, sure that as long as there was any danger of hitting him, Tiffany would hold her fire.

"Let go of my dog," Tiffany said, moving in.

Lydia crouched behind Lucky, who was straining to get back to Tiffany. The animal was surprisingly strong. She had to hold on to his collar with both hands. When Tiffany took a step forward, Lydia took a step back, dragging Lucky with her.

The dog struggled. He didn't like this game. With an enormous burst of energy, he broke away, racing to Tiffany, nearly knocking her down in his display of affection. His back foot hit the sunglasses on the floor and sent them skidding down the hall.

While Tiffany was trying to fend off Lucky's frantic leaps and kisses, holding the gun out so she wouldn't accidentally shoot her beloved animal, Lydia grabbed her wrist and twisted. Hard.

The kid was strong and wiry. She kicked, scratched, and screamed. Lucky interpreted their struggle as a game and barked enthusiastically, cheering for both sides. Lydia got a rigor mortis grip on Tiffany's wrist and kept twisting until the gun clattered to the cement floor. She snagged it up and poked it against the black leather jacket, between the wings of Tiffany's back. "March," she ordered. "Upstairs."

"You're too chicken to shoot me," Tiffany said, starting to turn around.

"Right. I wouldn't shoot you. I'd shoot your dog."

Her threat got Tiffany up the stairs while Lucky scrambled back and forth between them.

Up in Carolyn's kitchen, Lydia pointed Tiffany to a chair at the table by the window, where sleet pinged against the glass. "Sit," she commanded. "Both of you."

Tiffany sat, but Lucky made a beeline for the dish on the floor and polished off the Science Diet in one gulp.

"Hey, you," Lydia said. "That's Alf's food."

Wolfing down another animal's food didn't bother Lucky's conscience. He jumped up and down, begging for more.

"Who's Alf?" Tiffany asked, looking around as if she expected to be attacked.

"Carolyn's cat."

"I didn't see any cat."

Didn't, Lydia noted, not don't. "You've been up here before, haven't you?"

Tiffany clamped her mouth shut. She watched Lydia closely, biding her time for a chance to snatch her gun back.

"You could have at least fed Alf. The poor little guy was starving when I fed him," Lydia told her.

"Did you feed him for the kill?"

"What are you talking about?"

"The guilty always ask that," the girl said, looking at Lydia with green-eyed loathing. In the overhead kitchen light, Lydia saw that her left eye was nearly swollen shut. There must have been a lot of fury behind the fist that delivered those blows.

Lucky was running wild between them again. His distracting antics could cause her to lose the gun to Tiffany just as Tiffany had lost it to her. Keeping the gun trained on Tiffany, Lydia hooked a finger through Lucky's collar and dragged him into the dining room.

"Don't kill him," Tiffany pleaded. "Kill me instead."

"I'm not going to shoot him. I'm putting him in here so we can talk without interruption."

The minute Lydia closed the door on Lucky, he began scratching and barking for readmittance.

She ignored him, walked over, and stood across the table from Tiffany, keeping the gun on her. "Talk. Tell me what you're doing here."

"Not unless you let Lucky back in."

"Where are Carolyn and Amon?"

Tiffany pressed her lips together, jiggled a blue-jeaned leg, and looked beyond Lydia with her good eye. The kid tried to be cool, but she was jittery, always swinging a foot, twisting a strand of hair, shifting positions. She gave a jump at the sound of ice cubes falling from the freezer into the tray.

"You know, Carolyn's interest in Amon extends beyond her being his boss," Lydia said, hoping Tiffany would rise to the bait.

Tiffany scoffed. "He's not interested in her. She's too ancient."

"Young boys are often attracted to experienced, older women."

"I'm plenty experienced. I'm not worried. I trust Amon," Tiffany said. "Vashti, too," she added. Lydia detected a certain amount of bravado in her voice. "They have a platonic relationship," she insisted.

"So why are you protesting so much?"

Tiffany clammed up and regarded her suspiciously. Lydia wondered if Tiffany was suspicious of everyone in general or of her in particular. She grew tired of standing and sat down across from Tiffany at the table. The kid watched her and the gun from the corner of an eye and, jiggling a leg, whistled under her breath in an attempt to prove that the silence wasn't getting to her. Her message to the world was that she could take anything it dished out. Then: "This jacket's hot. Can I take it off?"

"All right, but no funny stuff. You try that, and Lucky gets it in the head."

Tiffany removed the jacket in slow motion, stalling, trying to figure out how to get her hands on the gun. She wore an acid-green T-shirt with Betty Boop's heart-shaped face, pouty lips, and long, curly eyelashes outlined in black. Carefully, she draped the leather jacket over the back of a nearby chair, fingers pressing out the wrinkles.

"Come on, Tiffany, stop stalling. Tell me how you got Carolyn to go along with you last night? What bill of goods did you sell her when she found you downstairs with Amon? How did you manage to get her to agree with your plot to steal Iggy Pop?"

"I didn't steal him. I rescued him. Vashti sees the truth. She believed me. Believes me," Tiffany amended. "*She* knows I'm not lying."

"Lying about what?"

Tiffany gave a comical imitation of a sneer, but that didn't mean she shouldn't be taken seriously. A jittery amateur could be as deadly as a cool pro. "About what that scumbag is up to."

"Scumbag? I thought you got fined a dollar for saying such words."

"Yeah. She's such a good friend of yours she tells you everything, right?" Tiffany said, still watching Lydia's every move.

Lydia laughed. "Last night was the first time I met the woman, believe it or not. I went there looking for Carolyn because that's where Amon had said she'd gone. You must have heard him. You were standing behind that door after you zonked me.

"Diandre Denvers isn't the real villain in this. She's afraid of Stuart Starr. Or maybe just afraid of losing him, I'm not sure which. You'll be glad to know that she doesn't want the iguana back. Or you. She considers you competition."

For the first time Tiffany looked at her as if she wasn't a creature from outer space.

"So how did you get Iggy Pop back?"

"Like you said."

"You'd get fined another dollar for that."

Tiffany smiled. "*As* you said. Hypocrites. They're so persnickety about how we talk but not what we do." She gave a small, bitter laugh, then heaved a worldly sigh as if this were just too much to explain to a simpleminded person. "Vashti called Amon and said the coast was clear and to get Iggy Pop.

We nearly got caught, though, when we went into the shelter."
Her face lit up. Obviously, she'd enjoyed the adventure.
"Someone was coming down the hall."

"Who?"

"I don't know. We couldn't see them—just heard the footsteps coming toward us. We barely had time to hide behind the
counter."

"Them?"

"It was just one person. I said 'them' because I don't know
if it was a man or a woman."

"No clicking heels or heavy footsteps? Nothing that might
tell you the difference?"

She shook her head. "As soon as they left, we grabbed Iggy
Pop and took off," she said triumphantly. "Boy, was he glad to
see me. I wanted to call and tell that filthy creep that I got him
back. But Vashti said I shouldn't. All the same, he'd better
watch it. One of these days he's going to climb into his car and
get blown to smithereens. Just like in the movies," she said,
humming the theme to *The Godfather*. Her eyes sparkled with
hate.

Lydia could see why Diandre found this kid scary. She was
a disaster waiting to happen. Biding her time to get back at the
world for what it had done to her. And at the moment Lydia
was the world to her. She tightened her hold on the gun.

CHAPTER 18

Sleet clattered against the kitchen windows, increasing in in-
tensity. Across the table Tiffany shot Lydia looks of pure,
unadulterated hate.

Lydia wished Carolyn would come back and take over. She

didn't want to spend the rest of her life sitting with a gun trained on a child. In the meantime she'd better find out all she could.

"What time were you in the shelter last night?"

"I'm not telling you anything as long as you have my gun in your hand."

"Do you think I'm crazy enough to put it down? If I'd decided to shoot you, I'd have done it by now. What time were you there?"

"I'm not sure. What do you care?"

Lucky had started up again, howling for company.

"Listen to him. He's lonely, and you don't give a damn."

"For the moment I'm more concerned about the murder last night at the shelter." She wasn't sure the murder had happened at night, but she wanted to see the effect on Tiffany.

Tiffany's good eye widened in either genuine or pretend innocence. "Someone was murdered?"

"A security guard."

"There wasn't any guard when we were there."

Lydia wondered if Carolyn had killed Bud so Tiffany could get her iguana back, until she remembered that Carolyn had been at Dresner's with Hank.

"They didn't steal the animals, did they?" Tiffany asked anxiously.

"They? You mean the person who killed the guard? No. What makes you think someone would?"

Another laser look of hate. "You tell me."

Lydia sighed. "The only animal who disappeared was Iggy Pop. You have a lot to thank your friend Vashti for."

"I will when I see her."

"You didn't see her last night?"

"We figured she went with the vet to his place."

"She was here."

"You saw her! Where?" Tiffany gave Lydia a suspicious look, as if she'd done Vashti in.

"I didn't see her. I heard her—them—in the bedroom when I went by."

Tiffany started giggling. "That was us."

"You and Amon?"

"His room is hardly the Plaza. And the first time should be romantic, you know."

The first time for this kid must have been many men ago. Lydia hated to think how many. She was still a child, with baby fat plumping out her cheeks. Dangerous and reckless, but nevertheless a child. "You mean it was you and Amon who ate my couscous and drank my champagne?"

"You made the couscous? It was super."

"Glad to hear it. So where is Amon now?"

Silence. Alf appeared and crept over to his empty dish.

"Don't move a muscle," Lydia whispered. She got quietly out of her chair, trying not to make any abrupt movement that would frighten the cat. It wasn't easy keeping the gun on Tiffany and spooning food in Alf's dish. He ducked into a narrow space between the stove and the counter, eyeing her as suspiciously as Tiffany. After she sat down, he came tiptoeing out, sniffed, looked around him, took a dainty bite, and settled down to serious eating.

"The poor thing's starved." Tiffany's remark sent Alf scurrying back to his hiding place.

"Great. You've scared him off."

"What's he so scared of?" Tiffany asked.

"He's not so much scared as wary. He was rescued, barely alive, from an experimental lab. Carolyn is the only human he doesn't run from."

"He didn't run from you."

"Yeah, well, you know, animals recognize the essential goodness in people." Lydia said it as a joke, but Tiffany took it seriously.

"Vashti says a person isn't trustworthy if animals don't like them."

"Vashti would say something like that."

"She was talking about you. She said animals didn't like you. That proved you were in on the deal."

"What deal, for God's sake?"

"The one the fat feeb talked about."

Lydia was trying to make some sense out of this talk about

deals and fat feebs and Carolyn's obvious lies, but it was hard to think with Lucky howling again. His whines were as pitiful as the plea in Tiffany's eye. "Okay, okay," she said. "If I let him in, will you tell me what this is about?"

Tiffany nodded vigorously.

Unlike his mistress, Lucky wasn't a grudge holder. He jumped up and kissed Lydia as soon as she opened the door.

"Lucky, come here, honey. Come to Mommy," Tiffany called, sounding jealous. Lucky bounded over. Tiffany hugged Lucky and talked. Having the dog at her side appeared to have a calming effect on her.

All it took was a little prompting. "The feeb," Lydia said.

"*Him!* I hated him. Even before I knew. Stuart made me"— she stopped and searched for a word—"go to bed with him," she ended up lamely. Hardly the expression Lydia would have expected from a hooker, even one so young, but apparently Diandre had done a good job of cleaning up her charges' language.

"Was Diandre in on this, too?"

"No. Yes. I mean she didn't try to stop anything. She just stood by wringing her hands and asking what was going on. Stuart gave her his credit card and told her to take the kids to Saks. He pockets all the money. She's *so* dumb. You'd think she'd at least have her own credit card."

"Does he pocket your money, too?"

"That goes for my higher education," Tiffany said defensively.

Lydia didn't argue the point, not wanting to risk the chance of breaking Tiffany's sudden talking spell. She didn't allow herself to ask any more questions when something wasn't quite clear. She forced herself to stay immobile, barely breathing, the way she had earlier when she hadn't wanted to scare off Alf, and listened to the pinging sleet and the high, excited child's voice.

"He was ugly and greasy and mean. And he had bad breath. Not like our usual trade. I mean, he just—shoved it in. At least it didn't last long," she told Lucky, hugging him to her Betty Boop T-shirt, as if she were comforting him.

"Then he started talking. Bragging. That's what they really come for," she said, one beautiful green eye on Lydia. "Talk. They pay us mostly to listen. Sometimes it's some big business deal they're trying to pull off. I bet I know more than *The Wall Street Journal*. Or what's really crazy, they talk about their wife and kids. Show pictures. A lot of times their kids are older than me. I mean, it's really pathetic, you know.

"Except the feeb didn't pay. I'm on the house, courtesy of Stuart Starr, so he'd do what they wanted and keep his mouth shut. But he talked anyway. Told me what they're doing. God, I couldn't believe it. He even bragged about it! It made me sick. I threw up. That's how I got the black eye."

"He hit you?" Lydia said, breaking her vow of silence.

"No, that was courtesy of Stuart Starr again. He thought I threw up because of what the feeb did, not what he said. Hey, getting beat up is no big deal—that's SOP, you know. Standard Operating Procedure. Army talk. My stepdad is a career soldier. *Him.*" She packed a lot of hate into that little word.

"Was he why you ran away?"

"Mom didn't believe me. She said I was always lying about something. So I got Iggy Pop and hopped on the bus for New York. And guess who I ran into when I arrived at the Port Authority Bus Terminal?"

"Stuart Starr?"

She shook her head. "Diandre."

"So Diandre said, 'Poor little girl, come with me. There are so many big, bad people in this city,' and took you to her town house."

"It was awesome. Like the pictures I'd seen of the White House. All that marble and so many rooms! And they were really nice, Diandre and Stuart. They let me and Iggy Pop have our own room and Stuart bought him a terrarium. Heather and Jamie were already there. Stuart said I could write romances, too. Diandre was so beautiful and he was so sweet and generous. I thought they were the two most wonderful people I'd ever met."

"Until they started giving you assignments."

"Yeah. But when they weren't around we'd talk about leaving, all of us girls. Diandre suspected. She told us scary stories about life on the streets and how Stuart had saved her, and how grateful she was, and how we should be the same—that we were getting an education and blah, blah, blah. And Stuart would always be extra nice to us. It may sound funny but we sort of considered him a father, someone who'd take care of us, you know? Then, when that feeb told me what he and Stuart were up to, I had to stick around to find out more so I could put a stop to it. My big mistake was confiding in Heather and Jamie. I thought they could be trusted. Instead they ran straight to Stuart and reported me. He locked me in my room and took Iggy Pop. I have this little balcony in my room. We each have one. I climbed from mine to Heather's. Luckily, Heather wasn't in her room. I managed to get out, but I couldn't find Iggy Pop anywhere, so I grabbed Lucky and got away. If he finds me he'll kill me." She hugged Lucky so hard he let out a yipe. She kissed him and apologized profusely.

All the love this kid had to give was lavished on the dog.

Lydia risked putting the gun down, but not within Tiffany's reach. Even if Tiffany wasn't a criminal but just another victim, she didn't quite trust her. On the other hand, if she were going to find out what Tiffany knew, delicacy was required. "What did the feeb tell you?" Lydia asked, as softly as when she spoke to Alf.

It didn't work with Tiffany either. All she got was that hostile look again.

"I thought we were friends."

"Vashti said you weren't to be trusted."

Lydia wondered if Vashti was whistling looney tunes again. "Vashti is sometimes mentally shaky. And extremely paranoid." Unfortunately, this kid seemed to fit the same description. Although, admittedly, Tiffany had more reason.

"Vashti said you'd say that."

Lydia tried logic. "If she thought I wasn't to be trusted, why would she invite me to stay in her house?"

"She said she didn't know the real you until yesterday when she talked to Ms. Exner from the shelter."

"Ms. who? Who is Ms. Exner?"

Tiffany suddenly looked stricken. Obviously, she'd let the name slip. "Vashti didn't say."

"I don't know any such person. The lady's mad."

"That's what you said about Vashti."

Lydia listened to sleet hammer the window, and tried to figure out who Ms. Exner might be. Had Carolyn conjured her up for her own twisted purposes? Then she remembered the copy of the list of nationwide shelters on Carolyn's desk with the name "H. Exner" written above PROPERTY OF NORA'S ARK. She also recalled the formula on Carolyn's desk—the same formula as in the *gazelle* article. Had this Exner person mentioned the formula to Carolyn? But what connection would a formula appearing in *gazelle* about a magic potion called Anima have to the shelter? And why would the mysterious Ms. Exner tell Carolyn not to trust her?

Lydia decided that if she was going to get any information from Tiffany, she'd have to convince her she was on the side of the angels—or rather the animals. Ignoring Tiffany's hostility, she casually mentioned the arrival of the buncher at the shelter yesterday.

"What's a buncher?"

"Bunchers steal animals and sell them to licensed dealers who pretend not to know the animals are pets stolen from people's cars or backyards. Dealers are the guys who supply labs with animals for testing. But the buncher might not resort to dealers. He might act on his own or with some cohorts, raid an animal shelter, and sell the animals to illegal labs or crazy religious cults that slash animals' throats and let them slowly bleed to death—"

"Don't!" Tiffany said, clapping her hands over her ears, in exactly the same way Lydia often did. Lydia took mercy on her and didn't go into further ugly detail. "Anyway, this pigtailed cowboy came in yesterday with a little girl for cover. He claimed he was getting the kid a dog for Christmas. But I saw him sizing up the place, suspected the worst, and threw him out."

"He had a pigtail! Was he fat?"

"Yeah, well, a beer belly—beer belly, beard, greasy pigtail, and cowboy boots. Why? Does he sound like someone you've seen before?"

"What kind of cowboy boots?"

Lydia tried to remember, then it came back to her. "Snake-skin. Joey Buttafuoco. Joey Buttafuoco is the guy—"

"It's him!" Tiffany yelled. Lucky jumped up and looked around as if he expected to see someone. "The feeb! You threw him out?"

The buncher was the feeb? What did that mean? Why would he show up at both Stuart Starr's house and Nora's Ark? Coincidence maybe. Other than the fact that both he and Stuart were ruthless men who subjected the innocent and helpless to ill use and abuse—and in the case of the animals, to slaughter—Lydia couldn't imagine what they had in common.

Suddenly, without warning, Lucky charged into the living room. Tiffany jumped up and ran after him, and Lydia ran after both of them. Lucky was barking like crazy at the door, where someone was knocking.

"That's not Amon. He'd come in from downstairs," Tiffany whispered, clutching Lydia's arm. "Maybe it's Vashti."

"She wouldn't knock. She lives here," Lydia pointed out.

"Maybe she forgot her key," Tiffany said hopefully.

Lucky danced around the front door, barking loudly.

"Don't open it," Tiffany said, her voice sounding small and scared. "See who it is first. Maybe it's *him*. He'll recognize Lucky's bark and know I'm here." She stood in the kitchen doorway, ready to run out the back way.

Unfortunately, Carolyn's door with the Palladian window didn't have anything as mundane as a peephole. Lydia hurried to the front window and looked out, recognizing the bulky shadow.

CHAPTER 19

"It's okay, it's Amon," Lydia called to Tiffany. But was it okay? Thanks to Carolyn assigning her the role of the evil one, Lydia wasn't sure if Amon harbored the same ill feeling toward her as Tiffany had. Would she and Amon team up against her? Well, she still had the gun.

Although Tiffany stood on the far side of the room, she beat Lydia to the door and flung it open, falling on Amon as enthusiastically as Lucky. Amon's blue parka was sopping wet, but Tiffany didn't seem to notice.

In the midst of the happy reunion, Amon spied Lydia. "You're trespassing. This is Vashti's place."

"So are you, kid. You're also dripping on her Oriental rug."

"Oh, yeah, sorry." He tiptoed across the rug and out to the kitchen, with Tiffany hanging on to an arm and Lucky nuzzling a hand.

"Lydia is okay," Tiffany told Amon. "She kicked that feeb out of the shelter yesterday. You know, that creep I told you about? The one I overheard talking to Melissa Starr in the greenhouse about their terrible plans." She shot a warning glance at Lydia to keep her mouth shut and not reveal where, or under what circumstances, she'd really come by her information. "He threatened to kill her," Tiffany added for good measure.

Amon hung his wet parka on the back of a kitchen chair while Tiffany continued singing Lydia's praises, telling him how brave she'd been in saving the animals. Less than a half hour ago Tiffany would have shot her if she'd had the gun.

Tiffany was one of those people who divided her world into heroes and villains. She saw everything in primary colors.

The phone rang suddenly. Lydia grabbed it. The voice at the other end was breathless and shaky, speaking before Lydia had a chance to so much as say hello. "Amon! Meet me at Nora's Ark. They've—"

The connection broke.

"Carolyn," Lydia said. "Either she got cut off or she had to hang up. She told me to meet her at Nora's Ark," she lied. "You can come along," she told Amon. "Let me grab my jacket."

"Me, too. I'm going with you," Tiffany said.

"Stay here in case she calls again," Lydia yelled over her shoulder as she started up the steps. Why was Carolyn going to the shelter and why did she want Amon there? Or maybe she'd called from the shelter.

Lydia flew into her apartment. While she scrambled into her ski clothes, she explained to Colombo why he couldn't go along. Her ski outfit was a North Face. They didn't come any better or more expensive, and hers had seen the action on the best and most exclusive slopes from Gstaad to Aspen. The trouble was that its vivid blues, greens, and purples, designed, for purposes of safety, for high visibility on the slopes, would be all too easily seen in the dark. But her long black coat would hamper her progress. She opted for speed over visibility and, after slipping the gun and a pencil flashlight into her jacket pocket, rushed back downstairs.

Amon was waiting by the door, parka hood pulled low over his head. Remembering the sleet, Lydia lowered hers. Tiffany clung to Amon as if he were going off to war. "Come on," Lydia called, halfway out the door. "Your Vashti could be in trouble."

"The animals, too," Amon said, extricating himself from Tiffany and Lucky and following her down the stoop.

"They'll be okay. Darryl's on duty."

"Who's he?"

"One of our security guards. The one who didn't get killed."

"Yeah, Tiffany just told me."

"I hope he's safe. Darryl's just a kid, not much older than you, but very responsible. He's studying computer programming at Baruch and—"

Amon wasn't listening, but walking, almost running, ahead of her down the block. The sidewalk was like a skating rink under the stinging sleet. Lydia skidded and righted herself. "You walk like you're used to this," she said.

"My Eskimo blood."

Always so damn careful not to reveal where he came from.

They crossed to First Avenue. The reflection of red lights wavered in the wet streets north toward Harlem. A cab ran the light, splashing water over them.

They made it to the shelter in record time, thanks to Amon's breakneck speed and Lydia's determination to keep up with him.

"Dammit," she said. "It's completely dark in there. Darryl forgot to turn the lights on in front. He's probably in back studying."

Lydia fished her keys from her jacket pocket, unlocked the door, and flicked on the light. The place was tomb silent.

Bouquets of red balloons and dangling silver streamers blew lightly in the draft of cold air coming down from the domed skylight; otherwise, nothing stirred.

Lydia saw that someone had moved the showcase cages back into the reception area after the party. Then she saw something else, and her heart took a dive. "Oh, my God, where are they?"

"We're too late," Amon said, his voice breaking.

She took in the details slowly, as if they were too much to grasp. The cage doors were open, and all the cages empty, except for the fighting cock who looked at them with fierce beady eyes. Emil and the puppies and kittens were gone.

"Darryl," she yelled. Her voice echoed around her. Goddammit, she was tired of calling people and not getting an answer. Then she thought of something hopeful. She'd intended to stop off and see Emil at the open house this afternoon, but after she'd found Bud's body, she'd forgotten. For all she knew Emil and the puppies and kittens might have been put in different cages temporarily. She explained this to Amon. "These are the special showcase cages that we keep up in front. Darryl must intend to move the animals into them later. He just hasn't moved them up yet." With the cage doors hanging open? With everyone gone but the fighting cock?

"Yeah, maybe that's it," Amon said, wanting to believe it as much as she did.

"Let's go back and check." She spoke in a deliberately loud voice to scare off any intruders. She stamped her feet noisily and told Amon to as well.

"Maybe they've got Carolyn back there," Amon said, forgetting to call her Vashti.

"Or she might not be here yet."

"I thought you said she was."

"She said to meet her here. I don't know where she was calling from."

"Maybe she got here before us and she's in trouble." Amon ran ahead calling, "Carolyn, Carolyn."

The echo repeated up and down the hall along with their footsteps.

"Maybe she only answers to Vashti," Lydia suggested.

He switched to Vashti. Neither name worked. And why didn't Darryl come out and see what all the noise was about?

Lydia switched on each light she came to, wishing that sweet, brave Emil was with her. He'd take a chunk out of anyone coming near.

Up ahead a door banged, back and forth, back and forth.

Amon dropped back. "Are you carrying?" he whispered.

"Huh?"

"Tiffany's gun. She said you took it. Do you have it with you?"

Lydia patted her jacket pocket. "In here." But would she use it? "How about you?"

"A knife."

Why didn't that surprise her? "One of those stiletto jobbies they sell on Forty-second Street?"

"Yeah, this'll really carve you up," he said dryly, and produced a Boy Scout knife. "My Dad gave it to me."

It was the first time she'd heard him mention anyone in his family but now was not the time to ask questions. It was far more important to find out about the animals than his father.

They reached the holding room for the dogs.

"It's locked," Amon said. "They couldn't get to them."

Lydia hoped he was right, and refrained from pointing out that it locked automatically. She got out a key. "Pray they're okay," she said. She stepped inside, holding her breath, reassured by the sound of barking, then had trouble breathing at all.

Amon let out a cry as if he'd been hurt.

Before them, row on row, wall to wall, were empty cages with doors hanging open. Only a few elderly dogs remained. They crowded forward in their cages, barking the kind of welcome they might have barked to the thieves when they broke in. "You don't know how lucky you are," she told them.

In their hurry to steal the dogs, the thieves had knocked over the food and water dishes. Small mounds of dog food and animal shit had been mashed underfoot, leaving footprints.

Amon reached in and stroked a grizzled muzzle. "Maybe they just took the dogs," he said hopefully. "Maybe they didn't take the cats and kittens."

But they both knew better. They checked all the holding rooms in order to make sure. It got harder with each door, knowing what would be on the other side. Except for the elderly and sick animals in the recovery room, all the animals including the cats and kittens were gone. The cats had put up more of a fight. Some of the cages were knocked over, and there was blood on the floor. She hoped it was the thieves' blood and not the animals'.

"They only wanted the younger, healthy ones," Amon said. "Just like—" He stopped.

"Just like what?"

"Just like what you'd expect."

"That wasn't what you were going to say."

He remained stubbornly silent. She became aware of the banging door again.

"They left the door open," Amon said.

"What does that matter? They got what they wanted. Come on, let's find Darryl. Maybe he didn't come in tonight."

"Maybe someone told him not to," Amon said. "Maybe that's how they planned it. Maybe he was in on it. Helped set it up. That's what they do, the fuckers."

It was the first time she'd heard him swear. "How do you know?"

"That's what I heard."

She'd ask him about that later. "I can't see Darryl doing this. He liked animals too much."

But what did she really know about Darryl? He worked the midnight-to-morning shift and was usually gone before she came in. All she knew was what Shantel had told her. Besides working here to pay his tuition to Baruch, he helped his grandmother support his three kid brothers.

They walked cautiously down the hall, passing the room where she, Allegra, and Hank had found Bud's body. The yellow police tape was still stretched across the door.

Up ahead, the ramp looked spooky in the shadows. Lydia remembered the loaded trolley rolling toward her. Had Bud been trying to kill her or scare her away? And had he been killed because he knew the animals were going to be stolen? Blackmailing somebody? Out of the blue, Lydia remembered the fragmented letter. *You said to write if the situation became desperate.* Heidi must have written that. Was Heidi really on an around-the-world cruise as Richard said, or hadn't she claimed her paycheck because she was dead? Richard had also said P.S. had talked to Heidi when she hadn't come back from lunch. But either he or P.S. could have been lying. Lydia decided to call Heidi. She didn't know her last name, but the number would be in the shelter phone book. If she'd sublet her apartment, the tenant would probably have seen her before she left on that cruise. "I'll call her tomorrow," Lydia told herself. "If I live through tonight, that is."

Reluctant to venture onto the shadowy ramp, Lydia played the pocket flashlight on the wall. "There's a light switch here somewhere," she told Amon. Then, pointing the pocket light toward the back, she saw sleet pellets blowing through the

swinging door and heard them bouncing on the cement before
the door banged shut again. She was hurrying to lock it when
she stumbled on something. Lydia aimed the pocket light at her
feet.

"Quick, find the wall light," she said, hoping it wasn't what
it looked like.

Her heart thumped in her ears. It seemed to take Amon forever to find the switch. Finally, light flooded the ramp.
Stretched out on the cement was a body. He was young and
dark and wore a blue uniform. It looked like open season on
security guards.

CHAPTER 20

Lydia pressed her thumb on Darryl's wrist, but her own pulse
was pounding so hard she had trouble finding his. And what if
he had no pulse to find?

"I think he's breathing," Amon said reassuringly. He placed
two fingers on Darryl's neck in a very professional manner.
"He's okay. His pulse is real strong."

She let Amon take over, since he was better at this business
than she was. Lydia stood by as Amon swabbed Darryl's forehead with damp paper towels. "You okay?" he kept asking.

Finally, Darryl moaned and opened his eyes. It took a while
before he focused on them. "What happened?"

"That's what we'd like to know," Lydia said. "How are you
feeling?"

"Dumb," Darryl said, sitting up. He looked woozy. He felt
the back of his head. "I got a lump back here big as an egg. Feel
it."

Lydia and Amon both felt the lump under his bristly hair. "I think you've got the dimensions right," Lydia said.

Darryl started to get to his feet and sat down again.

"Careful," Amon warned. "You might have a concussion."

After another try, Darryl managed to stand up to his full six-foot-seven. "Wow," he said, and shook his head.

"You didn't see who did it?" Lydia asked.

"Nah, they snuck up from behind. It wasn't long after Shantel left. She was keepin' me company. Lucky she wasn't here when it happened."

"How long ago was that?"

"I dunno. I dunno how long I was out. The cops were packing up when I got here, 'round seven, I guess. Judy and Shantel, they took the dogs out and exercised them. Then Judy went home."

"They had to have a long reach to hit you on top of the head," Amon said, gazing up admiringly at Darryl.

"Or a long-handled weapon," Lydia said, thinking of the three empty loops on Carolyn's bedroom wall. She remembered that one end of the missing weapon was an ax and the other end a hammer, handy for thumping someone. Also, the handle was fairly long. But it didn't make sense for Carolyn to clobber Darryl, since he was on the side of the animals. Except nothing made sense—especially Carolyn's actions.

"I was bending over when he did it," Darryl said.

"He?" Lydia asked.

"Whoever. Anyway, I was looking at the door lock to see if it'd been jimmied open." He gingerly touched the back of his head again. "Good thing you guys got here when you did. No telling how long I'd be out cold. How come you're here, anyway?"

"We got here too late," Amon said, unable to say anything more. Darryl looked puzzled. It hurt Lydia to say it, too. "They got all the animals," she told him finally.

"Aw, shit! They stole *all* the animals? *All?*"

"All but the old guys and the fighting cock," Amon said.

"Shit, I shoulda been more careful. I'm studying, you know? Up in front at your desk," he said to Lydia. "I don't like that hole of a guard's room. I hear some kind of noise back here and take a look. I don't see anyone, but I see the back door isn't shut tight. So I'm bending over looking at the lock like I tell you when something comes down on my head. Bam!"

"They jimmied the door open?" Amon asked.

"No one broke in. They had a key."

"They must have had a key to the gate, too," Lydia said. "Otherwise they couldn't have driven the truck out or whatever they used to transport the animals."

"Yeah, you're right. We keep a set on the board. Anyone could've grabbed them and made duplicates, I guess."

"Let me borrow your flashlight. I'll go out and look around," Lydia said. "Maybe they left some kind of clue. We're wasting time standing around talking. We've got to find the animals before it's too late. But you should go to the hospital," she told Darryl. "We'll do the looking."

"Nah, I'm okay." Darryl refused to relinquish his flashlight. "I'm going with you. It's my job."

They went outside into the punishing sleet. Lydia put her hood up. Darryl played his flashlight across the puddled dog run to the gate in the tall fence that separated the shelter grounds from the sidewalk. "Yeah, it's open, all right. They just unlocked that gate and drove in. Hey look, a white van! Over there!" He beamed the light to their left, where the trucks dropped off supplies. "It's not a van," he said, correcting himself. "It's an ambulance from East End Hospital."

Lydia heard Amon's sudden intake of breath.

"East End Hospital is two blocks away. Why is their ambulance here?" Lydia asked. "And where is Carolyn?"

"Yeah," Amon agreed. "She should be here by now. She didn't have that far to go."

"What do you mean? Where's she been all this time?"

"Tell you later," Amon said, and took off after Darryl, who was loping through the driving sleet toward the ambulance. Lydia followed.

The cab was empty, but there was a key in the ignition.

"Why would someone come here in an ambulance, leave the key, and go?" Darryl asked.

"We might have scared them off," Lydia said. "They knew we'd hear the engine start up, so they took off on foot."

"Maybe they left the animals in back when they took off," Amon said when they reached the van. "It smells like animals. Like they're scared." He whizzed past Lydia and Darryl to the rear of the van, swinging open the back doors.

"Phew! It stinks," Darryl said, joining Amon in a few long strides. He played the flashlight around, climbed in, then gave a low whistle. "Shit!"

The flashlight was suddenly shaking in Darryl's hand, skipping and darting around inside the ambulance. Lydia scrambled up into the van behind him. She didn't see the body until the light darted to the floor. A man with a red beard and a beer belly, wearing snakeskin cowboy boots, stared up at nothing.

"Is he dead?" Lydia asked, kneeling beside Darryl.

"If he's not dead, he's Superman," Darryl said. "Got him right in the heart. I can't find a pulse."

Blood spread like an ugly flower, blending in with the red plaid shirt. It looked like he'd been shot, but she couldn't tell what had happened because of all the blood. They looked at the man in silence while sleet pinged on the roof.

"Call 911," Lydia called to Amon, glancing over her shoulder. But Amon was gone. "Where did he go?"

"Maybe he's already calling them," Darryl guessed, looking up. "No, he's not. There he goes!" He beamed the flashlight on the figure in a blue parka speeding through the open gate.

"Hey!" Lydia yelled.

For a moment Amon turned toward her, his face white in the glare of Darryl's flashlight. Then all she saw was the back of the parka.

"Hey, come back here," she screamed. "You're going to be in serious trouble. I'm not going to lie for you." She was wasting her breath. He'd already disappeared from sight.

"Why's he running off like that?" Darryl asked.

"He's scared."

"What's he scared of?"

Lydia shook her head.

Darryl remained with the body while Lydia went inside to make the 911 call.

Drenched and shivering from the cold and the sight of two dead bodies in one day, Lydia hurried down the ramp toward the hall. She spied something glinting faintly on the cement floor, stepped over it, then went back and scooped it up—a stainless-steel guardian angel. Lydia remembered how proudly Carolyn had shown her the pendant, a Christmas present from Amon. Had Carolyn lost it last night when she was here with Diandre? Or tonight after she called Amon? If Carolyn had gotten to the shelter before her and Amon, where was she now? And what had Amon meant when he'd said Carolyn didn't have far to go to get here?

Lydia slipped the pendant into her ski-jacket pocket and hurried to the guardroom in search of the nearest phone.

She'd just called 911 when Darryl came in, his blue uniform soaked through. "I got spooked hanging out there with that dead guy," he said.

They hurried to the church part of the shelter in front, where they stood near the door waiting for the police, taking some comfort in one another's company.

Lydia averted her eyes from the depressing sight of the empty cages under the festive red balloons and silver streamers.

"Maybe we shouldn't mention the kid," said Darryl, who wasn't a lot older than Amon. "Like you said, he took off 'cause he's scared. I mean, that guy back there was dead before you two got here."

"Yes, okay." Lydia remembered Amon's surprised intake of breath when he'd seen the ambulance—how he'd been so sure the animals were in back. Not mentioning to the cops that he'd been with her would make things that much easier. If she mentioned him, she'd have to explain why Carolyn had hired, and sheltered, a runaway kid in trouble with the law. One question could lead to another and she'd end up having to explain Tiffany and Lucky and Iggy Pop and the romance-writing pimp and his orchids and their possible connection to Anima, a product mentioned in an article of a magazine she'd once edited. They'd find it all too farfetched, and question her sanity. But she'd certainly tell them about Stuart and Diandre's exploiting those little girls. See that those two were brought up on morals charges. She should have done that already—but things had happened so quickly. She'd also tell the cops about Carolyn, who might have been taken along as hostage, and could be in grave danger. The sooner the cops knew about this, the better the chance that Carolyn—and the animals—would be found.

Outside, police cars came to a screaming stop before the shelter. Plainclothes and uniform cops spilled out. The Crime Scene Unit was back, along with a man in a khaki jacket who greeted her at the door. "Well, we meet again," Lieutenant Larry Heller said.

CHAPTER 21

Lieutenant Heller found a parking space two doors down from Carolyn's place. He had a peanut head, otherwise he would have been attractive. But maybe his head looked so small because of the enormous khaki jacket he was wearing. Heller yawned, settled back, and stretched an arm along the back of the car seat, almost but not quite around her. Lydia edged toward the door. Heller shook his head as if trying to stay awake, and smiled over at her.

"You keep long hours," she said, ready to jump from the car. Trouble was, she was in no hurry to go home. Up ahead Carolyn's house lay in total darkness. She wasn't sure what awaited her. She was glad she had Tiffany's .38. If it's them or me, I'll use it, she assured herself, not sure who "them" was.

"I came on duty at four," Heller was saying. "Just in time to catch that first murder at the shelter. I'm supposed to be off at midnight, but there's paperwork to do. My wife is used to my coming home late."

"Where do you live?"

"Staten Island."

"Don't any New York cops live in Manhattan?"

"Who can afford it?"

He described the difficulties of making ends meet on a cop's salary. Lydia nodded her head and worried about Carolyn and the animals. Heller had put out an all points bulletin, but there wasn't much to go on.

Explaining how she happened to be at the shelter had been easier than Lydia thought. Too easy. For a cop, Heller wasn't terribly curious. He looked close to retirement age. Maybe he was just putting in time. Or maybe he thought she had an honest face and believed every word she said.

Lydia had left the shelter in charge of Judy and Hank, since the two people who ran it—Richard and P.S.—couldn't be reached. Neither had answered the phone.

"P.S. is spending the night with her creep boyfriend," Judy said. "And Richard is up at his vacation place."

"You mean he's left town?"

"He always goes up there after New Year's Day. He deserves a mini-vacation," Judy said protectively. "You didn't know he was leaving?"

"He didn't mention it to me." Probably too embarrassed to, taking off to have fun while she came in to work. "Where does he go? Do you have his phone number?"

"Vermont. I don't have his phone number, do you?" she asked Hank. Hank said he didn't either.

"Where in Vermont?" Lydia asked.

"In the ski area."

"That covers a lot of territory."

"P.S. probably has his number. I'll ask her tomorrow," Judy said. "That is, if she's talking to me."

According to a conversation Lydia had overheard between Detective Heller and a cop who'd checked with the East End

Hospital, the dead man in cowboy boots was Russ Tanner, one of their ambulance drivers.

"He had a reputation for using the ambulance as his own private means of conveyance," the cop had said. Lydia had already told Heller about Tanner's appearance in the shelter the day before. "I'd hate to be in the ambulance with that guy," she'd said, forgetting she wasn't supposed to be listening in on the conversation between Heller and the cop. "Remind me never to go to that hospital when I'm sick."

The cop had also taken Darryl to East End Hospital to get checked out, and said Darryl seemed to be okay. Before Darryl left, Lydia had coaxed him into facing the media and pleading the urgency of finding Carolyn and the stolen animals. The media had already gotten word of the murder, and were hanging outside Nora's Ark with their vans and bright lights and coils of cable, ready to pounce.

Lydia looked toward the dark house again. There was no guarantee that Tiffany wouldn't turn on her for some paranoid reason and, if Amon had returned, convince him that Lydia was the enemy. Lydia could handle one or the other's hostility separately, but together they'd be deadly.

On the one hand, if she invited Lieutenant Heller in to look around, and he found Tiffany and Amon and asked if they were related to Carolyn, she'd have a lot of lying to do. How else to explain the presence of two young teenagers except to say they were Carolyn's cousins or siblings?

On the other hand, this could be a good time to report Stuart and Diandre and their exploitation of the teenage girls. Tiffany could vouch for the fact. But Tiffany might deny it if Amon were there. She might want him to think she wrote romances and not know what she really did. It would be better to wait and call Heller tomorrow when he came on duty.

But at least she could have Heller check out her apartment. She'd just have to chance it that Amon and Tiffany weren't in Carolyn's part of the house.

"Would you mind checking out my place?" she asked. "I'm beginning to think that wherever I go, a body will show up."

"I can see why you'd think that," Heller said. "I was going to suggest it myself."

They ran through the sleet toward the house and up the stoop. "Carolyn lives down here," she said as they entered. "I generally take the elevator on the ground floor up to my apartment, but it's broken."

"Nice place," Heller said, looking around. "She must not be hurting for money. What's down below?"

"An animal spa."

"What the hell's that? She give pigs mud baths? Sounds nutty. People pay money for something like that?"

"You'd be surprised."

"Hey, I'm a cop, remember? Nothing surprises me. Let's check this place out. How do you get there?"

Tiffany would be down below with Lucky. Maybe she should tell Heller about Stuart and Diandre, after all. The sooner she reported them, the sooner they'd be out of business. "Listen," she said, "There's a young girl downstairs, a beautiful little fifteen-year-old redhead who ran away from a sleazy couple who lured her into service as a call girl. And she's not the only one, there are other young girls—four of them."

By the time she'd finished her story, Heller was seething with rage. A vein throbbed in his temple. "I have a daughter that age. I'll move on those two first thing tomorrow. Goddamn, I'd like to get my hands on that scum. I want to talk to the girl," he said, yanking open the door and starting down the steps.

Lydia laid a detaining hand on his arm. "If her boyfriend's there, don't mention it. She may not want him to know anything, and might deny it in front of him."

"Yeah," he said, "I hear you."

But would he do as she asked? Anger had already propelled him to the bottom of the steps. Lydia ran after him, wondering why Lucky wasn't barking. The place was quiet as a crypt. They checked out the storage room, the office, the waiting room, and found no presence, animal or human, except in the soundproof Tranquility Room, where a frantic Lucky, who must have caught their scent, greeted them at the door, barking wildly. An iguana, dozing on the gravel in the pool under the dry waterfall, raised his prehistoric head, and looked at them with heavy-lidded, ancient eyes.

"Who the hell are these guys?" Heller asked, trying to stave off Lucky's frantic kisses.

"The iguana is Iggy Pop, Tiffany's pet iguana. And this poor, love-starved animal is Lucky." It came to her that the reason Tiffany loved Lucky so much was because of their mutual need for love.

"Where's the girl?" Heller asked.

Lydia shook her head. "I guess we'd better look around upstairs." She promised Lucky his mistress would be back any minute, and closed the door on him.

Heller was thorough. After he'd checked out the kitchen, dining room, and living room, they went up to the third floor, where he looked in closets, under beds, and behind shower curtains. They proceeded to her floor. Colombo was the only one waiting in her place. He cozied up to Heller, sniffing his trouser cuffs.

"He smells Gotto," Heller said.

"Gotto?"

"My dog. You've never heard of Joe Gotto?"

"Isn't he some Mafia don?"

"Right."

"In prison?"

"Where he belongs."

"Why would you name a dog after a gangster?"

"He's a pit bull. He'll tear you apart if you trespass on his turf. Got any idea where that girl might have gone at this hour of the night—I mean, morning? She wouldn't have gone back to that scum, would she?"

"I doubt it. She hated him. Besides, she wouldn't go anywhere for very long without Lucky and her iguana. She took Iggy Pop with her when she ran away from home. That was before she got Lucky—her dog."

"Tell me about her," Heller said. "Got any coffee?"

"Decaf?"

"Nah, nothing keeps me awake."

She invited him into the kitchen. While she brewed coffee and fixed herself chamomile tea, she told him all she knew about Tiffany, Stuart Starr, Diandre, and their four little slaves. "Those kids are so emotionally needy, they'll do anything for love."

"Hey, you're making me feel guilty. I don't see as much of my two kids as I should." Colombo put his head on Heller's thigh as if to comfort him. "Nice doggy," Heller said. Colombo wagged his tail.

After Lydia set a cup of coffee before Heller, she joined him at the kitchen table, and sipped her chamomile tea.

"So what about Tanner and this guy Tiffany calls the feeb?" Heller prompted, spooning sugar into his coffee.

"They're one and the same person. And he told her of some deal that he and Starr had together. She told two of the other girls, Heather and Jamie, about it. They ratted to Starr, who locked her in her room. She climbed from her balcony to an adjoining one and got away."

"What was this deal?"

"I don't know. I think she was about to tell me when Carolyn called from the shelter," Lydia said, fudging the truth and not mentioning Amon. "And now she isn't here to ask. Tiffany, I mean. Even if she were here, I'm not sure she trusts me enough to tell me. But it has something to do with animals," Lydia said, surprised to hear herself saying what she hadn't been aware of thinking. "This kid is cynical where humans are concerned—with reason—but she loves animals. And she was nauseated by what Tanner told her to the point where she threw up."

Encouraged by Heller's nod, she continued. "It has to do with stealing animals," she amplified. "I'm not sure for what purpose. I thought at first Tanner was a buncher—someone who steals animals and sells them illegally. He might be, but there's more to what's going on if Stuart Starr is involved. He lives too high on the hog to be in anything penny ante. The payoff would have to be big. And it must have something to do with Nora's Ark. Tanner visited there yesterday, and tonight he's found dead in an ambulance parked behind it. In the meantime the animals are stolen."

"You said earlier that he had a pretty little girl with him you were sure wasn't his daughter. Maybe the person who killed the scumbag was doing us all a favor," Heller said. "Maybe that's the deal those scum are in on. Pimping children."

"Diandre wouldn't allow it. She might rationalize teenage call girls, but never a child of seven. She's a rotten person, but not that bad." Lydia hoped what she said was true.

"Maybe she didn't know about the very young ones. Any coffee left?"

"She knows something about something but not everything," Lydia said, refilling Heller's cup.

"Did you tell your boyfriend Kramer any of this?"

"How did you know his name?"

Heller smiled at her above the steaming cup. "I have my ways."

"You're pretty thorough."

"So what did he have to say?"

"I was so distracted by the security guard's murder that I forgot to mention it—to either of you. And I didn't talk with Tiffany until after Kramer left. But I still think that deal is connected to animals and Nora's Ark. Last night Starr got unduly upset when Diandre said she'd taken the iguana there. Not many people have heard of it. And something else . . ." She told him about the orchids in the greenhouse and the flower in the article about Anima in *gazelle*.

Heller looked skeptical.

"I'll show you," she said, getting the magazine from her bedroom. She handed him the article.

"Yeah, well, I'm not a botanist, but it looks like just another white flower to me."

"Yes and no. The petals have the same shape."

"Yeah, okay. So what are you saying?"

"Well, why would a guy have *gazelle*, a woman's fashion magazine, hidden in a greenhouse drawer?"

"Magazines are often put in drawers. That woman, Diandre Denvers, reads it. So what?"

"Well, she threw a fit when she found me looking in the drawer."

"She probably thought you were snooping. But for the sake of argument, say this orchid is connected to the flower in *gazelle*. They're flowers. What does Anima have to do with animals?"

When he said it aloud she had a "eureka" moment. "It's like *Ulysses*. Joyce's, I mean."

"You lost me."

"The meaning isn't clear until it's read aloud."

"We didn't read it at Rutgers. Enlighten me."

"Anima, animal. All you have to do is add the *l*. Get it?"

His look said he didn't.

She tried again. "Anima sounds suspiciously close to animal—and an article on Anima is found in Starr's greenhouse drawer." She limped to the end of the sentence. Her theory sounded weak, maybe a little wacky, when put into words. "Maybe it's a little farfetched."

Heller got to his feet. "Honey, you said it; I didn't."

"You don't have to be so bloody condescending."

"Sorry." He got his khaki jacket. "Thanks for the coffee."

"Thank you for checking out the place," she said coolly. "No bodies after all."

Heller smiled. "Don't sound so disappointed." He gave her his card and told her to call when Tiffany came back. "Don't worry," he said soothingly. "I'll find out what she knows about the deal."

Lydia returned his smile, fully intending to find out first.

CHAPTER 22

As soon as she was alone, Lydia felt an overwhelming sense of depression. Although she'd disliked Tanner from the minute he'd swaggered into the shelter, and liked him even less after what Tiffany had told her, she was still jolted by the sight of his body lying on the ambulance floor in the blood-soaked plaid shirt. He'd been shot twice in the chest, Heller had said. Two murders in one day were too much.

Who could have killed Tanner, and why? And why had Amon run off when he saw Tanner's body in the ambulance? Was Heller right in his guess that the connection between Tanner and Starr was pimping and had nothing to do with animals, which had even less to do with Anima? If only Amon hadn't interrupted her and Tiffany by his ill-timed arrival, she might have found out. And now she wouldn't know until Tiffany came back—that is, if she did.

Lydia's head teemed with questions. Sleep would be impossible. She made herself more chamomile tea and drank it seated at the kitchen table, listening to the wind and sleet rattle the window, knowing that somewhere a truck traveled through the night crammed with crated, terrified animals. And the horror had only begun. Soon they'd be tortured in some lab. She remembered Hank's graphic descriptions of brains cut open, blistered skin, and blinding by hair spray.

Maybe the animals had already arrived at their destination. The nightmare could begin in the morning. Colombo rested his head on her thigh to comfort her as he'd done with Heller. She thought of brave, loving Emil headed toward his doom, and kissed Colombo between his floppy ears.

The worst of it was that she felt so helpless to prevent the animals' slaughter. Dammit, P.S. and Richard should be doing something. They knew more than she did about animal thieves and illegal labs or, for that matter, legal labs who got their animals illegally. It annoyed her that Richard had taken off for a ski holiday in Vermont while expecting her to come in and work. Little wonder he hadn't mentioned his trip.

On the off chance that P.S. might not be spending the night with her boyfriend, after all, Lydia tried her number again, and got the answering machine. "While you were out the animals were stolen and someone else murdered," she said. That should get a response.

She turned again to the article in *gazelle*, and again wondered if Laura Haddon had been referring to Anima when she'd talked about repairing time's ravages. Lydia studied the dewy white flower that so resembled Stuart Starr's greenhouse orchid, and reread the definition of *anima*, whose first meaning was soul, life, specifically the animal soul. She was positive of a connection between Anima and animal, no matter how much Heller scoffed at the idea.

She was about to pour herself more tea when Colombo gave a sharp bark and made a wild dash into the living room. She followed him and stopped cold in the doorway. Colombo stood before the elevator door barking. Her pulse thumped as she listened to the sound of grinding and slamming in the shaft as the elevator rose toward her floor. The elevator that was supposedly not running. Someone was on the way up! Carolyn? She was the only person who had a key besides Lydia. Wrong. Amon must have a key in order to repair it. But he hadn't repaired it. Maybe it hadn't been broken after all. Maybe he'd lied.

Remembering that she'd left Tiffany's .38 in her jacket pocket, she ran to the closet, grabbed the gun, and trained it on the elevator door, ducking behind a fat chair for cover. Her heart banged against her chest as she listened to the creaking cables.

The elevator shuddered to a stop. The accordion gate folded back, and the door slowly opened. Colombo barked and danced up and down as excitedly as Lucky. How could she shoot without hitting him?

"Hey, hi, how's my pal?" a young voice whispered to Colombo. Amon dropped to his knees and gave the dog a hello hug.

"I thought you said the elevator was broken," Lydia said, rising from behind the chair and keeping the gun focused on him.

"I lied. Carolyn told me to," he said defensively. "So you wouldn't be going in and out and find Tiffany. Tiffany was supposed to keep Lucky in the Tranquility Room so you wouldn't hear him bark. But she said it was cruel to keep him shut up in one room, and let him out. That's when you heard him. Did she leave you a note?"

"Tiffany? Why would she?"

"She's disappeared."

"I'm aware of that."

"I thought she might, because she likes you. While you were getting your coat she said she liked you better than Vashti. When I got back here she was gone."

"When you got back after taking off at the shelter, you mean?"

He studied his sneakers. "I got scared when I saw that guy lying there."

"You recognized him, didn't you?"

"I never saw him before in my life. I swear on a stack of Bibles."

She knew he was lying by his reddening cheeks. "And you recognized the ambulance, too. I could tell by the way you reacted."

"Why would I lie about something like that?"

"That's what I'd like to know. So would Detective Heller."

"You told a cop I left the scene of the crime?"

He looked so frightened that she took pity on him. "I was tempted to. Where were you when Heller was here?"

"Hiding in the elevator. Do you think maybe Tiffany was kidnapped? She wouldn't leave without Lucky and Iggy Pop.

Maybe that creep guessed she was here and took her up there with the animals."

"By 'creep,' I assume you mean Stuart Starr?" Amon nodded, and Lydia's heart skipped several beats. She'd been right about Starr's connection to the animals. "Up where?"

"Nowhere. It's just, you know, an expression, something you say."

"I don't say it unless it's a direction. What is Starr's interest in this?"

Amon bit his lip and avoided her eyes. Lydia flopped down in the fat chair, pretending indifference. "The longer you hold out on me, the less chance there is of finding Carolyn and the animals alive."

Amon still stood by the elevator, the traitorous Colombo by his side. It occurred to Lydia that Tiffany might have been sent by Starr to spy on them—to find out how much they knew about what was going on. Ridiculous. She dismissed the idea. Tiffany genuinely hated Stuart Starr. And adored Amon. On the other hand, she'd seemed to adore Carolyn and had, according to what Amon just said, shifted her allegiance from Carolyn to her. As much as Lydia wanted to credit this shift to Tiffany's good taste and sound judgment, she was afraid that the word to describe Tiffany was fickle. She cared only for Lucky and Iggy Pop. But then she'd gone off and left them, too.

"Are you just going to sit there and not do anything?" Amon asked.

"How can I do anything as long as you lie? I know very well you know Tanner."

Amon looked surprised, then wary. "You know his name?"

"The cops checked his identification. He's an ambulance driver at East End Hospital. Makes you think twice, the next time you call 911 on an emergency."

"Did Darryl go to emergency? Is he okay?"

"Nice of you to ask."

He didn't miss the sarcasm. "Well, he seemed okay to me. I appreciate his not ratting on me."

"Hey, I didn't rat on you either," she reminded him.

"If I told you everything, you wouldn't believe me," Amon said. "You'd think it was your duty to turn me in. Hold that gun on me and call the cops."

"I don't consider you to be a killer, okay? You're too empathetic to be one. Look, my nerves are frayed and my patience is about to run out. Now, either you tell me about it or get out. I'm tired. In two minutes I'm going to send you packing and go to bed."

He hesitated, looked toward the elevator door as if he might take off, then sat down on the sofa and hugged Colombo. Like Tiffany, he needed an animal to cling to while he talked. The beginning was slow.

"Amon isn't my real name. That was Carolyn's idea. My real name is Gary. Gary Grillo."

Once Gary Grillo got started talking, he couldn't stop.

Lydia listened as he described the ambulance screeching up to a stone quarry in Vermont where he waited with his father in a borrowed truck. "The same ambulance as tonight. But back then it was filled with crates and the crates crammed with animals. I could smell how scared they were. The same smell as tonight. It brought everything back. That's another reason I took off.

"I took off back then, too. I wasn't going to help them do their dirty work—Dad and this guy Tanner. I headed for the woods. They chased me for a while, then gave up. When I thought it was safe to come out, I went back. The truck was there. Empty. I figured the ambulance driver had gotten mad and drove off and Dad was in the woods somewhere looking for me—if I went looking for him, we'd miss each other. So I sat on this big boulder called Suicide Rock and waited. It was getting dark but still light enough to see, you know?

"I looked down and saw something like a big fish floating in the water. It was Dad. I think Tanner must have stabbed him and shoved him into the quarry. He had a knife, I saw it. I knew better than to hang around and wait for him to come back and kill me, too, because I knew he did it. But I couldn't go home. I'd said a lot of times I'd like to kill Dad. The kids at school heard me say it. Mom, my friend Kathy—everyone. As soon as someone found Dad dead in the quarry, the cops would haul me in and accuse me of murder. So I took off."

"Most kids say they'd like to kill their parents at one time or another. You're not the first."

"Yeah, but their dads don't turn up dead. We fought, too, Dad and me. I nearly punched him out once after he beat up Mom."

This kid's father sounded like a real winner.

He leaned forward. "I think I know where they took the animals tonight. I figured it out. Dad told Mom we'd be back by supper. Supper's at six. It was about a quarter to four when we left. We reached the quarry around four o'clock. Say Dad figured it'd take another fifteen minutes to transfer the animals. That makes it four-fifteen. So in order to get back by six, including time to unload and the fifteen minutes it takes to get from the house to the quarry—the place must be about forty-five minutes from there."

"Your Dad didn't tell you where you were going?"

"He wouldn't tell me anything. Neither me or Tanner. I think that's why Tanner killed him. Dad wasn't supposed to know where Tanner got the animals, and Tanner wasn't supposed to know where Dad was taking them. Whoever was in charge didn't trust either Dad or Tanner. But Tanner got real mad when Dad refused to tell him."

"He must have choked the information from your father then killed him."

"Either that or he got the instructions Dad had in his pocket afterward. Then struck a deal with that creep Starr or someone."

"Are there others?"

"Ms. Exner told Carolyn there's several besides the ones at your place."

"Who's Ms. Exner?"

"Her Afghan, Greta, was Vashti's first client. She thought she was pregnant. Greta, I mean. Vashti convinced her it was a false pregnancy."

"How did she do that?"

"You're not going to believe this."

"When it comes to Carolyn, I'll believe anything."

"She sent me out to buy a pregnancy kit, ran a test, and showed Greta the negative results. And it worked!"

"You're right. I don't believe it."

"I wouldn't have either if I hadn't been there. Anyway, Ms. Exner thought Vashti was terrific and knew how much she loved animals. That's why she came in yesterday and told Vashti about all the weird stuff going on at Nora's Ark. She didn't know who else to turn to. Vashti was the only person Ms. Exner trusted, Vashti said."

Vashti would. "So what are the weird things going on at Nora's Ark?"

Gary's face became guarded. "You should know, you work there."

"I know there's a war going on between the owner and his office manager, but that's it. Tiffany was just about to tell me when you came back and pounded on the door," Lydia said, not quite sure if Tiffany would have told her anything.

"When Vashti discovered Tiffany downstairs yesterday, she was ready to throw us both out. But after Tiffany told her why she'd run away—about overhearing Tanner and Starr and their plan to steal the animals—Vashti said it fit right in with what Ms. Exner said and she'd help Tiffany get Iggy Pop back."

Lydia noticed that Tiffany had altered the facts, claiming she'd overheard Tanner discuss his plan instead of bragging to her about it in bed. She was right in guessing that Tiffany didn't want Gary to know the sordid details of her life.

"So what did Ms. Exner tell her?"

"You're not going to like this. Vashti said Ms. Exner— Vashti calls her Heidi—"

"Heidi? The woman who didn't come back to work at the shelter after lunch?"

"She was scared to."

"What did she say?"

"You're not going to like this."

"So you've said." Colombo left Gary and returned to her side. To lend sympathy for what she was going to hear?

Heidi's story sounded crazy to Lydia. Little wonder Carolyn

believed it. It was the sort of thing Carolyn would make up herself. Still, it began believably enough. Like Lydia, Heidi had
thought Bud had taken off from the shelter late one day only to
discover he was there all along. He'd also been drinking, and
he'd invited Heidi to go out with him, which she refused to do.

"He told her she'd change her mind when he came into
money," Gary said. "So Heidi asked how. And he said the shelter was a gold mine, and he knew what was going down and
was going to make it pay off."

"Blackmail?"

"Yeah, that's what Heidi thought. She couldn't get much
more out of him except that some snotty woman was coming
in and to watch out for her—she couldn't be trusted. So when
Heidi told Vashti that yesterday, you know what Vashti
thought?"

"I'm afraid to ask."

"Well . . ." he hesitated. "She thought the snotty woman was
you."

"But he didn't say coming to work, he said coming in."

"Vashti said that's what it meant. And Bud told Heidi she'd
better keep her mouth shut if she didn't want to end up missing
along with the animals."

"So she got scared and quit?"

"Yeah. At first she thought of telling someone there, but
when she came in the next morning, someone had let loose a
German shepherd who'd have torn her apart if the rescue squad
hadn't killed him."

"The rescue squad wouldn't kill an animal. They'd shoot it
with a stun gun. Besides, the German shepherd is Emil, a
sweet-natured animal."

"Well, that's what Vashti said Heidi said."

Lydia didn't know how much credence to give to Heidi's
story, if any. Shantel had said Heidi was a flake. But Bud had
ended up dead, and the animals had been stolen. Heidi might
have gotten things confused, but she'd been right about what
would happen.

It occurred to Lydia that Allegra had come in around the
same time she had. But Allegra was friendly, not snotty. Still

she might have seemed snotty to Bud, a man with an inferiority complex. Also, a dermatologist would be more likely to have heard of Anima than most people. Maybe Allegra saw a chance to enhance her appearance as well as her finances. Obviously, anyone who wore Donna Karan and Ralph Lauren was concerned about how she looked and needed money to indulge in her tastes.

"So what are you thinking?" Gary asked, waiting expectantly for her to come up with some kind of solution.

Lydia's head was in too much of a muddle to attempt to work things out. "How long does it take to get from New York to—where are you from?"

"Woodboro. Woodboro, Vermont. Maybe three and a half to four hours." His body grew tense. "Why do you want to know?"

Woodboro? She'd heard that name before. Except she couldn't remember where. But she was sure it wasn't too long ago. Within the last day or two.

"It will take longer than four hours to get there in this kind of weather," she told him.

"You're going up there?"

"So are you. As soon as I can get the car from the garage. It's supposed to be open twenty-four hours."

"No way. I'm not going. They'll pick me up and throw me in jail."

"I need you to tell me how to get there. You can duck when we go through town. If we're lucky and track down Carolyn and the animals early on, there's a good chance of finding them alive."

"And of me going to prison."

CHAPTER 23

She'd been white-knuckling it since Albany. The sleet had frozen, making the turnpike treacherous. She should be driving a Cherokee instead of her Corvette. But at least it was equipped with all-weather tires. And if she was slowed down, so was the animal transport. There might be a chance of catching up with them after all.

She'd done some heavy thinking on the way up, and remembering the events of New Year's Eve when she'd stayed late at the shelter, she'd come up with where she'd seen the name Woodboro—on the form requesting animal information that P.S. had become so excited about. It had taken her a while to remember Société chimique, and the name hadn't been listed in the all-in-one phone book she'd checked out when she stopped off at a diner for coffee. But it might have an unlisted number. It was hardly the sort of place that would advertise its presence, although a foreign name sounded strange in these surroundings, it sounded innocuous enough.

Why, she wondered, would someone transport animals to a place so far away? Why not find a nearby animal shelter to raid? Because those shelters had already been raided? Or because raids aroused suspicion?

The drive up had already taken close to six hours, and it was after ten when she arrived in Woodboro, a small, pretty town that surpassed Brigadoon, Ohio, in clinging to the past. The town square in Brigadoon had given way to a shopping mall, but this town square appeared to be thriving, supplying the essentials, including a general store, drugstore, bowling alley, and a luncheonette called Ruth & Ralph's. In the distance, a church spire pointed toward the clear blue sky.

Colombo stirred in the seat beside her, as if aware they'd reached their destination. It took about ten minutes to drive through the town.

Outside Woodboro, on Route 107, she pulled over to the side of the road to look at the map Gary had drawn in lieu of coming along. He'd appeared so genuinely frightened of being immediately thrown in jail that she hadn't had the heart to pressure him. "Now that Tanner's dead, there's no way of proving I didn't do it," he'd said. "They'll even say I killed him, too."

Colombo leaned in to take a look at the map, as if he might be of some help. Obviously, Gary had gone to great pains with the map. It was neat and detailed, drawn in red, blue, and green ink, and included footnotes and insets. One inset showed two blue-inked roads leading up to the quarry from either side of a shaded area he'd labeled "mountain." An asterisked footnote explained that the red ink indicated branches off the quarry roads and the green ink indicated branches off the red branches. "I don't know all of these," Gary explained in parentheses. A dagger footnote specified that the branches spanned a seventy-five-mile radius. Another set of parentheses said, "It shouldn't be more than sixty at the most, but I played it safe."

Lydia made a right onto the road leading up to the quarry and found herself inside a virtual-reality calendar scene of snow-laden pine trees and a winding mountain road. All that was missing was a little mountain brook. She opened the window and inhaled the cold piney air. She also opened the one on Colombo's side. He stuck his head out to better enjoy the passing scenery.

The trouble was, the road hadn't been cleared. If she skidded she might end up stuck in a snowdrift. Who would haul her out? Maybe it wasn't smart to drive up to the quarry. There were few houses around, and fewer in view. The only indication of civilization was a mailbox at the end of a snow-covered private lane, an occasional shingle on a post giving the owner's name, or smoke rising from a distant chimney.

Still, she had to take her chances on getting stuck to see if

truck tracks led to the quarry, if the plan were to switch drivers
as in the Labor Day arrangement that had ended with Gary's
father's death. But if that had been the original plan, Tanner's
murder would have changed things. All the same, she'd better
check out the situation. It would save a lot of time if another set
of tracks indicated in which direction the animals had been
transported. Then she'd know that what she was looking for.
The firm with that ambiguous name—Société chimique—
should be somewhere in the area.

Lydia glimpsed a familiar name on a shingle, slowed,
backed up, and took a second look. Stopped. DR. R. A. COATES.
So conveniently near the quarry. He could have taken off last
night around the same time the animals had been stolen.
Maybe the animals' destination was closer than Gary ever
dreamed.

She sat in the parked car trying to piece it together. Richard
worked at a research lab at Rockefeller University. During her
interview he'd stressed that his work had nothing to do with
testing animals. Was he protesting too much? And Boyd had
called him evil. With reason? Could mild-mannered Dr. Bean
Curd be part of the Anima project? Along with Allegra, whose
froggy eyes fit the description in the newsmagazine items?

Lydia had called Allegra last night at the shelter and talked
to yet another answering machine. Still, just because Allegra
was out for a while didn't mean that she was up to anything
sinister. Besides, Richard and Allegra didn't particularly seem
to like one another—but that could be a cover-up.

What was at the end of the lane? A building, besides the
house? She wasn't risking much by driving up there. After all,
Richard didn't even know she had a car, much less what kind.
She could pretend to be just another winter tourist who'd lost
her way, go up, and circle around. Just don't get stuck in the
snow, sweetheart, she warned herself.

She drove up a long, pine-shadowed lane, where only
glimpses of the clear blue sky were visible between snowy
branches. A gabled house hove into sight, a big old ramshackle
spooky place she'd have liked under different circumstances.
Smoke drifted up from two chimneys. There was no car in

sight, but a set of tire tracks led to the closed doors of a garage, the only building other than the house. Lydia didn't know whether to be relieved or disappointed. She certainly didn't want Richard to be in on this scheme, but she was in a hurry to find Carolyn and the animals, and finding them here would have saved time. She thought of knocking on the door and notifying Richard of the animals' disappearance. But that could be risky. If he was in on the deal, it wouldn't be smart to let him know she was here looking for the animals. Trust no one, she told herself.

The quarry was about three miles farther along, in an isolated, eerily beautiful area. But the only tracks in the pristine snow were some delicate bird tracks and the paw prints of small, wild animals. Lydia got out, stretched her legs, touched her toes, and trudged through a frozen crust of snow toward the quarry. A relief to be moving after so many hours of sitting. Colombo seemed to feel the same. Unlike her, the crusty snow bore his weight, and he galloped this way and that, stopped to pee, and galloped off again. The stillness spooked her. It was so quiet that she heard a chunk of snow slide off a branch and plop into the snow below. She arrived at a large boulder jutting out above the quarry, which she judged to be Suicide Rock. Down below, the quarry was iced over. Didn't kids ever come up here and skate? Maybe it was too dangerous.

She stood on Suicide Rock and gazed down at the quarry, trying to picture what it must have been like for Gary. She imagined him sitting in the twilight, skipping stones, and discovering his father down below in the black water. She thought of Gary's mother, who must go to bed every night wondering what had happened to her son. She'd like to call and tell her that Gary was okay. Did anyone truly believe he'd kill his father? Very likely. Patricide wasn't all that rare, unfortunately. And Gary looked guilty not only because he'd threatened to kill his father, but also because he'd run away. If it hadn't been a matter of life and death for her to find Carolyn and the animals, she'd go to the library or the newspaper office and read up on his father's death, and what the police had made of

Gary's sudden disappearance. How soon had his father's body been found?

Lydia drove down on the same side of the mountain she'd come up, passing Dr. R. A. Coates again. To reduce the sun glare on the whiteness, she put on dark glasses and spent another couple of hours following roads and side roads branching off from the quarry. She passed through resort villages with restaurants, gift shops, sports and rental shops, quaint country inns, chalets, and ski lodges, seeing few signs of industry.

It was after one o'clock by the time she'd explored all the branches and subbranches on the east side of the mountain. Deciding to conduct her search of the west side after lunch, she drove back to Ruth & Ralph's in Woodboro. If she ate in one of the more touristy places, it would probably take forever.

Despite the fact that it was lunch hour, the red-and-white-checked clothed tables at Ruth & Ralph's were empty. A leathery, weathered-looking man in a navy cardigan sat at the counter chatting up a big-breasted waitress who looked both motherly and muscular in her green uniform. Lydia chose a table by the window overlooking the town square, draping her jacket over the back of an adjoining chair.

The waitress plopped a glass of water in front of her, gave her a plastic-covered menu, and extracted a pad from a pocket and a pencil from graying, comma curls. Pencil poised, she stood by, silently waiting.

Lydia didn't take time to scrutinize the menu. She was hungry and wanted to eat quickly. She asked for today's special—chicken noodle soup and a meat-loaf sandwich—and where the rest rooms were.

The waitress pointed toward the back of the restaurant with her pencil. Lydia had always heard that New Englanders weren't talkative, but wasn't this carrying things to extremes?

She walked down a dark narrow hall to the women's room, a cold cubbyhole whose stingy paper-towel dispenser clamped its teeth down after releasing one sheet.

As soon as she returned to her table, the waitress appeared with her food. Large chunks of chicken floated in a golden broth with plenty of noodles. The meat-loaf sandwich was moist, thick, and tasty—a far cry from fast-food fare. She asked for three cheeseburgers to go.

The sphinx spoke. "For a skinny thing, you sure can tuck it away," the waitress said admiringly.

"That's for later," Lydia said. She didn't want to hurt the waitress's feelings and say that two of the cheeseburgers were for her dog. Colombo was crazy about cheeseburgers. She supposed his former master, Adam, had given him cheeseburgers when he came back from Megan's out in the Hamptons.

"How'd you like the meat loaf?" the waitress asked.

"It's great, and so was the soup."

"They serve the real stuff here," the leathery man said.

"I could tell," Lydia said, hoping the waitress would hurry with the cheeseburgers. She should have asked for them before. It would be dark soon up here. If she was going to do any more searching, she'd better get started.

But the waitress had different ideas. "Don't be in such a hurry. There's someone I want you to meet." She disappeared into the back and returned with a man who looked like her twin. "Meet the chef," she said. "My husband, Ralph. He likes to mess around in the kitchen. Tell him what you said."

"The noodle soup and the meat loaf were great, really inspired," she said, wishing that Ruth had stayed unfriendly and laconic.

Ralph beamed. "You ain't seen nothin' yet. You gotta try my specialty. Give her a piece of that apple pie," he said to Ruth. "On the house," he told Lydia, and winked.

Ruth brought what looked like half an apple pie, topped with ice cream, and served with coffee.

Lydia thanked them profusely, and tried to figure out how to eat fast with Ruth, Ralph, and the leathery man watching her every bite. The apples were sweet and tart and juicy, the crust fresh and flaky, definitely not supermarket stuff. Even the ice cream tasted homemade. "This is really delicious," she said, shoveling it in.

"Hear that, Ralph?" Ruth said.

Ralph beamed.

"Won't get pie like that in your big cities," the leathery man said.

Right. She figured she might as well profit from this sudden display of friendliness. "This is certainly beautiful country," she said. "I enjoyed driving around and just looking at the scenery. Ended up at an old quarry. It was kind of spooky, though."

"Stay away from that place," Ralph warned. "A man was killed up there last summer. Found him floating dead in the water."

"Did they find who did it?"

"Nah, he was an ex-con, and kept bad company," the leathery man said. "They figured the killer might've been one of them child molesters. He kidnapped the son at gun point or something."

"How old was his son?" Lydia said.

"A kid. Fourteen years old, not a baby. Tall for his age, too. But he wouldn't be no match for a grown man with a knife. His daddy sure wasn't," Ruth said.

"Fought a lot with his dad, people say," Ralph put in.

"That trash was a bully," Ruth said. "Ask anyone. He beat up his wife, that boy's mother. She came in here all bandaged up once. That boy was just protecting his mother. He's a good boy."

"Boy's no criminal," the leathery man agreed.

"No one's accusing him of anything," Ralph said.

Gary would be glad to hear that.

"His neighbor saw him leave his house with his dad," Ralph added.

"That don't mean anything," Ruth said. "You know what I think? I think he ran away. No one would've blamed him. There's a lot of teenage runaways. You see them on those afternoon talk shows."

Their attention was diverted by the entrance of a touristy-looking family, winter pale in brand-new ski outfits, a couple with two little boys. Ralph returned to the kitchen and Ruth went over to the table with water and menus.

Lydia looked at her watch. Almost two-thirty. Damn. To

think she'd thought she'd save time by eating in a mom-and-pop place. Better get going. She polished off the ice cream and wrapped the rest of the pie in a napkin. She was just reaching for her jacket when she spotted a familiar figure emerge from the drugstore on the opposite side of the square, wearing a white fur hat pulled down over her red hair, sunglasses, and a white designer ski outfit. So she hasn't disappeared from planet Earth after all, Lydia thought, watching the figure cross the square to her side of the street.

Lydia was about to tap on the window and call out her name when something held her back. She dug a ten-dollar bill from her wallet, threw it on the table, and grabbed her jacket.

" 'Bye and thanks," she called to Ruth, and stepped out into the cold air, but stood in the doorway watching as the woman unlocked the door of a silvery-blue British Range Rover, her back to Lydia. Lydia made a beeline for her car.

"Hey, don't forget these," Ruth called, running out and waving a brown paper bag. Shit. Lydia snatched the bag and gave Ruth a twenty, since all the rest of her bills were ones. "Keep the change," she called over her shoulder, jumped into her car, and drove off, following the Range Rover. In the rearview mirror, she saw Ruth standing coatless, looking after her, hugging her arms against the cold.

CHAPTER 24

Gillian barreled down the road in her Range Rover while Lydia kept a Ford pickup truck and tan Volvo between them. She'd talked to Gillian about buying a red Corvette last fall before leaving *gazelle*. She didn't want to take any chances on Gillian's seeing her car and suddenly remembering.

The pickup dropped out a quarter of a mile later, turning down a snowy lane lined with fence posts and an occasional skeletal tree, black against the white snow. Robert Frost country. Lydia wondered if she should drop out like the pickup. Was she making a mistake following Gillian? The shadows were already lengthening. Shouldn't she be searching the west side of the quarry instead of acting on a hunch? No. Instinct had taken over before her brain had worked it out back there at Ruth & Ralph's. Gillian was a beach baby, not a ski bunny. If she'd run into Gillian on some tropical island, she wouldn't be surprised, but never once had she heard Gillian mention skiing. Another thing—if Gillian had taken up skiing, she'd go to Gstaad or St. Moritz, or at least Vail or Aspen, certainly not to a place as unfashionable as Woodboro, Vermont. And that designer ski outfit she wore looked brand-new, as if it had never seen the slopes. Fitted jacket with pants that flared over her boots. *Très chic* and *très* inappropriate for serious skiing. Anyone the least bit familiar with the sport would know better than to wear something that blended in with the snow in case of an accident.

Lydia swerved to avoid a New York–sized pothole, then went back to her musings about Gillian, remembering that Bud had described the woman he intended to blackmail as snotty. To Lydia, Gillian had been charming and agreeable, but then she'd been Gillian's boss. Come to think of it, Gillian had treated the secretaries and clerks in a high-handed manner, as if they were servants instead of coworkers. But friendly Allegra could also be bossy. Bud might not have known that she bossed everyone around and taken it personally. And an upper-crust British accent like Gillian's often sounded arrogant to Americans.

How far was Gillian going? They were already a good distance from Woodboro, and climbing a mountain. Lydia glimpsed bits of bright color between clumps of trees as skiers glided downhill. Maybe Gillian was headed for the slopes, after all. Lydia saw no sign of skis, but then there was plenty of room for skis in the Range Rover. Maybe someone had told Gillian that skiing was good for her thighs. Gillian was always big on self-improvement. But she was also prone to shortcuts, resorting to a dermatologist for lipo instead of working on problem areas with a personal trainer. And she went in for all the latest beauty trends. Like Anima?

Wait a minute, Miller, you're forgetting that Allegra is a dermatologist, she said to herself. The dermatologist Gillian had gone to for her lipo? No. Lydia couldn't remember the dermatologist's last name, but she was sure it wasn't St. John. And how to connect either Gillian or Allegra with Stuart Starr, who was a part of this slimy operation?

Maybe it was just another example of six degrees of separation. In New York, circles overlapped like an Olympics symbol: someone's ex-husband, a painter who showed at the Nimbus Gallery, was now dating an actress appearing in an off-Broadway theater, who was friendly with her director, who often invited the actress to her parents' summerhouse on Martha's Vineyard, next door to an editor whose brother-in-law was a Wall Street broker, who'd bought a painting from the ex-husband and attended his new show at the Nimbus Gallery, meeting the ex-wife (still on friendly terms with her ex-husband), and started dating her.

Lydia had learned to be careful of what she said at parties, restaurants, art galleries, and theater lobbies. In a small town, where everyone knew each other, gossip was the expected thing, but she hadn't been prepared for the complicated relationships of New Yorkers, radiating out to Long Island, New Jersey, up to all the states in New England, and down to Washington, D.C., or out to L.A.

Ahead of her the Rover made a right. Lydia followed, her heart thudding as she wondered if Gillian would lead her to the animals, while simultaneously telling herself that Gillian was a nice kid who would never be involved in such a cruel business. The road was actually a paved driveway. Up ahead a discreet sign announced THE INN OF THE SEVEN PINES.

Lydia felt both relieved and depressed. Relieved that Gillian was just another tourist, probably up here with her boyfriend, Nigel, who preferred skiing to sunbathing. Depressed that she was no closer to finding the animals than before she'd left New York. And time was running out.

It was almost three-thirty and growing darker by the minute. She'd have to hurry if she was going to explore the roads on the other side of the quarry. Gillian turned off the driveway, drove about fifty yards, and drew up before the kind of log cabin Abraham Lincoln would never have dreamed of. Behind the cabin were thick woods. Similar cabins, irregularly spaced, were partially hidden behind snow-draped firs. Lydia kept to the driveway, passing a building marked OFFICE and a glass-enclosed restaurant overlooking some magnificent pine trees. Seven, of course.

When she circled back, she saw Gillian unlocking a cabin door, the white ski outfit blending in with her surroundings.

Lydia debated stopping off and questioning her about Trish Ackers and Anima or continuing her search. Colombo, aware that she'd slowed down, sat up, ready to jump out for a romp. "We'd better search for your brothers and sisters while it's still halfway light, sweet stuff," she told him, and after pushing his paws off the map spread out beside her, headed back for the main road.

A half hour later she was once again wending her way around mountains, back in tourist country. She passed inns, motor lodges, motels, condominiums, and resort villages, and skiers shouldering their skis, returning from the slopes and eager to lounge before a crackling fire with après-ski drinks. And then she remembered. Kramer! Early tomorrow morning they were supposed to be leaving for Quebec. She couldn't cancel on him. She'd done that all too often. She would follow all the roads on the map, pay Gillian a brief visit, and take off for New York. She sighed, already weary from the drive up and circling the countryside after a night without sleep. She'd be even more exhausted after the drive home. And to make matters worse, it had started to snow again.

Lydia wended up mountains and down into valleys, running into very little traffic. After the holidays, things were probably quiet until the influx of weekend skiers. She switched on her headlights, lighting a white-on-white world. The flakes came at her, sticking to the windshield. She turned on the wipers and drove past the blurry yellow lights of a quaint chalet that looked like something out of Disneyland. There was no sign of what she'd come looking for.

By 6:35, she'd followed all of Gary's roads and found nothing. Zilch. Either his map was incomplete or the animals were somewhere else entirely. Maybe she'd made a mistake jumping to the conclusion that just because Tanner had come this way once, he would have done so again. A mistake that might have cost Carolyn's and the animals' lives. While she searched for them here they could be in New Jersey, Pennsylvania, Connecticut, or even back in New York. Tanner could have conducted his deadly dealings anywhere in the northeastern area. But what about the form from Woodboro?

All of a sudden she remembered that the form had dealt with animals. She also remembered that P.S. had grabbed the form away from her, declaring it was something meant for Richard. But P.S. might have intended to cover up any connection between the form and herself.

Lydia decided to call Gary from Gillian's cabin on the off chance that he might have heard from Tiffany or, by some miracle, Carolyn. Too bad her car phone had gone on the blink on her return from Ohio. She gave it a try just to be sure, but all she got was static.

Back at the Inn of the Seven Pines, Lydia drove by dark, silent, and carless cabins. She hoped the inn did a better business on weekends. She was pleased to see that Gillian's Range Rover was still in front. At least she was still here. Trouble was, it looked like Gillian was having a party. Lights blazed forth from inside, yellowing the snow. Besides the Range Rover there was a sleek white Porsche and a cream-colored Jag. She bet the Porsche was Nigel's.

Since there was no parking space for her Corvette, Lydia pulled up by a Subaru in front of the cabin opposite Gillian's. A faint light shone behind a plaid-curtained window, but no one peered out to see who'd arrived, so Lydia decided it was okay to leave her car. She wouldn't be staying long anyway. Lydia wondered why, with such a wide choice of cabins, and all of them closer to the restaurant and lounge, the Subaru person or persons had chosen a place at the far end across from Gillian's. For that matter, why had Gillian chosen such an isolated spot? Maybe she'd arrived on the weekend when the place had been crowded. And maybe the Subaru person wanted to be near someone.

Lydia let Colombo out to explore the territory, and knocked on Gillian's door. No one answered. It seemed unusually quiet, considering the number of cars parked in front. She knocked again and waited. All remained silent except for an occasional call from a night bird in the woods behind the cabin. Spooky. She pictured dead bodies sprawled under glaring lights. All that was missing was the blare of loud music. You've seen too many horror movies, kid, she told herself.

After another several minutes' wait she peeked in the window. A dying fire burned in a stone fireplace with a fake bear rug in front. Two friendly chairs sat on either side of the rug, each with plaid pillows matching the sofa under a far window. No bodies sprawled in the chairs, on the sofa, or the floor.

A blond square of light shone on the snow from a rear window. Lydia went around to the back, plunging through deep snow, glad she'd thought to change into her tall boots before she'd left home. Two white terry robes were flung on the unmade bed, neither blood-soaked. Another robe lay on the floor in front of an unlit fireplace. Three robes? A ménage à trois? Lydia wasn't sure she wanted to know. And maybe she wouldn't know anyway, since no one was back here either. Where were they? Romping naked in the woods? At the restaurant?

Deciding to let Colombo explore the territory, Lydia tramped through the snow toward the glass-walled restaurant that curved gracefully in front. All lit up, it looked like a ship's prow in a sea of white. Only a few cars were parked beneath some of the seven pines.

She decided she'd join Gillian, Nigel, and the third guest, since she needed something hot to warm up, as well as some kind of sustenance to get her back to New York. And she'd get something for poor Colombo to fill up on. The cheeseburgers had been gulped down hours ago. She should have brought along some dog food.

Lydia stopped short in her tracks. Up ahead, just beyond the reach of the lights outside the restaurant, a black-caped figure darted from behind a car and stationed itself behind a tree trunk near the restaurant, peering in at the diners. Almost simultaneously, Colombo gave a short bark and whizzed past Lydia to the tree, jumping all over the caped Peeping Tom in a friendly greeting. But his reception wasn't the least bit friendly.

"Hateful thing. Get away from me." The onetime animal lover kicked a booted foot in Colombo's direction.

CHAPTER 25

Colombo slunk off, his feelings hurt.

A minute later Carolyn was running after him and apologizing. "I'm sorry, sweetie, but you shouldn't sneak up on people. You scared me to death," she said in a breathless whisper. Spying Lydia, she got to her feet and hugged her. "Lydia! Oh God, I thought you'd never get here. I'm terrified, and my feet are frozen."

Carolyn was shivering, either from cold or fear, maybe both. The hood of her cape had fallen back. With her long pale hair scattered over her shoulders and huge dark eyes, she looked like an Edward Gorey rendition of a damsel in distress. Her black velvet cape was inadequate for New England exposure and she wore city boots—short, pointy-toed, and wet from the snow.

"I didn't even know I'd be here," Lydia said. "How did you know I would?" This was the sort of thing that made Lydia wonder if Carolyn possessed the supernatural powers she claimed.

"I called Amon to tell him where Tiffany and I were. He said you were on your way. I just knew you'd show up at the inn. You're such a wonderful sleuth."

Lydia ignored the obvious flattery. She should have checked back with Gary. Now that she knew Carolyn was alive and out of danger, she could return to being furious with her for her lies and transgressions. "You mean Tiffany's up here, too? Where is she?"

"I don't know. I'm scared something might happen to her. Or has already." Carolyn shuddered. "Get out of the light or they'll see you," she added in a whisper. "That man in there is a killer." She nodded toward the restaurant. "I saw him do it. He shot a bearded man twice through the heart and hauled him into the back of an ambulance. And now Tiffany is missing. The last I heard from her she was tailing him."

"What man?" Lydia asked, hoping that Carolyn was exaggerating about Tiffany as she did about most things.

"*Him*. The one with the longish black hair. Sitting at the table by the fireplace with that vile Stuart Starr and some woman. Who is he? Have you ever seen him before? And who's the woman with him?"

Lydia peered in. Although the restaurant would easily seat a hundred diners, there were only four occupied table besides the one where Starr sat at ease, an arm hooked over a chair. He was smiling his regular-guy smile at the man Carolyn pointed out as Tanner's killer, who sat with his wide-shouldered back to Lydia. His beautifully blow-dried black hair grazed the neck of his fisherman's knit sweater. Lydia's heart slumped when she saw the woman seated next to him.

"I don't know who the man is. At least not from the back. But the woman is Gillian Smith-Markham. You must have heard me mention her—my former assistant at *gazelle*."

Carolyn gasped, as if her worst opinion of Lydia had just been confirmed.

"No, we are not in this together," Lydia told her.

"Heidi said you couldn't be trusted."

"And being a loyal friend, you took the word of a stranger."

"I didn't know who or what to believe. Not after I heard all the terrifying things that happened to her at Nora's Ark. She told everyone there that she was taking an around-the-world cruise so they wouldn't come looking for her. But someone did. The bearded man killed at the shelter almost killed her. He'd been following her in an ambulance, but she hadn't noticed. Not until she was halfway across the street. Then he turned on the siren and suddenly she looked up to see this monster vehicle bearing down on her. She was petrified and couldn't move. Some man pushed her out of the way. Her description of the woman at the shelter sounded just like you."

Carolyn, like Milke, frequently resorted to non sequiturs. Lydia didn't have to ask her what she meant since Gary had already explained it.

"If I were in on the deal, I'd be in there, not standing out here," Lydia said.

"I know." Carolyn spoke in a small, apologetic voice.

"I've seen the black-haired guy somewhere before. Not with Gillian, though. I'm pretty sure he isn't her boyfriend, Nigel. There's something brutish about this guy despite his blow-dry. He's not Gillian's type." But then, who was her type? What kind of people did Gillian hang out with? The last person she'd expected to see her with was Stuart Starr.

Lydia had always considered Gillian a decent kid who'd come over from England to find adventure and rich playboys and eventually marry. Gillian was a fluffhead and basically out for fun. But, after all, she was only twenty-four. Twenty-four and already terrified of losing her looks. Of aging. Was that what had led her into the scheme with a scummy person like Starr? But how had she met him? The cold must have sharpened Lydia's senses or maybe it was just seeing Gillian again. She immediately came up with the connection—the words Gillian had spoken before leaving for her lipo: *He's a first-rate doctor with an international practice in the states and in Switzerland, where he runs a very posh spa.*

Lydia also remembered that the New Year's Eve call to Stuart that Diandre had listened in on had come from St. Moritz.

But now that she'd found the connection what good did it do? It brought her no closer to finding the Société chimique, the animals, or Tiffany—wherever she might be. Also, Lydia couldn't think of the name of Gillian's dermatologist, although she was sure Gillian had mentioned it.

Inside the restaurant, the unholy three had stopped talking while fresh drinks were set before them, only resuming their conversation after the waiter had left.

"What happened to Tiffany?" Lydia asked. "How did she get up here? Why did she come?"

Carolyn wrapped the cape around her and shivered. "I can't answer all your questions when I'm freezing. I've been standing here for hours. I'm going back to my cabin. You keep watch."

"You have a cabin?"

"I took one just across from that ghastly Stuart Starr and that woman. This is their second round of drinks."

Lydia figured they must have been in the restaurant for forty-five minutes at the most. Even so, Carolyn plainly wasn't dressed for this kind of weather. She'd bought the black cape after she'd seen Lydia's long black trench coat. She often bought something similar, if not identical, to Lydia's. The trouble was, Carolyn's cape was much thinner.

"I'll bring my car up here, turn on the heater, and you can tell me what happened, okay?" Lydia asked.

Carolyn reluctantly agreed. Lydia went back to the cabin to get the Corvette. Even through the layers of clothes, she felt the cold leather when she slid in behind the wheel. Colombo flew past her to the passenger seat. "You're going to have to sit in back," she told him.

She drove up to the restaurant and parked the car where she could keep watch on the three inside, turned off the lights, and turned on the heater.

Carolyn jumped in beside her. Colombo obligingly jumped in back. "Feel," Carolyn said, touching icicle fingers to Lydia's cheek.

"Maybe you'd better go to your cabin and take a hot bath instead of sitting out here."

"I'll be perfectly all right," Carolyn said stoically.

That was the paradoxical thing about Carolyn, Lydia thought. She could whine and carry on about some minor discomfort, but if it came to something really serious, she'd take it in stride. "You haven't told me how Tiffany got here. She was at your place the last I saw of her."

"She absolutely insisted on following the truck with the animals. Refused to let them out of her sight."

"Wait a minute. You omitted a few facts. What put you onto this to begin with?"

"It was who, not what. Heidi. She came to the spa on the morning of New Year's Eve with a fantastic story about some dreadful international conspiracy to steal the animals and make millions. 'It involves a cast of characters you wouldn't believe,' she told me. I remember exactly. I have a gift for total recall *and* a photographic memory. I can repeat anything I've read or heard, ten years later, verbatim. Word for word," Carolyn translated, as if Lydia didn't know what verbatim meant. "People think I'm brilliant, a genius. But that's not the case," she said modestly. "I'm merely endowed with these totally marvelous gifts."

Lydia had heard Carolyn variously described as charming, poisonous, or crazy, but never brilliant. She didn't, of course, reveal this. "Who was this incredible cast of characters?"

"In there," Carolyn said, nodding at the unholy three. "Except at the time I didn't have the faintest idea who they were. Neither did Heidi. Bud had said some snotty woman on a magazine, an international financier, and a millionaire entrepreneur who grew orchids in his greenhouse."

"Millionaire entrepreneur? Stuart Starr's a pimp."

"Well, I didn't know that until I discovered Tiffany hiding out at the spa. When she told me that the man she ran away from grew orchids in a greenhouse and was dealing with this man about stealing animals, I suspected that he was linked to the conspiracy. So the four of us—Heidi, Amon, Tiffany, and I—kept watch on his place, spelling one another. In fact, I was sitting in my Subaru when you called on him last night, which made me sure you were involved."

"I was looking for you."

"Well, how was I to know that?"

"By checking with Amon. You don't have a Subaru."

"I rented it. We alternated between my Subaru and Heidi's BMW. Tiffany drove the BMW up here later, since Heidi was terrified of these people and refused to come. That was after I called Heidi on my car phone to get her help—have her follow us. I knew the killer and that vile Stuart Starr would take separate routes eventually. Heidi commandeered Tiffany."

"Tiffany's too young to have a driver's license."

"Yes, but she knows how to drive. And the police aren't very likely to be out in the sleet writing traffic tickets in the middle of the night.

"The last I heard from her was just outside of Woodboro after the truck driver turned onto a side road. We drove up here together, kind of like a caravan—Stuart led the way in his Jag, the killer following in the truck with the animals, I was in the Subaru, and Tiffany in the BMW. It was like some spooky funeral procession—sleeting and slow driving, too slippery to go fast. Luckily, those two were so busy looking where they were going that they didn't notice they were being followed."

"Why did you let the killer get away in the first place? You could have had him brought in and saved the animals if you'd called the cops immediately."

"The police would have been no help. They'd be far more interested in a dead body than in saving some animals. Besides, he'd have been miles away by then. The police would never have found him. And anyway, I was too upset to think clearly. Are you going to let me tell this or keep interrupting?" Carolyn asked. "What's taking them so long in there? When are they ever going to eat? This is their third bloody round."

"I think they're waiting for someone. We'll have to wait with them and see who turns up. What happened last night when you called Amon? Did you get cut off or hang up?"

"I hung up. I'd followed Stuart Starr to the shelter and was calling from the security guard's room when I overheard two men arguing over who got to drive the animals in the truck. I slipped outside thinking I might free the poor things, but the men came out, too, still quarreling. I barely had time to hide behind the outside door. It was horrible. I was wet to my skin and shivering and I could hear the animals barking and mewing and wasn't able to help them. Stuart stood out of the sleet in the doorway enjoying the argument. I think that's what he wanted. The next thing I knew I heard a shot, and the man with the beard pitched over. Stuart told the man with the gun to make sure the other one was dead, and he shot him again. I was terrified they'd find me and kill me, too. I'd armed myself with this, but it would have been no contest against a gun."

From under her cape, Carolyn pulled out the wicked-looking blade-and-hammer weapon that was missing from her room. "Stuart and the killer dragged the body into the back of the ambulance. Then the killer jumped into his truck and started up. Stuart ordered him to wait until he got his car so he could lead the way. While they were talking I slipped out from behind the door and jumped into the Subaru and followed the truck which followed Stuart's Jag. That's when I called Heidi and she got Tiffany. Tiffany caught up with us long before Albany. It was after we got here that I lost her on the phone. All I heard when I called was an eerie kind of humming. I guess one or both of us had run into a dead spot. I dialed to make a different connection, but it didn't work. Two hours later the truck driver drove up in a Porsche and joined Stuart and Gillian."

"So what do you think happened?" Lydia asked.

"I don't know," Carolyn wailed. "I was hoping you'd tell me."

"You come crying for help after all the damage has been done. If you'd told me sooner, this could have been prevented."

"That's an unkind thing to say."

"So were your lies. They nearly got me killed. Tiffany thought I was in on the scheme to steal the animals."

"I was only repeating what Heidi told me."

"We've gone into that already. And where were you yesterday when Gary was running all over Manhattan searching for you?"

"Gary?"

"He told me his real name. Amon was your invention."

"A definite improvement. He knew where I was, he just didn't tell you," Carolyn added with a smug little smile. "Both he and Tiffany are extremely loyal."

"Certainly far more loyal than you were to me. And all this time I was stupid enough to worry about you."

"Duck! He's looking our way."

"He can't see us in a dark car," Lydia said. Obviously, Carolyn was trying to change the subject. True, Stuart was looking in their direction—casually, in his regular-guy way. But there was something alert behind that laid-back pose. Lydia cut off the engine.

"Why did you do that? I'm still shivering."

"I was afraid he'd hear the motor running. How did you manage to hang around here without his seeing you?"

"Easy. Practically everything was vacant. After he disappeared into the cabin, I went to the office and told the desk clerk that I wanted a cabin near the woods. I knew Stuart wouldn't recognize the Subaru."

Lydia tried to put it all together, wondering how much to believe of what Carolyn had told her. Certainly, Carolyn wouldn't lie about losing track of Tiffany. What had happened to her? Worrying about the animals wasn't enough. First she had to worry about Carolyn, now Tiffany. "Tiffany might have tried to reach you by car phone when you were in the cabin," Lydia said.

"Oh God!" Carolyn clapped her forehead with the heel of her palm. Always the grand gesture. "I should have thought of that. I'll call her now." She was reaching for the door handle when the headlights of an approaching car beamed in.

"Wait a second, Stuart might look out and recognize you," Lydia said as a red Cherokee pulled in beside them.

The headlights shut off, and two people climbed out, wearing hooded anoraks and trousers tucked into boots. It was hard to tell what they looked like, or if they were male or female. Whatever the case, they were all over one another in a long kiss. Then, holding hands, they made their way to the restaurant. Suddenly Lydia thought of Kramer. It was too late to start back. Anyway, she couldn't leave now that she knew the animals were up here. She felt a blast of cold air as Carolyn opened the door.

"Give me the keys to your cabin. I have an important phone call to make," Lydia told her.

"But I was going to try to get Tiffany on the car phone."

"Okay, I'll wait. I have to call Kramer soon. We were leaving for Quebec early tomorrow morning." She sighed. "He'll never forgive me when I cancel."

"He always forgives you."

"That's just it. This will be the last straw." Lydia's eyes fell on the hostess, a plump woman in a turquoise suit, who led the newly arrived couple toward a table. They'd doffed their anoraks and were wearing matching red ski sweaters with white reindeer. Lydia got a jolt when she recognized the couple. Never would she have expected those two to be friends, much less lovers. She got a further jolt when she saw the table the hostess was leading them to.

"My God, they're sitting with the unholy three." Lydia watched transfixed as more chairs were added to the table. Starr exchanged seats so that the bull-necked, blow-dried man could sit opposite P.S. and Richard. And seeing the bull-necked man's surly face, she realized where she'd seen him before. Crime made even stranger bedfellows than politics.

Carolyn, who was about to get out of the car, paused. "They're involved, too?"

"Looks like it," Lydia said grimly. "He runs Nora's Ark. I thought they hated each other. Now here they are, as thick as the thieves they are. The two people supposed to protect the animals are behind their destruction. And the man with Gillian and Stuart is Boyd, the vet Richard fired from the shelter. Richard said he wasn't a real vet, and he said Richard was evil."

"He's the evil one," Carolyn said, opening the car door.

"They all are."

"Oh God, I hope I can reach Tiffany."

"If you can't, call Gary and see if he's heard from her. After all, she doesn't know where you are. And take Colombo with you. Put him in the cabin. Sorry, sweet stuff, but you might be in the way," Lydia told him.

"You don't want him with you?"

"If they leave while you're gone, I'm following them. No telling where they're going."

Carolyn was about to protest. "Go," Lydia said, to both her and Colombo. "Hurry. When they leave, they'll probably take off in different directions. So we'll each have to follow a car."

"But if I reach Tiffany, it could change everything," Carolyn said.

Lydia had the horrible feeling that any change would be for the worse, although she didn't know how much worse things could get. In the rearview mirror, she watched the caped figure fly across the snow.

CHAPTER 26

She was starting to get a headache. Lydia leaned her head back against the car seat and tried to relax. Impossible. It wasn't that she was new to worrying. Worrying was a hobby of hers. But that was over small things—such as had she turned off the coffee or left on the iron? These were big-time worries about Tiffany, the animals, and who provided some ingredient Starr et al. considered essential to Anima—a product said to promote youth yet resulted in facial paralysis, a product for which, nevertheless, thanks to Gillian, women were clamoring for.

Cosmetics, like fiction, require the suspension of disbelief. The cosmetic industry was based on it. But in this day of protests over the use of animal-tested products, Anima was literally getting away with murder. If nothing else, she'd write an exposé. But she needed facts. Who had come up with the formula? Richard the biochemist or Boyd the phony vet? Lydia doubted that Milke would publish a piece showing *gazelle* had steered its readers wrong. She'd have to go to a competitor's magazine. Or was this too hot for any of the women's magazines to handle?

The five people sipping drinks at the table by the fireplace appeared restless. P.S. smoked, Richard smiled inanely, Boyd kept an eye on both of them, while Gillian kept an eye on him. Stuart frequently looked toward the door and checked his watch. They must be waiting for a sixth party to join them. Lydia shuddered to think who it might be—perhaps the most improbable person she could think of: Hank the Hunk, Milke, or Paul and Linda McCartney.

It was a good half hour before Carolyn returned. "I tried and tried and couldn't reach her. I called Amon. He said he hadn't heard a peep."

Lydia doubted if Gary said "peep," but that wasn't important. More important was Tiffany's disappearance.

"Here, have some chocolate," Carolyn said, tossing a bar of Cadbury's into Lydia's lap. "You might need your energy later." Lydia bit into it hungrily.

"You'll be pleased to know I called Kramer."

"You what!"

"I called your true love. Don't look at me like that. I thought I was doing you a favor. Anyway, he wasn't home."

"Good. Otherwise, he'd think I was trying to avoid talking to him."

"I left a message with his little girl. I told her where we were, and that you couldn't make it. She's so adorable. She insisted on writing it all down."

"Shit. Why can't you stay out of other people's lives?"

Carolyn sniffled. "Everything I do is wrong. It will be my fault if you and Kramer break up. And if something happens to Tiffany or the animals, I'll have blood on my hands. I can hear their cries. It's all so horrible, horrible, horrible." Her voice became higher and more hysterical with each horrible.

Lydia could have cut out her tongue. She'd forgotten how the slightest bit of criticism could set Carolyn off when she was

in a shaky state. She hoped Carolyn wasn't going to freak out
the way she sometimes did when life got to be too much for
her. Lydia tried to come up with some palliative while Carolyn
carried on, castigating herself for doing everything wrong and
castigating others for wronging her.

"I've had dreadful luck ever since I lost my guardian angel.
The one Amon gave me. She scared off the evil spirits. The
moment I lost her a man was murdered, the animals stolen, and
now Tiffany has disappeared. Nothing, nothing, nothing has
turned out right." Carolyn began to weep.

The guardian angel! Quickly, Lydia dug into her jacket
pocket. "Here." She handed over the pendant. "I found this at
the shelter. On the ramp."

"Oh, Lydia, bless you. Never never never will I think of you
as anything but a dear dear friend." She kissed the angel and
then Lydia. "Never again will I doubt you. I will trust you forever."

"Let's hope it changes your luck."

"I'll pray to her. She's helped me before in times of adver-
sity."

Lydia heard a soft murmur and glanced over. Carolyn held
the chain the way she'd hold a rosary, and gazed up at the car
roof as if her guardian angel were flitting around up there.

In the middle of her prayer, a long, black limo that looked
like a hearse drove up and came to a stop before the restaurant.
Lydia watched as a uniformed driver got out and opened the
back door. A man wearing a top hat and long overcoat stepped
out. The driver hurried ahead to the restaurant door and held it
open. He needn't have hurried, since the man walked slowly,
limping.

Despite the limp, he walked straight-backed and head up,
with a military arrogance in his bearing. Somehow Lydia
wasn't surprised when the turquoise-suited hostess led him to
where Stuart Starr sat with the others. She was merely relieved
that it hadn't been Hank, Milke, or the McCartneys.

Lydia was sure who this was, if only by the deference being
shown to him. Gillian sat straighter, and the men jumped to
their feet. P.S. put out her cigarette. Boyd gave the man a

hearty handshake and Starr practically bowed him into a chair, following what looked like introductions to Richard and P.S.

The man had a beautiful head of white hair and chiseled features. Soon all six were involved in an intense conversation. The flames flickered over the faces of the devil's henchmen.

"He's the one behind this whole hideous plan to kill the animals. I know it, I know it, I know it," Carolyn chanted. "This is a man to beware of," she warned.

Since Carolyn had warned Gary and Tiffany against her, Lydia wouldn't ordinarily have taken this warning too seriously, but for once she knew Carolyn was right. Suddenly the name came to her. The name that meant "mishandle" in French. Malmener. Still, instinct told her Boyd was the one to follow. Dr. Malmener would let someone else do the dirty work, and Boyd looked like just the person to do it.

Carolyn went back to praying to her guardian angel while the group inside went about ordering and eating. They concentrated on their food and talked little throughout dinner.

"It's still snowing," Lydia said a half hour later. "That won't help matters any. Can't you get your guardian angel to put a stop to it?"

"They mocked Jesus, too," Carolyn told her, and returned to her prayers. Lydia grew tired of sitting. It was another half hour before the diners got up to leave. They hadn't lingered over coffee. Maybe someone had noticed the snow.

Richard and P.S. were the first out of the restaurant.

"Why are they leaving ahead of the others?" Lydia asked.

"They finished dinner. Now they're going home to make love," Carolyn said.

"I'm not so sure."

Lydia ducked as P.S. and Richard headed for the Jeep. They drove off in a hurry. Her eyes followed their headlights down the road. Was she making a mistake by not tailing them?

The limo didn't take Dr. Malmener anywhere except to Gillian's cabin. Gillian rode with him while the two men walked.

"Maybe he plans to stay the night," Lydia said.

Carolyn was undaunted. "He came in answer to my prayers,"

she said. "A signal from my angel. I'm following him wherever he goes." She was on her knees in the seat looking out the back. "Stuart's going into the cabin, too, but Boyd is just getting into his Porsche."

"You'd better get out, then. I'm following him."

"I hope you don't disappear like Tiffany," Carolyn said, jumping from the car.

CHAPTER 27

The Porsche swung out onto the highway, then veered left. The snow that had fallen so haphazardly just a half hour before had become serious. All Lydia could see ahead of her were speeding red taillights winking in a cloud of white.

Lydia kept a good distance behind Boyd, in case he glanced into the rearview mirror, although he'd probably see no more than a blur of yellow headlights.

Soon they were in the mountains, the red taillights ahead of her going up and up, wending 'round and 'round a snowy road. Boyd had sped up, executing curves that could be tricky under ordinary circumstances, but turned treacherous on a low-visibility night like tonight. The flakes flew toward her from the other side of the windshield where the wiper worked efficiently but ineffectively, leaving behind a fan-shaped smear. Rows of snow-clad firs loomed at her from either side of the road, pristine and perilous.

What she could make out of her surroundings looked faintly familiar, reminiscent of this morning when she'd driven up to the quarry. But all mountain roads probably looked alike. Every once in a while she'd see the distant lights of some small touristy inn, twinkling red, green, and yellow like Christmas-tree lights, then disappearing, as if a mirage.

They had the mountain road to themselves. Everyone else had had the good sense to stay in. Suddenly a horn sounded abruptly from behind. Lydia swung slightly to the right as a big dark hulk hurtled by, a fleet, black shadow in the silvery night. A second later the horn sounded again. Headlights sprayed the Porsche, then shot by. It looked like the limo. But no Subaru followed in hot pursuit. She knew that once Carolyn decided to do something, she did it. If Carolyn wasn't following the car, it wasn't the limo. She'd no sooner had the thought than another horn sounded, and a second car came up from behind. Carolyn? Hard to tell, since it passed in a shadowy blur. Christ, it was getting to look like the procession the night before when Carolyn and Tiffany tailed the Jaguar and the truck. It must have been the limo and the Subaru that had passed by, after all. Why else would they be going in the same direction on a lonely mountain road under practically blizzard conditions?

Lydia felt a shiver of excitement. She'd been on the right trail after all. Her instincts had played her true, and now the search was narrowing. But what would she find at the end of her search? Would Tiffany be okay, or would it be too late to save her and the animals? Lydia saw Emil's brown dog's eyes looking hopefully at her. Hang in there, boy, she ESP'd, I'm coming.

On the other hand, she could be totally wrong. She didn't really know who was in the other two cars. And Boyd just might be on his way to some touristy place for an overnight stay. Or for that matter, he might live here. She didn't even know if Tiffany was with the animals. Suppose Tiffany, held up by a stoplight, had lost sight of the truck in early-morning traffic. Suppose she'd taken a wrong turn in the road after the truck had disappeared, and didn't know where to reach Carolyn. Suppose she gave up and went back to New York. A million things could have happened. Also, Tiffany wasn't the most dependable person in the world. Most kids weren't, except for Gary.

Lydia went on red alert. Something strange had happened.

Both sets of taillights had disappeared. Ahead an empty road narrowed into the night. She sped up and shot forward. For a dangerous moment the car skidded and headed for a tree. She regained control of the wheel, eased the car in the opposite direction, slowly straightened out, and moved forward, this time more cautiously. She drove for what seemed like an eternity but registered only a mile on the odometer. Boyd couldn't have gone too far, could he? He'd appear as soon as she went around the next curve—or the one after that. But what if he'd turned off a road she'd overlooked? While she'd been so smugly congratulating herself on tracking down the animals, she'd managed to lose sight of the car that would have led her to them.

Now, don't panic, she told herself, you didn't lose Boyd. He just dropped out of sight. Yeah, and off the edge of the earth. There was no place for her to turn around and go back. She could end up stuck in a snowdrift, stranded near a mountaintop where she wouldn't be discovered until the spring thaw.

Lydia shifted into reverse and backed up the Corvette, looking for a turnoff that Boyd might have made and she might have missed. Boyd hadn't acted as if he thought he was being tailed, but maybe he'd suspected something, seen that constant snowy blur of yellow in his rearview mirror, and caught on. She'd thought the heavy snow would be a proper camouflage, but she could have thought wrong.

And then she saw it—scarcely a road—more like a wide path with the snow packed down by tire tracks. A lane through a woods. A lane that led to nowhere, or to the animals? Why would the snow be so hard-packed except for unusually heavy traffic, especially since it was still snowing and the tracks should have been covered up? And why would there be unusually heavy traffic up here at the top of the world?

Lydia took the chance and turned off. A quarter of a mile farther she realized she was gradually headed downhill into a valley. Five minutes later her headlights hit an iron gate in a high stone wall. Behind the gate stood a guard hut that looked dark and uninhabited.

All the same she cut off her lights, drew up to within five feet of the gate, and stopped. She wondered if she'd made a mistake dousing her lights. It would give the lie to claiming that she'd innocently taken the wrong road. But she needn't have worried. No one appeared. Maybe it was a private home, although that seemed peculiar since she'd passed no sign of civilization for miles.

Lydia dug through the maps and detritus in the glove compartment and found the big flashlight. She slipped it into the same jacket pocket where she kept the penlight and stepped out of the car into snow country. Sky and earth were an eerie white. Hushed. Silent. Not a branch stirred. Falling snowflakes melted on her cheeks. She stretched her legs and took deep breaths. The cold air chilled her lungs. Somewhere in the distance a dog started barking. Or was it a wolf baying in the night?

Snow crunched underfoot as she made her way to the gate in a high stone wall. No guard dogs came howling up to tear a leg off. She shone the flashlight on the guard hut and then down the road, where she saw what looked like an enormous tombstone—gray and slick, and almost windowless—a five-story-tall slab. Probably few people knew it existed except those living in the immediate vicinity. Sheltered and secluded, high up in the mountains—this had to be it! Her heart bumped against her chest.

A row of cars was parked in front of the building, but it was too far away to see if there was a Porsche or a limo. She knew if there were a Subaru, it would be parked out of sight. Boyd and Dr. Malmener must be here.

The chain-link gate looked climbable, but how did she know that she might not be electrocuted if she touched it? Or it could be set for an alarm. Maybe she should try for the stone wall. She slogged through a snowdrift and inspected it. Enough stones jutted out so that she could get a tenuous toehold. Good!

Next, she walked a short distance beyond her car and found a place behind trees wide enough for her purposes. Treading toe to heel, she made sure the ground was level, with no ditch hidden under a snowdrift that she could get stuck in. She climbed into her Corvette and backed into the chosen spot so that the car faced the main road in case she wanted to make a fast getaway. All she had to do was find the animals, get away, and get help. It would be foolhardy to attempt to rescue them single-handedly.

She inspected the eight-foot stone wall looking for a place that appeared surmountable, and ended up back where she'd started, the place she'd originally inspected. She found a toe-hold for her right foot and started up. Her boots turned out to be more of a hindrance than a help, but after a lot of grunting and swearing and telling herself she could do it, she made it to the top. She dropped to the ground on the other side and crept forward, keeping to the trees.

Nearing the gray building, she made out an occasional figure passing by one of the few lighted windows. The place was uncannily still, although close to a dozen cars and vans were parked in front of the building—one a white Porsche, and the other a limo. No chauffeur sat behind the wheel. She wondered if he was inside the building, or if Dr. Malmener had driven here himself. Neither seemed likely. And what had happened to Carolyn and her Subaru? Had Carolyn done the same thing as she, hidden the car? Was she already in the building? Or hadn't it been Carolyn following the limo, after all? Lydia felt a feverish excitement, her heart drumming loudly in the still night.

Bingo! There it was, the name she'd been looking for! Above a stone arch jutting out from the building entrance, curlicue blue neon tubing spelled out the words *Société chimique*. She'd first seen neon tubing twisted into odd shapes five years ago at a gallery opening she'd attended in Paris while she was there for a spring show. She'd spoken to the artist, who'd said it was a painstaking and expensive process. Lydia wondered why someone had put up an arty, costly sign announcing a clandestine company. No doubt Dr. Malmener complimented himself on his exquisite taste and sensitivity. Maybe he even played the piano beautifully, like the Nazis in late-night movies.

Finally, she was here—the place she'd been searching for! But what could she do now? She couldn't very well walk in the door and demand the release of Tiffany and the animals—

provided Tiffany was even here. Provided the animals were as well. But she could get an idea of what she was up against if she peeked inside. She crept forward, trying to make herself small, wishing she'd worn something white like Gillian that blended in with the snowy background.

She stationed herself behind a pillar supporting the stone arch and peered through the glass double door into a vast, blindingly white entrance hall that looked like a high-tech nightmare. The fluorescent ceiling lights reflected on shiny ivory linoleum. Everything was white except for a huge panel where blue lights burned steadily and the green uniform of a security guard tilted back in a swivel chair, feet propped up on a white steel desk, ankles crossed, face hidden by a girlie magazine.

A switchboard was positioned at the guard's elbow and a TV monitor angled in his direction. The wall panel with its glowing blue lights was directly above the monitor. The panel looked as if it had something to do with building security. She studied it carefully. There were six rows of small lights—blue, green, and red—each above a number. The blue lights burned steadily, but the reds were unlit, while eight greens shone among the blue—one green in the top row and seven in the bottom. She remembered that the building was five stories tall. The top row could be the executive offices and the bottom row the basement. The green lights might mean that the rooms were occupied, while the blue lights meant empty. Did the red light signal intruders? Of course, she could have gotten it all wrong, but it seemed logical. It was reassuring that the guard paid no attention to what was going on.

Lydia tried the door. Unlocked. She considered sneaking past the guard, who would conveniently keep his nose poked in the girlie magazine. Somehow she didn't think it would work. Only V. I. Warshawski got away with such feats.

Moving away from the door, shielding the flashlight with the palm of her hand, she circled the building looking for a way to get in, trusting the falling snow to cover her tracks. The windows were either too high to see into or so low they were half-buried in the snow. The low windows were made of frosted glass, so that she couldn't see into them either, but they provided her only hope of entry. She started digging away at a bottom window. Soon icy particles stiffened her mittens and her fingers grew numb from the cold. When she finally succeeded in uncovering enough of the window to open it, she found it unmovable. It was either locked or frozen shut, as was each window she tried.

Toward the back of the building, Lydia found a curious demarcation—a recessed level of snow covering a six-foot-square area. When she kicked away some of the snow, her heel struck metal. Kneeling, she brushed off the snow with a frozen glove and found two metal doors set into the ground, similar to metal doors leading to basements in city sidewalks. She put her gloves back on, grasped the handles with icy fingers, and yanked. Hard. Neither door yielded. Frozen shut at best, locked at worst. Was this where the animals had been unloaded from the truck? She put her ear to the metal and heard nothing. She tried yanking at the doors again, and realized after a bad fifteen minutes that she was wasting time.

Lydia got to her feet. After kicking snow back over the doors to cover up, she walked to the next window, where she began her routine scooping and tunneling. Like the other windows she'd tried, it was unbudgeable.

By the time she reached the back of the building, she was beginning to think it was a lost cause. Had Carolyn been able to get in? Or had she been caught in the attempt? Was Carolyn in there now, both she and Tiffany held captive? But what exactly could she do about it if she couldn't get inside? Besides, her fingers would soon be so frostbitten from futilely scooping snow away from immovable windows that she'd have to give up.

She'd try one more window and—what—go home? Now that she was nearly positive that the animals were here? Lydia scrabbled again in the snow. No luck. She eyed her snow boots with their reinforced toes, gave the window a good hard kick, and held her breath as she listened to the glass clink and clatter to the floor. She expected an alarm to go off any minute, pictured the red lights flashing like crazy up on the wall near where the guard sat with his girlie magazine. Nothing happened.

After a long wait she got down on her stomach and played the flashlight around inside. Stacks of unopened cardboard cartons stood on the far side of the room, stamped with the names of pet food—Alpo and Nine Lives. Open and empty cartons sprawled haphazardly on the side near her. Her heart beat an irregular tattoo. So many opened food cartons signified the animals had eaten and were still alive. She might still save them! Wrong. The fact that they'd eaten didn't mean they hadn't been slaughtered later, but it didn't preclude the animals being here, either. She'd have to get inside and take a look around.

Lydia beamed the light directly beneath the window on the broken and splintered glass. It looked like a long drop. Also, there was no guarantee that the door was unlocked. Even if she got in, how would she get out again? Simple. Pile up some boxes and climb on top of them.

After nearly pulling an arm from its socket, she managed to grab a box flap and drag it under the window so that it not only covered the broken glass but would break her fall. She played the flashlight on the window. The glass was jagged. She could get badly cut. Then she spotted the window lock. By pushing a lever to the right, she was able to unlock the window and pull it up. Again, she waited for the alarm to go off, and again nothing happened.

It looked like a tight fit, but maybe she could make it through the window by divesting herself of her bulky jacket. She unzipped the jacket and flung it inside, immediately feeling the cold cut through her sweater. She wiggled through the window on her stomach. It was easy going until she got to her hips. After much twitching and writhing and a good pep talk, she managed to get through. Hanging from the ledge, she lowered herself gently, dangled above the carton for a half second, and let go.

It was then that all hell broke loose. She must have nudged a button on the inside ledge. The noise numbed her brain. Dive-bombers, exploding grenades, and earsplitting gunfire slammed at her from all sides, creating instant paralysis.

Stupid, she told herself, You can't just stand here and wait for them to find you. Move. She headed for the door, remembered her jacket, sprinted back, snagged it up, and made another dash for the door. She was just reaching for the doorknob when she heard voices and a key turn on the other side.

CHAPTER 28

Lydia barely had time to dig in behind a pile of cartons when two uniformed guards burst in, on the run. A blinding light flashed on overhead. Crouching behind the cartons, she held her breath but couldn't control her wildly beating heart.

"Hey, look. The window's up. Someone came in," a whiny voice said, sounding high and excited.

"Or some dumb moron left it up and a wild animal got in," a gruff voice told the whiny one.

"Don't look at me, I ain't been in here since yesterday." The whiny one again.

"Yeah? Well, maybe it was a two-legged animal triggered that alarm. Guess we better check things out."

"Sure is a mess in here."

Lydia heard the sound of boxes being overturned or crunched underfoot. The footsteps grew louder, came closer.

"You don't suppose one of those animal people over in Burlington snuck in here?"

The voice came from the other side of the cartons she hid behind. If the guard tore away the boxes, she'd be exposed. Lydia crouched and got ready to spring, aware that she'd be no match for two guards.

"They wouldn't be smart enough to break in tonight."

"Smart? You call that smart? I'd call it dumb. What fool would go out on a night like this?"

"That's when you do it. Show up when you're least expected."

"Nah. Anyway, I don't see why we're wasting our time discussing it. They don't know about this place or they'd have been here by now," the whiny one said.

"You're the one brought the subject up," the gruff voice told him. There was a slight pause before the voice continued. "Someone over there in Burlington knows something's going on. They just don't know who's doing it. That's why the powers that be are getting animals so far from here."

"How do you know where they come from?"

"I got my ways."

"You snooping around? You'll be in deep shit they catch you," the whiny voice said, sounding farther away. "Come on, let's go."

Lydia let out the breath she'd been holding, but she'd relaxed too soon.

"First we find what set off the alarm," the gruff guard told the whiny one.

"You're stalling 'cause I got the winning hand."

"It's not cards I'm interested in. It's that little bit of cargo in the back room I'd like to get back to," the gruff voice said.

Cargo? Lydia was puzzled. What did he mean? Drugs?

"We can't do nothing till they leave. We already had one close call," the other guard whined. "Who'd of thought they'd be coming back?"

"They're not going to stick around forever."

"Then we have ourselves a ball." The whiny one snickered.

The "they" they referred to must be Boyd and Dr. Malmener, Lydia thought.

"Okay, close the fucking window, let's go."

Lydia's heart banged against her chest. She'd be lost as soon as they noticed the broken glass. They'd know no animal could have done it. And she'd never beat them to the door.

"I'm leaving it up so what got in here will get out by itself. I don't wanna get bit by some rabid squirrel. Wait for me," the whiny voice called.

The light went off and the door closed.

Lydia's hand shook as if she had Parkinson's. She didn't hear a key turn. Did that mean the door was unlocked, or that it locked automatically like the doors at Nora's Ark?

After giving herself a few minutes to recover, she tried the doorknob. The door opened easily. She was in luck. Or was she? Did she really want to go through with this? Risk her life for some crazy kid she might not be able to save? Who might not even be here? Yes. She couldn't have a child's life on her conscience. And then there was Emil and the other poor bewildered animals slated for slaughter. Twenty years from now she'd still be lying awake nights, torturing herself with the thought that she could have saved them.

Lydia stepped out into the hall. A strong smell of antiseptic assailed her nose. There were as many corridors as in a dream—or a nightmare—glaring and shadowless under the bright fluorescent lights. She stepped back into the storage room. After removing the flashlight and penlight from her jacket pocket, she tossed the jacket into a carton. Her white turtleneck sweater was better camouflage.

She tried to figure out where the double metal doors were in relation to where she stood. She was sure the animals had been unloaded there and put into nearby rooms. Unfortunately, she was cursed with a poor sense of direction. All she knew was that she was at the back of the building and the metal doors were on the side to her right. Okay, she'd head toward the front and not make any left turns. That should be simple enough.

She tiptoed down the shadowless corridor, peering left and right wherever the main corridor intersected, making sure no one was coming from either direction. All the doors were closed. She had no way of knowing if anyone was behind them except for the occasional door with the frosted-glass windows where she could see if there was a light on. So far they'd all been dark. She checked her watch. 10:17. The employees should all be long gone by now, but judging from the number of cars parked outside, a skeleton shift remained.

She became aware of the squeak of rolling wheels and footsteps. They grew louder and louder. No one was in sight, so that meant someone was coming from a side corridor. She had no choice but to duck inside the nearest door and pray no one was in the room. No one was. The room was pitch-black and cold. She regretted not having her jacket with her.

A minute later Lydia opened the door a crack and peered out. An albino-pale man in a green hospital jacket wheeled a laundry cart down the hall. A few seconds later another man appeared, dark-haired with a skimpy mustache. He carried a mop and bucket. "Bitch of a night out there," he said to the laundry-cart man.

"Yeah, I'd just as soon be in here working," the cart roller said, and went on his way down the corridor.

The bucket man set his bucket down and started swabbing an already spotless floor, which was, unfortunately, in the direction she'd figured the animals were kept. It was as if he knew what she was up to and deliberately set out to thwart her.

Lydia closed the door and was about to flick on the light when she remembered the wall panel. If she'd figured it out right, switching on the light activated a green light upstairs indicating the room was inhabited. Best not to risk it even if that guard ignored the panel. There might be a similar panel down here, and the guards would be on the lookout after the alarm.

She played the flashlight around. Its yellow beam glinted on the gray stainless steel of what appeared to be a many-doored, floor-to-ceiling refrigeration system lining one side of the room. On the other side, a stainless-steel counter held dozens of uncapped, milky-opaque bottles. Lydia's heart jumped. The bottles were just like the one she'd seen in the greenhouse. Except these were labeled: ANIMA.

The bottles stood within reaching distance of a sink where a thin rubber tube snaked through the wall from an adjoining room. The nozzle was just slightly larger than the openings of the milky-opaque bottles. On the other side of the sink was a motionless conveyor belt that ran to the refrigeration unit. Apparently, the so-called magic potion was poured into the tube from the adjoining room and emptied into the bottles over here, the bottles set on an activated conveyer belt that ran to the refrigerator. She'd love to see that other room. Or would she? Maybe that was where the butchering took place. It sickened her to think of it.

She found two freshly laundered white lab jackets in the cupboard below the sink and slipped on the smaller one. Still a little large, but okay. At least she'd look more like she belonged here.

Opening a refrigerator door, Lydia found shelf after shelf and row on row of milky-opaque labeled bottles with printed instructions. She'd just pocketed a bottle of Anima when she heard a voice in the hall, uncomfortably close. In fact, it sounded like it was coming from just outside the door.

"Wait a sec. Be right with you," a man was saying. Blood slammed in Lydia's ears. Please don't come in here, she prayed, but a minute later she glimpsed blunt fingers and the sleeve of a white lab coat as the door opened.

It was foolhardy to clobber someone with her flashlight while someone else waited outside—her only way out was to bluff. Lydia headed for the door and came eye to eye with a skinny man in his late thirties with thinning blond hair.

"Who are you?" he asked.

Lydia smiled her most winsome smile. "Oh, I'm new here. I thought I might score some extra points by working late," she said, attempting to slide by. But the man didn't yield an inch. "Working in the dark?" he inquired.

Damn, she should have turned the light on. "I just popped in for a minute to get this for Dr. Malmener," she said, producing the bottle of Anima she'd pocketed. "He wants a test run on it to see if it's up to standard before making a new shipment." She was talking too much and too fast.

"The good doctor is here? I haven't seen him."

"He just got in tonight."

"In this weather?" The man looked her over. Lydia realized with a sinking feeling that whatever credibility the lab coat might lend her was undercut by her neon ski pants. She held the flashlight behind her, hoping he didn't guess she was hiding something.

She looked down at her ski pants and laughed. "I'd just gotten dressed to go home when he asked me to get this," she said.

"Isn't that always how it happens?" the man said, laughed with her, and stepped aside for her to get by. The last she heard was the sound of a refrigerator door opening and some toneless whistling. She walked down the hall, passing an attractive plumpish brunette who must have been the one the man had told to wait. The woman was leaning against the wall with her nose poked into a paperback mystery. They smiled at one another as Lydia went on her way. The floor swabber was no longer around.

Three minutes later Lydia began to tremble from aftershock. Then she felt a surge of anger at the two people she'd just encountered. Neither seemed to give a damn. Trouble was, they hadn't seemed like villains. But most villains didn't or there'd be more caught. Probably they gave no thought to the slaughter of animals. Might even have pets they were fond of. Maybe people committed evil deeds so effortlessly because they lacked imagination. They couldn't conceive of suffering unless it affected them personally.

Ahead of her a mustached man in a lab coat popped out of the door, giving her a curious look as he walked toward her. "Working late," she said, and smiled. A split second later she was aware that the footsteps behind her had stopped. Was he having second thoughts, wondering who she was? She forced herself to keep the same pace while wanting to break into a run. Finally, the steps moved on. Lydia risked looking back and saw that the man had disappeared. What if he ran into the other guy and they asked each other who she was?

She was worrying about this when she heard a small army of footsteps approaching from a side corridor. She reached for the nearest door and was about to go in when she heard a man's voice on the other side. Quickly, she zipped across the hall to the opposite door with a dark, frosted-glass window and managed to slip inside before the footsteps came around the corner.

When she heard the voices, Lydia eased the door open and listened as they came her way, hoping this room wasn't their destination. She didn't have time to look for a hiding place—

they'd stopped just outside her door. Her heart stopped with them. After a few minutes when nothing happened, she again opened the door and peeked out. There were three of them— Dr. Malmener, Starr, and Boyd.

"Please God, don't let them come in," she prayed.

"I thought he would arrive with you," Dr. Malmener was saying. "What time will he be here? There has been too much delay already." He spoke in a clipped voice with only a trace of an accent.

"There's something I neglected to mention," Starr said in a voice that sounded more humble than hearty.

"What is it you neglected to mention this time?" the clipped voice demanded.

"He's dead," Starr said.

"Dead! How did this happen?" Malmener's voice echoed up and down the corridor. "Who killed him?"

"We had to," Boyd broke in.

"*We*? Where do you get that we? You're the one who shot him," Starr said.

Boyd started talking—fast. "I had to do something. He was reckless—dangerous. We were already headed for trouble after the lunatic way he got rid of that botched job. They have hundreds of cops assigned to the case. Why'd he have to go and hack her to pieces? A famous model—shit."

Lydia's head began to spin. The famous model had to be Laura Haddon! Boyd was still carrying on. " . . . on the front page of every newspaper," he was saying. "On the TV news every night and all the TV talk shows. Bad enough that the job was botched, but the way Tanner handled it was—"

"*Tais-toi,*" Malmener said in a voice shaking with emotion. If Boyd didn't understand French, he must have understood Malmener's tone of voice, for he immediately shut up. "The man was acting on *my* orders. And *I* did not botch the job. Such accidents happen. The injection took an unpredictable path to the brain, with the unfortunate consequence of an embolism."

Malmener was holding himself unaccountable for Laura Haddon's death. Poor Laura. She'd been terrified of undergoing the knife for a face-lift but had died by a simple injection.

"I could not risk her going to a hospital," Malmener went on. "That would have been extremely foolish. Even if she had not been well known, there would have been questions. An investigation. My orders were to conceal the lady's identity so that she could not be traced. Tanner, unfortunately, did not succeed in that. Everyone makes mistakes. And your mistake was to kill him," Malmener told Boyd.

"He came at me with a knife. I had to defend myself," Boyd protested. "He could have killed me."

Peeking through the crack, Lydia saw that Malmener's look said that might not have been such a bad thing. "Now I will have to find someone else to take his place. Immediately. We must not waste any more time."

"Agreed. It's risky waiting. Also, expensive feeding the animals. You'd be surprised how the cost mounts up. But I've already got someone else lined up to take Tanner's place," Starr said proudly. "He'll be here tomorrow morning."

"I do the hiring here," Malmener said. "The hiring *and* the firing." He let that sink in a minute before he went on. "I need someone who knows how to kill. Watching Monsieur Tanner was always such a pleasure. Killing was in his blood. He killed slowly, relishing the act. A slow and painful death stimulates erotic feelings in the animals, you know."

Stimulates your erotic feelings, you bloody sadist, Lydia wanted to shout.

"Practice makes perfect," Malmener continued. "Especially in the execution of either the human or four-legged animal. As with anything else, this is a form of art." His voice had become that of a lecturer in love with his subject, his accent more pronounced as he raved on, so that it was nearly impossible to make out half of what he said. Lydia felt a chill like ice water pour down her spine. The man was mad. Certifiably insane. But Boyd and Starr listened to his ravings reverently, nodding in agreement with each pronouncement, whether they could understand his words or not. Finally, the mad lecturer wound to a halt—returning to the original subject. "I will take care of this matter promptly. We do not worry about money. We will soon be making millions, even billions, on our little project. It does not pay to do things on the cheap, as you say here. There will be no further discussion of this matter. I will consult my list for a proper executioner."

"What if he draws the line and refuses to take care of the girl?" Starr asked.

"I'll take care of her," Boyd offered, eager to please.

Malmener turned on him. "*You?* You have already blundered by letting her follow you."

Tiffany! She must have been who the guard meant when he'd referred to that little bit of cargo in the back room that he intended having fun with. Tiffany was alive! Lydia's heart took a simultaneous leap and dive. She was happy to learn no harm had come to her, but saving Tiffany took precedence over saving the animals. She might be able to manage one, but both?

"I do not wish any more mistakes to be made," Malmener said, opening the door across the way and entering. "You amuse yourselves with your card games?" he asked someone inside.

"Just passing the time, sir."

Lydia recognized the whiny guard's voice.

"We keep a close watch on them, sir. Both the animals and the girl," the gruff voice put in.

"What caused that alarm to go off earlier?" Malmener inquired.

"Nothing much. Some wild animal got into the supply room."

"What do you mean 'nothing much'?" Malmener did a surprisingly good imitation of the whiny one's voice.

Silence.

"Well?"

"We're not sure, sir. A squirrel or something. We thought we'd let it get out the way it got in. Didn't wanna get bit by some rabid animal. Those shots can hurt something awful, I hear."

"Find that animal and kill it," Malmener ordered. "Leave the body on my desk before you go."

The man was mad. She was sure of it. Even so, Lydia shivered, thinking that the body on the desk could end up being hers.

The guards sped down the hall while Malmener, Starr, and Boyd walked toward the front of the building. From what she'd gathered of the guards' earlier conversation, Tiffany was within their groping distance.

Lydia listened anxiously to the departing footsteps of Malmener and his cohorts. She didn't have much time. If the guards came across her ski jacket, she'd have even less. She could enlist Tiffany's help with the animals; that is, if Tiffany hadn't been harmed. They'd let the animals loose, then get out of here and go for help. It seemed cruel to turn the animals out into the cold, chancing their getting lost in mountainous country. But they had a better chance of survival outside than in.

The sound of footsteps faded. Now, she told herself, and sprinted across the hall. She turned the doorknob and entered, fearing what she might find.

Nothing—just a guardroom similar to the one at Nora's Ark, but smaller. Shabbier, too. Dust and cement. A brightly lit cubbyhole. Cards lay scattered on a table, where they'd been abandoned. A keyboard hung on the wall next to a massive, dungeonlike door. But a key wasn't needed. The door was bolted shut. Lydia tried yanking the bolt, but it refused to slide back. All she could do was wiggle it a bit. She went at the bolt from the other direction, hitting it with the heel of her palm, and succeeded only in hurting herself. Shit, she couldn't waste precious time on a stupid bolt. She felt like howling in frustration. She leaned in on the door, and kept working the bolt until it moved infinitesimally. After nearly biting off her tongue in the effort, she managed to slide the bolt back.

Lydia had no sooner stepped through the door of a dark, musty-smelling room than an object came hurtling at her head. It would have hit her if she hadn't ducked. Something crashed against the wall inches away from her.

"Stay away from me, creep," a young voice called, sounding shaky but fierce.

"Hey! this is an improvement. The last time you held a gun on me."

The prisoner made a noise between a sob and a cry of joy. "Lydia! Is that you?"

Lydia aimed her flashlight in the direction of the voice. Tiffany stood with her back to the wall, white-faced and wild-haired. A second later something else came hurtling at Lydia. Tiffany. She clutched Lydia and started crying. "Oh God, I thought this was the end."

"It might be if we don't start moving. At least they didn't tie you up."

"Yes, they did. But I got them to untie my hands so I could eat that swill they fed me. Let them cop a feel. They were doing it anyway," Tiffany said. She spoke fast and breathlessly, running words together, as if she had to tell everything at once or burst. "They tied my feet to the chair. They thought I couldn't untie their knots. I couldn't. I broke my nails trying. Look! Then I found this little nail cutter with a file in my shirt pocket and sawed through the rope."

"You're a wonder," Lydia said.

"Yeah, tell me about it. If I wasn't so dumb, I wouldn't have gotten caught. I didn't know the truck dri—"

Lydia interrupted. "Save it. We don't have time to schmooze if we're going to save the animals." She became aware of the faint sound of barking. "Where are they?"

"On the other side of the wall."

Another dungeon door. It muffled the barking so that it appeared to come from a distance.

"It's locked," Tiffany said. "I tried to pick it with my file, but it didn't work. It kills me to hear them and not be able to help. What are we going to do?" she wailed.

Lydia remembered the keyboard in the guardroom. "Be right back," she said, but Tiffany stuck to her side. "Don't leave me," Tiffany begged. Then: "Damn," she said, looking at the numerous keys hung on the board. "We'll have to try them all."

"We don't have time for that," Lydia told her. "The guards will be back any minute." In fact, she was surprised they weren't back already. They must be turning all the empty boxes upside down looking for a raccoon or a squirrel, whose dead body they could leave on Malmener's desk. Maybe they'd have to go out and hunt for one.

"These are what we want," she said, sweeping two keys from their hooks.

"How do you know?"

"I don't, but they're not numbered, and the others are numbered like the doors in the hall. Come on, let's see."

They raced back to the other dungeon door. The first key didn't fit, but the second worked. Lydia swung the door open.

Tiffany let out a sob. "Look what they've done!" Her words became lost in the cacophony of yelping and howling. Lydia nearly passed out from the smell of feces and fear, the reek of urine.

"Shut the door behind you, and make sure it locks," Lydia called to Tiffany, who looked about to gag.

"I'm already having trouble breathing."

"Hold your nose," Lydia advised. "How do you think these poor guys feel? And where are the cats? Do you suppose they're in another room? And the steps leading to the metal doors, where are they?"

Lydia realized she was asking questions Tiffany couldn't possibly answer. Pull yourself together, she advised herself. You can always fall apart later.

"What doors are you talking about?" Tiffany asked.

"Some doors set in the ground outside. That must have been how they brought in the animals." She beamed the light around; if she'd had any dinner, she'd have lost it at the sight of outthrust bloodied paws and small black noses pressed between the flimsy slats of wood. The cages were cheaply made to save a few bucks out of the millions that slime Malmener planned to make. Well, at least the crates would break apart easily, so they could get the animals out. But how long would that take? There were hundreds of crates stacked one on top of the other. And suddenly, in the chorus of pleading barks, she heard a welcoming woof.

"Emil! Where are you, baby? I'd know your bark anywhere!"

The woofs sounded again, this time in the midst of a more ominous sound of banging on the far side of the door.

"They're outside," Tiffany screamed. "They're going to break in."

Lydia looked desperately about for Emil. He'd be some protection at least. She spied an ear and an eye between the slats of a crate, third up from the floor. He was with a shivering puppy and a cringing half-grown dalmation. Lydia set her flashlight on top of a crate and tugged at the slats with her bare hands. "I need help over here," she screamed to Tiffany in order to be heard above the chaos of howling, wailing, and door smashing.

Tiffany grabbed a slat and yanked. "How are we going to get out?" she sobbed.

The lower slats gave way enough for the dalmation to squeeze through. Next came the puppy. "Oh, look at this poor baby," Tiffany said, picking it up and crying into its fur. Emil broke the final slat by himself and leaped into Lydia's arms, licking her face with a corduroy tongue. Lydia hugged the dog she'd never thought she'd see again, then gently pushed him away. "Okay, enough of the mushy stuff. We've got to get out of here."

It sounded as if they were using a battering ram against the door to get in. "Try to open more crates," she yelled to Tiffany, who stood crying and hugging the puppy to her chest. "If they get in, they won't be able to handle the animals and us, too," she added, hoping that wasn't merely wishful thinking.

She grabbed the flashlight and beamed it along the wall, searching for a way out as the battering continued. Any minute now the door would give. Lydia became aware of cold air leaking in at almost the same moment she heard a sudden ecstatic bark from Emil. She flashed the light in his direction, just in time to see him bound up the steps. "Come on, hurry up. We found a way out," she screamed to Tiffany, and got no answer.

Emil stood by the door, woofing and wagging his tail. He

could find the doors, but he couldn't open them, after all. That was her job.

Lydia managed to climb one step up before bumping her head on the metal doors. These, too, were held shut by a thick black steel bolt. Surprisingly, this bolt yielded easily, perhaps because it was used more often. Behind her she heard a scream from Tiffany as a burst of light came from the far side of the room when the door fell in.

Lydia shoved against the metal doors with the strength of fear, and flung them open. She started up the stairs, surrounded by a half-dozen animals besides Emil. She was gratefully gulping in fresh cold air when she spied a dark figure standing above her in the white night. A woman. A woman in an anorak, pointing a gun at her. P.S.—the last person Lydia saw before the shot cracked the night and she crumpled to the steps. The animals bounded over her and out to freedom.

CHAPTER 29

Lydia opened her eyes and stared up at a fluorescent-lit ceiling. A woman stood over her. "We're awake," the woman said. Lydia knew that by "we" she meant her, and sensed the presence of a third person in the room.

"Give us your arm," the woman said, holding up a hypodermic needle.

"I don't want that poison. It freezes your face."

"We're out of it," the woman in white remarked to an unseen bystander. "We'll get some sleep and be a new person tomorrow," she told Lydia.

Which was what Lydia was afraid of. She struggled as the needle came toward her.

"I could use some help here," the woman in white called. "We're putting up a fight."

The unseen person stepped forward. Lydia recognized Dr. Malmener, even though he was disguised in a mask and wire-rimmed glasses. She'd be butchered and buried under the George Washington Bridge.

"Stay away from me!" she screamed.

"Hold her still."

Her arms were pinned down. "Help!" she called. Her voice was weak. The needle went in.

"There, there. It's all over. All that fuss over nothing."

Lydia tried to keep awake, but a white fog rolled in and over her.

CHAPTER 30

The first thing Lydia saw were the anemones. Beautiful, luscious velvety reds, purples, and whites. Her favorite flowers. Where did they come from? She looked out on an unfamiliar snow scene where a cardinal with a red top notch sat on the branch of a fir tree. Anemones and cardinals. I don't believe this, Lydia told herself. I'm dreaming. Or maybe it's a trap. Not a dream but a nightmare.

She turned on her side to escape the sun's glare and felt a piercing stab. Looking down, she saw that she was mummified in white tape and gauze extending from her elbow to her upper arm just below the sleeve of an obscene-green hospital gown. Looking up, she saw two people sitting on a bed opposite her, watching. Both wore identical red ski sweaters with white reindeer.

"What are you doing here?" Lydia demanded. She started to

sit up in bed, felt a sharp twinge, and slid back down onto her pillow. "For that matter, what am I?"

"You all right?" Richard asked.

"Hey, kid, I'm sorry I shot you," P.S. said. "But it's nothing mortal. I just winged you, that's all. You're lucky I'm such a lousy shot."

"Why did you do it?"

"Wait a minute," P.S. said, and got up. Lydia wondered if P.S. had gone to get her gun to finish her off. P.S. disappeared into the bathroom, leaving the door open. A second late she reappeared with a paper cup. She lit a cigarette and dropped a match into the cup.

"You can't smoke in hospitals," Lydia informed her.

"They have to catch me first. How was I to know you hadn't helped steal the animals?" P.S. asked, returning to their original discussion. "There you were hotfooting it out of that slaughterhouse, just after we moved in on Dr. Malmener and his crew."

"He's insane," Lydia said. "Certifiable."

Richard nodded. "Thanks to him, there are thousands of women out there who've let that poison be injected into their systems. Their faces will be turning into frozen masks if they haven't already."

"At the cost of all those slaughtered animals, they deserve it. They've got blood on their hands," P.S. said darkly.

"Oh, come on now, honey," Richard said. "Be fair. They didn't know what was in it."

"Do you?" Lydia asked Richard.

"I just got a bottle last night after our raid. The cops don't know I have it. I'll run an analysis as soon as I get back to my lab at Rockefeller. But I already have a good idea of what's in it since one of the detectives asked me to look over Malmener's notes when he found out I was a biochemist."

"What was in them?"

"A list of ingredients and their application. One's a toxin from mushrooms, *Amanita muscaria*."

"Tasty but deadly, I'm told," Lydia said. "Stuart Starr supplied them from his greenhouse. Some at least. But how about Botox? That's botulism, too."

"Yes, but not in the reckless amount Malmener used in his formula."

"And what about the orchids, what did they contribute?"

"You know about those?" Richard said, eyeing her through horn-rim glasses.

"Ladies' tresses, *Spiranthes cernua*, but I don't know what they're supposed to do," she said hoping she'd gotten the genus name right.

"They're reputed to have aphrodisiac qualities, and they're very rare. An endangered species. I don't know where in the hell he got them," Richard said.

"Also from Stuart Starr's greenhouse."

"You've been busy, I see," P.S. said.

"It's how I spent my New Year's Eve instead of living it up at the Rainbow Room."

"The evening turned out to be one big yawn," P.S. said.

At the sound of footsteps in the hall, she dropped her cigarette into the paper cup, jumped up, opened the window, and doused the smoking cup with snow.

The nurse came in sniffing. "Who's been smoking in here?"

P.S. set the paper cup on the outside window ledge and tried to look innocent.

"It must be next door," Richard said, gallantly coming to her rescue. "We had to open the window."

"Next door left this morning," the nurse said.

"Time for us to leave?" P.S. inquired, sounding hopeful.

Maybe it's hospitals she doesn't like, not me, Lydia thought.

"This will only take a minute," the nurse said. She jammed a thermometer in Lydia's mouth, took her pulse, and wrote something down on the chart at the bottom of the bed. "You'll be out of here tomorrow morning. Of course, we have to get doctor's okay first, but I'm sure he'll give it. No more smoking," she said, giving P.S. a warning look.

"Nurse Ratched lives," P.S. said, and turned to Lydia. "We'll be over to pick you up tomorrow. You can stay with Richard and me at his house."

"You can't leave. There are things I don't know yet."

P.S. sat down with a martyred expression. "Such as?"

"You didn't say what else you found in the notes," Lydia reminded Richard.

"It's sickening," Richard said. "He thought a combination of male and female sexual fluids kept the skin youthful because sexual activity was a youth-activating factor. And that a slow and painful death stimulated erotic feeling."

Lydia vaguely remembered overhearing Malmener lecturing Starr and Boyd on the subject.

"The cops confiscated some videos," P.S. said. "One told us about them when Richard dropped off the notes this morning. He said he threw up after viewing it for thirty seconds. Malmener enjoyed watching the animals die. He made videos of the torture."

"Don't talk about it, honey. You're upsetting Lydia," Richard said. "She's turning as green as her hospital gown."

"Yes, let's change the subject." Lydia was aware that Richard didn't want to hear about it either. "Tell me how you two got together. You were always at each other's throat."

"I came up here gunning for him," P.S. said, patting Richard's arm. "I'd been keeping in touch with some animal people in Burlington since September. They told me something was going on in this neck of the woods, but New York seemed to be the home base. Since I knew Richard had a vacation house nearby, I became somewhat suspicious."

"To put it mildly," Richard said.

"Well, when I checked my machine last night and heard Lydia's message, and knew you were here, what else *could* I think?" P.S. bristled.

Lydia was sorry she'd asked. She didn't want the war to start up again. "*You* could have at least told me you were coming up here. I didn't know what the hell to do."

"I didn't know if I could trust you any more than Richard," P.S. told her. "I thought you just might be covering up. So did Allegra. She's the one who brought me the newspaper clippings on Anima. She'd started collecting them after she'd tried it, using herself as a human guinea pig. She'd gotten the stuff from a distributor who'd said it was a fantastic product but warned her up front that it had yet to be approved by the FDA. But he assured her that was merely a matter of time, that the FDA is always slow to act.

"About three months after her injection, Allegra noticed her eyes looked rather poppy. But she wasn't sure if that was from Anima or stemmed from a thyroid condition she'd had as a child, which had made them somewhat poppy to begin with."

P.S. reached into her bag and took out a pack of Marlboros.

"Nurse Ratched," Richard said.

P.S. put the pack away.

P.S. and Richard already seemed to be developing their own language, as so many lovers do. Lydia felt a little envious. After all these months she and Kramer hadn't reached the point that P.S. and Richard had reached in twenty-four hours.

"Allegra contacted the distributor, who said no one else had complained, and they'd been using it in Europe without any harmful results. Besides, they'd warned that using it would be at her own risk. She asked other dermatologists about Anima and encountered a wall of silence. Of course, those who used it weren't going to admit it since it wasn't FDA-approved. But she started picking up things here and there. Someone mentioned a pharmaceutical company, someone else a magazine, a third someone an animal shelter. Gradually, she narrowed it down. The pharmaceutical company was foreign-owned, the magazine promoting Anima some tony women's magazine, and one of the people involved a male vet at an animal shelter called Nora's Ark.

"So she came aboard the Ark," P.S. continued, "and since I was neither a male nor a vet, decided I was trustworthy. She pointed out that Richard was a biochemist at Rockefeller, and a likely suspect."

"I knew there was something about her I didn't like," Richard said.

"Well, you have to admit you looked suspicious," P.S. said, giving his earlobe an affectionate tug. She turned to Lydia. "Allegra also pointed out that you'd quit a power job at *gazelle*, a chi-chi fashion magazine, for no valid reason, and come to work at the shelter. That's what Gillian told her anyway."

"For God's sake, Gillian was the guilty one, not me."

"Well, you can't blame Allegra for not knowing that. Gillian told her the piece praising Anima was your last contribution before quitting, and that you'd written it under the pen name Trish Ackers."

"Blaming me for what she did. And Allegra believed her? How gullible can you get, for God's sake?"

"Well, how was poor Allegra to guess? So that just made it look more suspicious when Richard hired you."

"He didn't hire me, I volunteered."

"Which made it worse, not better," P.S. pointed out.

"And I suspected Allegra," Richard said. "A dermatologist who was afraid of blood." He shook his head.

"Me, too," Lydia said. "I thought she'd killed Bud."

"That was Boyd," P.S. said.

"How do you know?"

"His partner Stuart Starr ratted on him. The original plan was to steal the animals on New Year's Eve. Boyd knew we all left early that day and had scheduled a raid before Richard got there, since he also knew Richard worked late at the lab. But you spoiled it by hanging around," P.S. told her. "Remember when Allegra and I tried to get you to leave? Good thing you didn't. So they delayed it a day, but Bud got nervous because of the open house and refused to go along. This made Malmener mad, so he had Boyd take him out, or so Boyd says. Malmener denies it. He's the one who ran the show, and the one who'll get off. He can't be pinned for a murder committed when he wasn't even in the country. They've got him in custody, but they won't be able to hold him for very long."

It was then that it came back to her. How could she have forgotten what Malmener had said out in the corridor? Maybe getting shot had given her temporary amnesia. "They'll get him for murder, all right," she said grimly. "He let Laura Haddon die. You've heard of her. That gruesome murder with the body buried under the George Washington Bridge. Or rather near it," she amended, reaching for the phone. She called the

Woodboro police and told them what she knew. "They're coming over," she said, hanging up.

"Too bad we can't get him for the mass murder of animals, too," P.S. said. Then: "At least you saved ours. They're already en route to the shelter."

"Where things will be much improved now that you and Richard are friends, right?" Lydia asked. "I still don't know how you two got together."

"Well, since we didn't trust each other, we didn't let one another out of sight. And the next thing we knew it was love," P.S. said, with a dreamy look in her eyes.

"I think it happened out on the slopes," Richard said. "I thought I'd shake P.S. downhill skiing—I've been skiing since I was six, and considered myself pretty good. But she was right behind me. I couldn't lose her. And that's where we ran into Boyd. I wondered what he was doing in this area. I thought maybe he was out for revenge. Followed me up here to kill me. He said he was working at a shelter in the vicinity."

"So I called the animal people in Burlington to check it out," P.S. kicked in. "They said he came in as a volunteer vet but worked full-time at Société chimique—a place high on their suspect list. They'd heard of mysterious goings on there with something to do with animals, but they didn't even know where it was.

"Naturally, they asked Boyd about this. He said it had nothing to do with animals, and what people considered mysterious were merely projects of a highly sensitive and explosive nature relating to governmental security between France and the U.S."

"Implying that it had to do with bombs not animals," Richard scoffed.

"As if Russia were still the evil empire. He said he couldn't discuss these projects or reveal the Société chimique's location. The Burlington people didn't buy that phony story. Also, they checked with Cornell University and found out he wasn't a real vet. He didn't fool them the way he did the people at Nora's Ark," P.S. said, as if she hadn't been one of them. Richard didn't correct her. It must be love.

"They put a tail on him, but he always managed to elude them," Richard put in.

"He didn't elude us," P.S. said smugly. "We tracked him down that very afternoon."

"But we couldn't figure out how to get in undetected," Richard added. "We called the Burlington people and they agreed to join forces, waiting until they heard from us. Then we tailed Boyd to the Inn of the Seven Pines, where we showed up later and invited ourselves to join him at his table. We knew he wasn't the only one in on this and we wanted to get everyone involved."

"You didn't tell us how you caught on to them," P.S. said to Lydia.

"It's a kind of complicated story involving an iguana and a kid named Tiffany. You might have met her last night."

"Oh, yes, isn't she a dear?" P.S. said. "As of this moment, she and a fascinating woman named Vashti, who's driving the truck, are returning the animals to Nora's Ark."

"How about their cars?" Lydia asked.

"Their cars weren't theirs. Vashti returned hers to the Hertz people up here."

"What stunned me was Heidi turning up to claim her BMW," Richard said. "She's the woman who didn't come back from lunch. You don't know her."

"I feel as if I did. Or as much as I care to, anyway. She spread some nasty rumors about me. Said I was in with the people stealing the animals. By the way, do you happen to know what happened to my dog?"

"Vashti left him with us," P.S. said. "That must be the police," she added, at the sound of heavy footsteps out in the hall. The nurse appeared in the doorway with two men in tow: one looked to be in his early twenties, the other in his midfifties; both were burly, red-cheeked, and wearing parkas.

"You the one who called?" the older one asked Lydia.

It was noon by the time Lydia had finished her story. P.S. and Richard stuck around to hear what she had to say, leaving shortly after the police.

"Don't forget you're staying with us tomorrow," P.S. said, giving her a brisk kiss on the forehead.

It was only after Richard and P.S. left that Lydia realized she hadn't thanked them for the anemones. Anemones weren't easy to get this time of the year. And how did they know they were her favorite flowers? She took the card from the envelope and read it, and was filled with instant euphoria. "All my love, Kramer. See you soon."

But how did he know where she was? Carolyn must have called him again. Lydia went to sleep happy.

CHAPTER 31

Instead of being on the outside looking in at the restaurant of the Inn of the Seven Pines, Lydia sat inside looking out at the snowy night landscape. Blue-and-yellow flames danced in the fireplace in a kind of nervous ballet, reflecting in the glasses of the person across from her. They drank after-dinner brandies from balloon glasses, she held the glass in the hand of her good arm. She was still taped up but no longer resembled a mummy.

"I should have known the moment I saw the anemones," Lydia said. "But I thought I'd never see you again."

"Well, when Andy told me that the lady who'd called sounded weird I got worried."

"A perceptive child. Just like her father."

Kramer traced her finger with his, then went on with his story. "So I called the number Andy had written down and got your ditsy friend. She was hysterical. It was hard to get the story straight. She said something to the effect that you, Tiffany, and the animals were about to be murdered by some people in the cabin across the way because she'd been praying."

Lydia glanced outside and remembered sitting in the car with Carolyn and keeping watch on the unholy three. "She must have been praying to her guardian angel when Stuart Starr slipped off with Dr. Malmener."

"Well, I knew that muddled though Carolyn's story might be, I had cause to worry, or you'd have called. It made me feel so damn helpless not knowing what was going on. So I stuck my neck out and called the Woodboro police with the intention of asking them as a cop-to-cop favor to see Carolyn and find out what was wrong.

"The cop who answered said the other two guys were out on an emergency call—something to do with animals. I immediately guessed you were involved. Later, a Detective Caruso called and gave me the story. A hell of a nice guy. I'm stopping by the station house to thank him personally."

"They were great about Gary, too. Very understanding. I called Gary and assured him no one up here thought of him as a murderer, and if he didn't call his mother, I would.

"I was there this afternoon when he arrived on the Greyhound." Lydia toyed with her glass and smiled at the memory. "There wasn't a dry eye in the bus station. Everyone was crying, including me. He's going back to school. Tiffany's replacing him at the spa and staying with Carolyn—thank God, I'm moving out. The other runaway kids are being sent home, Tiffany said. Whether they stay or not is anyone's guess. As for Gillian Smith-Markham, I don't know what happens to *her*. Did Caruso tell you how large a part she played in all this?"

"The kid who took over your job? According to Caruso, she wept and told all. Naturally, she claimed she was innocent and didn't know what her pals were up to."

"Once I'd have agreed. Now I'm not so sure. I hold her partly responsible for Laura Haddon's gruesome murder. She had to be the one who sold Laura on Anima and sent her to Dr. Malmener. Gillian isn't dumb. She'd have at least asked herself some questions when the body was found so soon after Laura had seen him."

"She was probably afraid to. You said she was bright but a reckless, impulsive kid."

"Kramer, you scare me. You have such a good memory."

"Oh, but I only remember the good things about you."

"What else is there? I didn't let you finish your story—or rather Caruso's."

"That's pretty much it. Caruso said all hell had broken loose when they arrived on the scene, with people getting shot and animals running wild."

"The only one shot was me."

"It must have seemed like that to him. As soon as I heard you were okay, I decided to take Andy up to her aunt Ellen's. That way you and I could drive back together, more or less sticking to the original plan."

"Except I wasn't supposed to be an invalid. You wanted to put in some ski time."

"Actually, I'm not the athletic type. I just thought it would be a good way to get some exercise. I'm sure we can come up with some other form of entertainment. And I brought Steinbeck along just in case."

"Did you really?"

"His short stories. I can read you *The Red Pony.*"

"My bedtime story," she said. "And I'm beginning to feel sleepy."

"Good."

They got their coats and left the restaurant, walking a snowy path to her cabin at the Inn of the Seven Pines, where Lydia had decided she'd rather stay with Kramer than with Richard and P.S. She wanted Kramer to herself.

IF WISHES
WERE HORSES . . .

by Tim Hemlin

Neil Marshall is a twenty-eight-year-old graduate student who moonlights as a chef.

When Neil is thrown out of his house one night, he takes up temporary residence with his horse-breeder friend, Jason Keys.

Then Jason is violently murdered, and Neil finds himself in the dark underworld of horse theft and illegal breeding. And as prime suspect in the ensuing murder investigation, Neil begins to do some sleuthing of his own.

IF WISHES WERE HORSES . . .
by Tim Hemlin
Published by Ballantine Books.
Available in bookstores everywhere.

Out of the starting gate comes
a champion mystery!

HORSE OF A DIFFERENT KILLER

by Jody Jaffe

When a quarter-million-dollar show horse and a top trainer are found brutally murdered side by side, Natalie Gold, a reporter for the Charlotte *Commercial Appeal*, seizes the chance to get out of the fashion beat she so detests and back to her beloved world of horses.

She knows that Wally Hempstead, the stiff in the stable, was not only a talented trainer but also an A1 cheat, skilled in blackmail and extortion.

As Nattie makes the rounds of the Carolina show horse circuit, she closes in on the truth and becomes the target for a series of increasingly savage death threats, not only to herself, but to her beloved horse, Brenda Starr.

HORSE OF A DIFFERENT KILLER

by Jody Jaffe

Published by Ivy Books.
Available in your local bookstore.

In the African wilderness,
the hunt is on . . .

to find the killer!

KARIN McQUILLAN

brings you suspense and action, set amid
the beauty of the African terrain and the
tragedy of endangered wildlife. Join **Jazz
Jasper,** amateur sleuth and safari tour
guide, in these three suspenseful mysteries:

DEADLY SAFARI
ELEPHANTS' GRAVEYARD
THE CHEETAH CHASE

"Everything anyone could want: suspense, real people
as characters, and real untamed Africa out there in the
darkness."

—TONY HILLERMAN

Published by Ballantine Books.
Available in your local bookstore.